"Tell me to let you go," he said, his voice balanced on a keen edge and soaked with desire. "I can be your shoulder, Cooper, but...I'm thinking things that are probably not a good idea. Have been thinking these things since I laid eyes on you."

She smoothed her palm up his arm and covered his hand. "You do things to me that have never been done before, but we work together, so I was trying to keep it professional, and I have history. Not fair to you. So...so..."

A nicer guy would have helped her to fill in the blanks.

Beau was not a nice guy.

He brought up his other hand, bracketing her face between his palms, delving into all that tantalizing red hair. He leaned down and kissed her, opened his mouth over hers and gave in to that hard, utterly decisive need to feel her heat. He felt as if he'd just jumped from a plane and was free-falling.

She melted against him, opening herself even more to the kiss. It was such a tease of what he really wanted: more *her*.

Be sure to check out the next books
in this exciting new miniseries:

To Protect and Serve—A team of military operatives
and civilians are called to investigate...

* * *

If you're on Twitter, tell us what you think of
Harlequin Romantic Suspense!
#harlequinromsuspense

Dear Reader,

My To Protect and Serve series continues with *Joint Engagement* pairing up a southern Louisiana Cajun charmer NCIS agent and a by-the-book special agent in the coast guard to investigate a drifting coast guard cutter with six dead men aboard.

Coast guard special agent Kinley Cooper starts her workout on a foggy morning that brings back memories of the day her father was murdered when she stumbles on a drifting cutter. Once the ship is piloted to the Hamptons Road docks, it's discovered that the six men on board aren't coast guard at all. They are civilians in black-market fake coast guard uniforms—except for one naval petty officer. Enter special agent Beau Jerrott. Once they lay eyes on each other it's a volatile mix of heat, conflict and danger as they each wrestle with their own demons. The investigation takes them first to the Bahamas, then Cuba, where the danger escalates. With only each other to trust, national security and their lives hanging in the balance, they race against time, terrorists, a ruthless drug cartel and their own hearts.

Best,

Karen Anders

JOINT ENGAGEMENT

Karen Anders

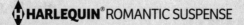
HARLEQUIN® ROMANTIC SUSPENSE

Recycling programs
for this product may
not exist in your area.

ISBN-13: 978-0-373-27915-9

Joint Engagement

Printed in U.S.A.

Karen Anders is a three-time National Readers' Choice Award finalist and an RT Reviewers' Choice Award finalist, and she has won a prestigious Holt Medallion. Two of her novels made the Waldenbooks bestseller list in 2003. Published since 1997, she currently writes romantic suspense for Harlequin. To contact the author, please write to her in care of Harlequin, 233 Broadway, Suite 1001, New York, NY 10279, or visit karenanders.com.

Books by Karen Anders

HARLEQUIN ROMANTIC SUSPENSE

Five-Alarm Encounter

To Protect and Serve Series

At His Command
Designated Target
Joint Engagement

The Adair Legacy Series

Special Ops Rendezvous

Visit the Author Profile page at Harlequin.com for more titles.

To CDR John R. Barrett, USCG, retired, 23 years on active duty, for his invaluable help and insights.

Chapter 1

United States Coast Guard special agent Kinley Cooper stretched as she rose at the annoying sound of her 5:00 a.m. alarm. She rubbed the sleep from her eyes and turned off her alarm, dreading this day. She reached for her dark gray jogging bra that was draped across black Lycra cotton shorts on the back of the chair near her bed.

Yawning, she pushed back the painful memories that clogged her chest and twisted her heart. They were always there, especially the one of that terrible morning. It sat at the back of her mind as she gathered up her dark auburn hair and pulled it into a tight ponytail. She grabbed the shorts, wiggled into them, then donned socks and her running shoes.

Exactly twelve years ago, her father had been murdered outside their London residence as he was taking her to school before heading to work at the American embassy.

She took a deep breath. She had been active in the Coast Guard for eight years now, and had been accepted into the Coast Guard Criminal Investigative Service two years ago. The good-ol'-boy system had taken one look at her and assumed she was a pushover, but she'd taken care of that. She'd conducted investigations and had done a fine job.

She lived in Kroebuck Beach, Virginia, and drove in to the CGIS office that was geographically located in the southeastern corner of the state. The area was known as Hampton Roads to the residents.

Heading for the back door, she pressed the timer on her sports watch and stepped through the screen door. She stopped dead.

Fog. Thick, cloying and cold, like it had been that fateful morning. The mist brushed up against her face and she recoiled from it like she would from a cold hand. A shiver racked her.

Just like that, she was back on that familiar London street, panting hard, running through the fog away from armed men, one in particular, his eyes cold and calculating, obviously the leader. His voice. It chilled her, the flat inflection in Arabic. She would never forget how it sounded.

Kinley stood in a pocket of fog, but it didn't seem like a pocket to her. She tried to shake the feeling of being swallowed, erased and eradicated by this enveloping whiteness. It was so white, it hurt her eyes. Staring at it made her feel like she was staring at herself, staring at nothing. Her mind fought hard to get away from the visions and the memories. But the insubstantial wisps mocked her. Each thought she had seemed loud and exposed, just as every movement she made in the silence that wrapped like the fog around her seemed to gather attention. And her father. Oh, God, her father. Maybe the fog was somehow in her, just as she was in it?

There was no reason to be afraid of fog. Mist was created when warm air hit cold air. It was a weather pattern, and didn't hide memories, ghosts or the chunk of herself from when she'd lost her father. She'd been so sheltered, protected and her world had been safe and secure. Since then, she'd found out that the world was a hostile and tough place to maneuver, and had developed a thick skin.

Her next-door neighbor's dog woofed as he usually did every morning when she ran, but he sounded distant, as if she was hearing his barking underwater.

Everything looked and sounded unreal. The fog was so thick she could just barely make out the shoreline across North First Street. Whiteness obscured the ocean. It swooped in and skirted around the homes and the trees like a giant eraser.

Just like the day that those men had robbed her of her father. And the US government had robbed her of justice. They hadn't been all that forthcoming with details of the investigation. All they would tell her was that they were looking into it and it was terrorists who had murdered him. She'd only been a child then with no pull whatsoever. Even now, they were still vague with the details.

She made herself move, took off into a slow lope. The sun would be up soon and burn a lot of this off. She wasn't worried. She knew this beach like the back of her hand. But as she hit the soft sand, her house was swallowed up like a great white whale had just opened his maw and devoured it. She even lost the feeling of being on land. The fog and the sea joined with each other; even the waves lapping against the shore were quiet. And her heart was heavy as she ran, as if the ghost of her father ran with her, trying to catch up from that sixteen-year-old to the woman she was today. As if he was always one step behind her.

Muffled popping noises suddenly sounded over the water. Kinley slowed down, her breathing harsh in her ears. She attempted to quiet it. Stopping completely, she turned her head and looked out, remaining still and listening intently. Her heart lurched and then started pounding. She couldn't be sure of what she was hearing. The fog or her mind could be playing tricks on her. Damn these doubts. She wasn't going to panic. Trying to stay calm and in investigator mode, she waited. The burst of sound came again in rapid succession, but with the fog blanketing everything and the visibility almost nil, Kinley couldn't see anything but light flashes in the distance.

Flares? she thought, scanning back and forth. *Fireworks?*

Cocooned in the eerie opaque cotton, she strained her eyes trying to detect what it could be. The sounds seemed to be coming from everywhere, leaving her disoriented and unable to quite tell from which direction the noises originated.

She waited, listening intently and almost holding her breath. She tried to identify those softened explosions.

She took a step closer, the water lapping at her feet, and peered out into the dense mist. Her stomach was tied up in knots. She'd heard that sound in the fog before…on a London street. Was it her imagination or real automatic gunfire?

It came again and a chill raced over her skin. Her breathing went shallow. Without concrete proof, she was not going to guess. She never guessed. Not anymore.

She heard a terrible scraping sound, like metal against sand. Thumping and muted voices.

The fog cleared suddenly, a patch of it misting across her eyes, and she saw…something whiter than the fog loom out at her, and a bright red splash of color before it was quickly covered and obscured again.

Her stomach dropped. Everything went dead still, deader than the deadening fog—the sounds, her hands, her heart—and it felt as if every drop of blood had drained from her head.

Suddenly the muffled sound of a boat's engine, gunning away fast, surrounded her.

She turned back the way she'd come and took off at a run, kicking up sand as she pounded back to her house, momentarily stumbling around until she got her bearings. After streaking across the street, she slammed into her house, rushed to her nightstand drawer and grabbed her holster, clipping it to the back of her shorts. She stuffed her ID into her sock. Snatching her cell phone off the nightstand, she was on the move again, back to the beach and the small dock where her former boyfriend had left a small motorboat. He'd hoped they would fish together. But that was never going happen as she'd refused to have him move in with her, which had pretty much killed their relationship.

She jumped into the boat and started the engine, heading to the vicinity where she'd heard that ominous scraping and popping noise. She searched the thick haze, and caught another glimpse of something large, white and red.

White…oh God, red. Her stomach plummeted to her toes. "No, it can't be. Much too close to shore."

Guiding the light fishing boat over the slightly rocking sea, she moved slowly through the dense fog, her attention caught by the sound of an outboard motor. She looked to her left to make sure she wasn't going to hit anything.

With a weird sense of something looming right at the corner of her peripheral vision, Kinley wrenched her gaze back to the front and the now impending white/red monster careening out of the fog. She jerked hard on the throttle and swerved to the left at the last moment. The small boat rocked madly as it grazed the side of the hulking silhouette, making a loud screeching sound. Adrenaline sizzled through her blood, her heart beating hard against her chest wall.

"My God, what the hell are they doing running without lights?" she murmured to herself.

She looked back at the ship that had suddenly materialized out of the fog. "Cutter, Point class. Eighty-two footer," she said absently. *They wouldn't run without lights, not in this kind of fog.* Her heart accelerated from alarm. Something was wrong. She felt it in her bones when she looked at the vessel. That ship should be alive with movement, lit up. Then it struck her. There was no thrumming—the engines were silent.

Kinley twisted the throttle and sent the small boat revving back toward the massive and eerily quiet ship.

There was a Jacob's ladder hanging on the side of the ship. That ladder was only lowered when people were getting off. Otherwise it was stowed. There was no one around, the ominous absence of the engine and the fog that still lay thick around her completely muffling all sound. That persistent chill seeped through her. A chill of apprehension.

She cut the engine and anchored the little boat. Pulling out her cell, she tried to find a signal so that she could call her boss. No luck. "Damn," she swore under her breath, torn between investigating herself and persisting in reaching her boss. What if there were CGs up there in distress and her inaction inadvertently caused someone to die? After setting down the phone, she grabbed the knotted rope sides, set her sneaker onto the first rung and pulled herself up. She looked up the side of the vessel but there was no visibility whatsoever. It looked like the fabled ladder that led to the clouds and heaven.

The churning in her stomach left her clammy, but she swallowed hard and climbed, pressing the foreboding back with a sheer wall of determination.

It was the fog and the anniversary of her father's death that triggered the haunting memories, the fear, the pain and the realization that she wasn't really safe in the world. Ever. The terrorists would have killed her, too, had chased after her, but the fog had deterred them. It had saved her life, yet it wasn't a friend. All she'd heard were the gunshots.

She'd never even seen her father die.

The boat dipped in a swell and her eyes popped open. She took a breath and heaved it out as she started to climb again. When she reached the rail, she hauled herself over, pulling out the SIG Sauer handgun at the small of her back. She flipped off the safety and chambered a round.

She still couldn't see a damn thing. Crouching low, she sidestepped her way across the deck, heading for the bridge. She kept quickly checking her six, leading with her slightly bent elbows and the black-as-hell weapon.

"CGIS! Is there anyone aboard? Identify yourself!"

Only her voice echoed back to her, sounding tinny in the thick fog that enclosed her.

Then suddenly she tripped and flew forward, and

she was back on the London street again, stumbling and falling to the pavement, landing right alongside her father's frozen face and his open, dead eyes.

It took her a moment to push back the panic and turn her head. As she did, the fog lifted on a sudden breeze. She cried out and scrambled backward.

Blood was on her hands, smeared on her weapon and down the length of her body. Staring at her with open dead eyes was a man dressed in a Coast Guard uniform. She turned to look behind her and was met with a similar grisly scene. Another man lay prone, more blood, more staring eyes.

"Ohmigod," she said softly, rising and trying her best to ignore the metallic smell of the blood and the red. Pearled drops dripped off her forearm as she raised her firearm and moved again, this time stepping over the body and checking the deck in front of her.

She was breathing hard, clammy sweat beading and running down her temples and her back.

As the sun rose, the ship became more visible. Crouching, she circled the bridge and approached the open door. Another no-no on a ship at sea. All doors were always closed and secured. It was a hardcore CG rule.

When she breached the door and glanced quickly inside, she found no threat. Just more bodies, obviously deceased. Without pausing, she did a check of the rest of the ship, and found one more dead. She lowered her weapon and headed back toward the bridge and the radio, stepping over each body. Six in all.

She searched for, but couldn't find, the logbook that would identify the vessel. Walking back outside, she leaned over the side of the railing, but there were no call numbers on the hull. No name, either. Back inside the bridge, she picked up the mic. Taking a breath to calm the trembling in her body, she pressed the transmission button and said, "Mayday, Mayday, Mayday. This is Special Agent Kinley Cooper aboard the unknown Coast Guard vessel, unknown Coast Guard vessel, unknown Coast Guard vessel at position 37.0431°N, 76.2933°W. The vessel is drifting on the tide. I repeat. The vessel is drifting on the tide. No call numbers, no name, no logbook. Request immediate aid to secure the vessel. No medical personnel are required. All crew aboard are dead—six in all. Request contact of Coast Guard Investigative Services special agent in charge Kirk Stafford. Engines are silent. But there is no visible damage to the vessel. It is intact and has not yet run aground. No hostiles aboard. Over."

A male voice responded, the quality distant with a humming sound each time the speaker pressed the mic. "Unknown Coast Guard vessel, this is the United States Coast Guard vessel *Point Sharon*. Break. Break. Request the description of the vessel. Over."

"Eighty-two-foot Point-class cutter. Over."

Kinley rested against the console, attempting to collect herself. She was more than rattled. Was there ever a time when such a scene wouldn't faze her?

"Special Agent Cooper, sit tight. United States Coast Guard vessel *Point Sharon* is en route. Alerting United States Coast Guard, Sector Hampton Roads. Alerting SAC Stafford. Over."

"Roger that, United States Coast Guard vessel *Point Sharon*. Over and out."

She set down the mic and took up a position near the door. The bridge had a clear view of the bow, but the starboard wasn't visible. Better to keep her guard up just in case she got company.

Even as she stood watch, her mind was going fast and furious. How could this have happened? This was an elite, combat-ready force. It was hard to believe that someone could have gotten the drop on them, boarded a United States Coast Guard vessel and murdered everyone aboard. It was a light crew for this class of vessel. Normally, fifteen men manned a ship of this size. Were they also looking at a possible hostage situation with nine men missing?

As soon as the *Point Sharon* pulled up next to the drifting ship and the preliminary introductions were out of the way, the crew got the engines started and piloted the ship over to the Hampton Roads docks for crime-scene processing.

Still on the *Point Sharon* to keep the crime scene as pristine as possible, Kinley stood at the rail as the ship docked. Her boss, Kirk, waited on the dock with a crime-scene team. He was a tall, compact man, a runner like her with a buzz cut and even though she knew he was older than her, he had a boyish face with a set of intelligent brown eyes. Once the gangway was lowered and he was aboard, she briefed him on how she'd found the ship.

He took her arm and drew her away from the team. "Are you all right?"

"Yes," she said immediately.

"You shouldn't have boarded that ship without backup."

"I tried to call you, but they had a wireless jammer on board on the bridge. No cell signal and I was concerned about casualties."

He searched her eyes for a moment. Gave her a nod of approval. "You did good. Why don't you use the head to clean up? Then get on identifying our guys so we can notify their families and get this investigation under way. I want to know what the hell happened here." He shrugged out of his jacket and handed it to her.

She took it and nodded. Her running clothes weren't the ideal outfit at the moment and she was grateful for his thoughtfulness. She walked to the head and turned on the tap, taking a deep breath. She looked at her face in the mirror, one she had lived with for a long time. The delicate features were blank and controlled. It had been a long, long time since she had felt the emotion she'd felt today. The combination of the fog and the memories had seriously shaken her.

She was good at compartmentalizing; she shoved everything into a box and tamped down the lid. She had a job to do. That was the most important thing she could do for her father right now. He was gone, but she would be damned if she'd let terrorists or drug dealers kill her comrades and get into the US without a fight. She needed to do her job, not just for herself but for him.

She set the jacket down, slipped a paper towel under the stream and wiped at the dried blood on her arms until it was sponged clean. After that was complete, she cleaned the blood off her weapon and set it back in her holster before shrugging into the jacket.

When she came out of the head, she snagged one of her team members and got a mobile fingerprint scanner. Now in front of the first victim, a black man, the one she'd initially tripped over, she took in the position of his body. He was lying facedown and obvious bloody gunshot wounds peppered his back. Caught by surprise was her first thought. Sympathy for him and his family made her sigh softly. Her throat tightened. Losing

a family member was so…devastating. He was someone's son, and a husband according to the ring on his
left hand. She frowned. No weapon. Anywhere. Had
the hostiles taken it? Using the device, she crouched
down and reached for the dead man's hand, separating his fingers and pressing his index finger against
the pad of the reader. She looked down at the screen
and waited for his identity. Nothing showed up. Figuring she must not have gotten a good reading, she
repeated the process, but the reader still returned no
information.

She walked over to the next victim and followed the
same procedure. Again, no reading. Kinley moved to
the next victim, but this time the reader returned an
identity.

Cameron Dixon, Petty Officer Third Class, assigned
to the USS *Matthew Robinson*, destroyer. She looked
for a laptop and typed in the information, and found
out that the *Matthew Robinson* was currently docked
at Naval Station Norfolk. She checked the remaining
dead men.

She approached Kirk and said, "Sir, these men are
not showing up on the reader as Coast Guard personnel. The only victim that I got a reading on is a naval
petty officer."

His eyes went bleak, his body stiffening. "What is
a petty officer doing on a Coast Guard cutter in one of
our uniforms?" he growled.

"Could be there was some kind of undercover joint
operation, but that seems unlikely considering his low
rank."

He nodded. "Contact NCIS at Naval Station Norfolk
and alert them."

"Yes, sir," she said.

"Looks like our ME has his job cut out for him today," he murmured.

Special Agent Beau Jerrott turned over and smiled at the sweet blonde who was getting dressed in the light from the rising sun. Her name was Daisy, just like the pretty flower.

"You sure you have to go back to DC today, Beau, honey?"

"Aw, *chérie*, duty calls and I've gotta get back to the city."

She thrust out her bottom lip and finished zipping up her dress. "Too bad," she said, softly dropping down on the edge of the bed and pressing a kiss to his mouth. "You are simply one of the most gorgeous men I have ever laid my blue eyes on. Face of an angel."

He chuckled. "I'm no angel," he said.

She pulled away the sheet and looked down. "Nope, flesh-and-blood man. Much better. Ooh, look, you have something special for me."

He laughed and looked down at himself. He was a man and waking up with an erection was routine. "I'd say we had a good time last night." She sent her hand through his hair, her blue eyes full of carnal lust. He smiled, one hand slipping to the zipper on her dress, the other hiking it up on her thigh. "I don't have to leave exactly right now—" His cell phone rang just as he was pulling her back down on the bed.

She sighed and gave him another kiss. "I'm so tempted to stay and be very late for work, but it looks like duty is calling right now, Mr. Special Agent. You ever in Norfolk again, give me a call."

He grabbed his cell and smiled at her, cupping her

jaw and running his thumb along the plump curve of her cheek. "Jerrott," he said into the receiver as she rose. Giving him a look of regret, she picked up her purse and slipped out his hotel room door. She paused and blew him a quick kiss. He covered his heart and smiled.

"You left yet?"

Beau sighed, his eyes following the pretty blonde to her car, then focused on what his boss, Special Agent in Charge Christophe Vargas, was saying. "Just about to. What's up?"

"Just received a call from SA Michael Steele back at Naval Station Norfolk. There's a situation over in Hampton Roads. Dead petty officer on a CG cutter. They requested that you do a look-see and report back to him."

"Roger that."

Beau pushed back the covers and rose, stretching. Padding to the bathroom, he took a quick shower and dressed. After pulling out a power bar from his stash, he opened the wrapper and took a bite as he grabbed up his firearm. He tucked it into the shoulder holster and snagged the handcuffs and his ID. He stowed one in the case next to his weapon, and the ID in his back pocket. He pulled up the handle of his suitcase as he grabbed his black leather jacket off the hotel coatrack and left the room.

Once he stored his bag and polished off the power bar, he settled into the driver's seat. He entered the address for CG HQ into his GPS and pulled out of the parking lot.

The trip was quick. He parked and pulled out his ID to make his way to where the cutter was docked, CGIS guys crawling all over it.

Walking up the gangway, he stopped the first person he saw. "Who's in charge?"

The tall blond guy pointed to a trim man with a buzzed military cut in blue slacks and a white button-down, standing at the bow of the ship. "Special Agent Stafford."

Beau walked up to him. "Special Agent Stafford. Special Agent Beau Jerrott, NCIS. I hear you have a dead petty officer aboard?"

"We do." His cell phone rang and when he looked at the number, he said, "I've got to take this. See SA Cooper." He immediately turned away and spoke into the receiver, "Yes, sir?"

Beau turned to look for SA Cooper, whoever the hell he was. His eyes snagged on a woman in a CG jacket, running bra and black shorts standing near six covered bodies. He was confused by her for a moment. Not exactly professional gear, but the jacket threw him. Was she a witness?

There was something about her that kicked him right in his solar plexus and almost made it hard to take his next breath.

Her hair was a deep, burnished auburn.

Kryptonite.

Redheads were his Kryptonite.

What a freaking knockout, and that wasn't an overstatement. He guessed five-seven, one-twenty. Was she trying to play down her looks with that pulled-back hair and no makeup, no jewelry, nothing to enhance or draw the eyes? She'd failed. It only heightened her natural beauty. Her bone structure was lovely, delicate, feminine, her features equally so, her skin flawless, improved by the freckles across her cheeks and nose. There was something in her stunning face, some kind of…struggle. Her fists were clenched, her jaw tight. He immediately wanted to wrap his arms around her but didn't understand why.

His eyes traveled down her curvy, gorgeous body, the skin of her midriff creamy and soft looking. He took a breath. Her belly button was pierced, but he couldn't make out the pin. He wanted to get closer, but shook his head to clear it.

Protective instincts didn't normally surface unless he was in rescue mode. This woman seemed a little out of her element, a little lost, and for some damn reason, that made him want to be her knight. Immediately wary of those types of feelings, he took a mental step back. Not exactly the role he was used to playing. The one that suited him was a complete and utter rogue. That was why he normally went for the tough, confident women who knew how to play his game. Like Daisy. Easier that way.

Compelled, he stepped away from the occupied Stafford and toward the woman and the bodies. As he approached, she looked up, and it almost stopped him in his tracks. Her eyes were green and he had to reassess his little-lost-waif impression after seeing the steel in those thickly-lashed, straightforward emerald eyes.

Her gaze locked on his and for a moment they just stood there, the intensity of the connection almost tangible.

He was surprised to see the way she sized him up, the flash of censure in her face and then her eyes narrowing just slightly, as if he was some kind of threat. She intrigued him all the more and that was damn bad. He didn't want to be intrigued. Good thing he was heading out and back to DC after he was finished here.

"Who are you?" she said, taking in his leather jacket

and tailored pants, the steel from her eyes threaded through a voice that was both commanding and sultry.

His ID was still in his hand and he brought it up. "Special Agent Beau Jerrott, NCIS. I was invited to this shindig. Who are you?"

She straightened, realizing that she'd been rude. "This is a crime scene, so I'm being a hard-ass to protect evidence. I'm Special Agent Kinley Cooper."

She didn't offer her hand, but he liked that she didn't apologize. "Cooper? I was told to speak with a Cooper." He might like to charm the pants off the ladies, but when it came to his job, he was just as hard-core as he'd been on the teams. He switched gears. She was a professional and a fellow agent, which made her off-limits.

"You found her, then."

He'd found her all right, he just had to think of her as an investigator and not as a woman. It was not going to be an easy task. "Could you brief me?"

She explained how she'd just gone running—which explained her attire—when she'd heard the popping noises and the metal scraping.

He looked down at the bodies. "Which one is mine?"

She indicated the covered body at the end. He walked over and removed the sheet. He swore softly in Cajun French. He was just a wet-behind-the-ears kid. His black hair was military regulation, Caucasian, strong Roman nose and jaw, all and all a nice-looking kid, just barely a man. His lips tightened, a mixture of anger and regret for the loss of life. No matter how many times he looked at a body, it never got easier. He took in the Coast Guard uniform. "It's a fake," he said softly, examining the ribbons.

She looked at the ribbons wordlessly, then said, "You're right." She crouched down next to him to get a closer look, the heat of her body drifting over him, the light scent of her intoxicating. He turned his head and realized that she was too close for him to maintain any kind of balance between work and…play.

She must have realized that she was closer than was professionally acceptable. She wobbled and he reached out, snaking his arm around her waist to keep her from falling. Dragging her inadvertently against the length of his body. She was a pleasant weight against him. The skin of her bare stomach was soft against his hand, the warmth of her enticing. The top of her head fit right beneath his chin and the smell of her shampoo tickled his nostrils.

Startled, she made a soft sound, her head dropping back as her green eyes slammed into his. He rose with her to ground her completely before letting her go.

"Steady there, sailor," he said, his voice coming out huskier than he meant it to.

She gave him a quick, tight smile. "My fault. I was too eager to point out my findings."

"No worries," he replied and crouched down again. She walked around the bodies so that she was a fair distance from him. "These ribbons don't mean anything, just colored tape, and the CG emblem is missing."

She peered at the ribbons and gestured toward the sleeve where the emblem was absent, then looked up at him. "Exactly. Good eye, Jerrott."

"It's Beau," he said, and for a moment she stared at him before she dropped her gaze. "At first glance this might fool someone from a distance, but it's not going to fool anyone who's active-duty CG."

Using a pen he plucked from the inside of his leather jacket, he dug around the neck and came up empty. "No dog tags. They must have been removed after he was dead. Look at the abrasion here along the neck."

"Yes, I figured out he and his dead friends were posing as Coast Guard members."

"Looks that way, but when they executed their witnesses, they must have checked them over. Do you know who these other guys are?"

"No. There were no hits on them. They definitely aren't in the military database. We're going to have to identify them through forensics."

He nodded. "So, we have six dead men on an unidentified CG cutter. It's a good-size ship. What exactly were they trying to get to shore? Contraband? Illegal immigrants? Weapons?" he asked. Or even worse. "Terrorists?"

"Terrorists?" Her jaw clenched. He could see that was a definite button pusher for her. She looked out over the ocean, deep sorrow in her eyes.

"It's our job to make sure to find out," she growled, the sorrow replaced by a snapping anger that went deep. Personal deep.

He had to wonder how this warrior waif had come into contact with terrorists.

His gut clenched at the thought of how many unknowns there were in this grisly case already, and how he was lucky he was going back to DC and getting away from the lovely and complex Kinley Cooper.

Chapter 2

There was no denying how simply drop-dead gorgeous Special Agent Beau Jerrott was. A woman would have to be dead to not be affected by his tousled black hair, those penetrating eyes and that just-French-enough accent he had going.

He caught her first with the magnetic quality of his dark blue eyes, glittering with devilish light. When their eyes met, something tangible sizzled between them.

A grin unfurled, slowly, easily, cutting a pair of dimples into his lean, tanned cheeks. Kinley felt as if someone had just gut-punched her. The smile transformed a face that had only moments ago looked stern and unapproachable. His mouth was wide and mobile, the lips wonderfully masculine and full, accentuated by the faint stubble across his upper lip and around his chin. His thick, dark hair lay across his forehead, the rest tapering down in a medium layer cut that framed his striking face.

First off, she wasn't going to give in to an attraction that could spell disaster for her professional career. That was her one and only focus. Rising in the ranks to eventually run her own team. She knew how the boys' club worked. Sleeping with fellow agents regardless of what alphabet-soup agency they belonged to wasn't smart. She'd discovered that the hard way.

"What else did you find?" he asked as he rose.

"I was just going to search the bridge and gather evidence if you'd like to tag along," she said, keeping her voice neutral and cool. She grabbed some evidence bags and headed toward the bridge as he followed.

"What other info do you have on Dixon? Where is his family located? You're going to want to interview them," Beau said.

"I'm aware of that. I'm not some novice," she said, turning on him, her words sounding more than a little snappish. She didn't need him telling her how to run an investigation.

He stopped when she did and shifted his weight. He didn't say anything and Kinley realized that she was reacting to the previous pressure, the anniversary of her father's death, and the horrific find she'd literally stumbled on in the fog.

But it was best that he realize he wasn't dealing with any kind of pushover.

"I wasn't suggesting you were. Just thinking out loud," he said, his voice very calm.

Of course he wasn't suggesting that. What an easy backtrack, but instead of just viewing a strong woman as assertive, *bitch* was the watchword. She didn't care.

"His parents live here in Norfolk. My plan was to finish here and go over to their residence and…break the news along with questioning them." She again kept her voice neutral and cool to counteract the heat the man generated. She entered the bridge and he followed, and the expansive area felt smaller with his presence. He smelled so good, a combination of spicy and male.

"Breaking the news is the worst part of the job," he said, crowding her enough that she felt the need to back up so he could look around. She was all for a second pair of eyes as long as they were scoping out evidence and not on her.

She was momentarily distracted by the unusual color of his eyes and the sadness there. She couldn't seem to stop her immediate reaction to that emotion. It was both a personal sadness and a general one. She knew nothing about him, but the fact that he was affected made her heart beat a little harder.

"It's tough," she said noncommittally, not allowing herself to even bend that much.

"Not to get you all riled up again, but have you handled many murder investigations?" He tilted his head and his unruly hair tumbled down over his forehead. He shoved it back carelessly. "Not sure about the stats, is all."

She stiffened, taking a steadying breath. The fact was that she'd handled all of two murder cases and one turned out to be suicide, which she'd proved. She'd spent the past eighteen months on a drug-smuggling task force with the DEA. "I may not have handled as many murders as you have, but I do have experience," she said.

He nodded. "I'm not here to challenge you, Agent Cooper. It's all about those dead men. We are all that stands between them and justice. I'm just taking notes for now."

"Got it," she said. "It's been…a tough day, and I don't envision it getting any easier. No offense."

"None taken," he said, pulling on the latex gloves she offered him. Walking over to the captain's chair, he searched around it, and then moved to the console. "How many crew members were found in here?"

"Three. That's less than the bare minimum required to pilot the ship." She watched him, finding it difficult not to. The way he moved with such grace was a pleasure to look at. "Agent Jerrott," she said with curiosity, blatantly ignoring the weird rhythm her pulse had taken up. "You said pretty much what I thought out on the deck about those dead men. They were posing and I agree. It must have something to do with evading us. We fiercely guard this coast. We just broke up a huge drug-smuggling operation with a tanker and go-fast boats using the bay to transport drugs into this area, then up and down the East Coast."

He nodded. "I haven't dealt with drug smuggling. It's been mostly murder and high-profile cases. We prevented a security breach with one of our navy scientists just recently, a kidnapping." His eyes traveled over her and she got the distinct impression that he got momentarily distracted. His eyes were frank and appreciating. This was not good. She had no intention of making the same blunder again.

"Sounds like you're the best person for this detail if drugs are involved," he said.

She didn't know what to say to that. As a way to get her to lower her defenses, that was a good move and very effective. He was charming, that much was clear.

His attention was diverted from her to the deck. He crouched down and examined an area near the back of the bridge. "Bring an evidence bag over here," he said, reaching out to her as she moved closer to him.

A bit peeved by his request for her to be a fetch-and-carry, she asked, "What did you find?" She was still feeling the effects of his words and not trusting herself. She'd trusted once before and had gotten terribly burned.

He brushed something into the bag and rose. Standing this close, looking into his eyes, she saw no sign of manipulation, no wavering. He was either very, very good at it or he was being sincere.

His eyes sparkled with the discovery. He seemed to love this as much as she did. The puzzle, the mystery, the unraveling of threats to the US. "A white powder. Could be cocaine or heroin."

She took the bag out of his hand. "I'd rather not jump to conclusions. Guessing gives me hives."

He chuckled. "Ah, methodical, huh? I personally detest red tape."

Kinley narrowed her eyes. "Not very PC of you."

He smiled and, again, got much too close for her comfort. "I don't exactly worry my pretty head over being PC," he said, bending a little closer, holding her gaze with his. His eyes followed the path of a curl as it escaped her tight, pulled-back hair.

His voice was low and smoky, Cajun spiced and as tempting as sin itself. Kinley felt that voice, like his smile, had the power to touch her. It trailed down the side of her neck and caressed like a fingertip down the length of her arm. She stiffened against the urge to shiver. The man was an absolute seducer. She had no business reacting to him on such a...a...carnal level. She was a self-respecting, self-sufficient woman who expected—no, demanded—to be treated in a manner that didn't involve hormones.

She was on the job, for God's sake.

Drawing in a slow, deep breath to steady herself, she raised her chin and said, "You cut corners?" She shook her head. Her middle name was control. "I prefer to adhere to the rules. It's better that way." Dammit, she sounded so defensive. But look what had happened when she'd let her guard down once. Just once.

He laughed. The sound was as captivating as his voice.

"There's nothing wrong with following the rules…" He shot her a look as he moved to the far end of the bridge, his eyes trailing along the console. "Up until the point it becomes necessary to break them, no."

"In my experience that leads to nothing good." Kinley searched around at the rear of the bridge.

He continued to search and didn't respond to her. "There's something behind here."

"What is it?"

"Another bag."

She grabbed one and headed over to where he was. Darn, she wasn't his gofer. He reached behind the metal bolted to the side of the bridge and pulled out gauze bandages. "There's blood on them." He set them into the bag and she closed it up.

"Good find," she said.

He pulled off the latex gloves. "The ME has his work cut out for him." She got caught in his intense, dark gaze, was held captive and mesmerized. He leaned over, giving her a challenging look, all the time his eyes locked on her. Everything suspended, time, movement, breath; even the ocean seemed to go…still.

The experience was seductive, intimate and unnerving.

She stared right back at him, refusing to be seduced or intimidated. Refusing to admit to either, at any rate. He grinned, as if amused by her spunk, and broke off the eye contact to step back.

"He's up to the challenge."

His mouth curved. "I've no doubt." He looked at his watch. "I've got to get going."

"All right. Could you keep me posted on your petty officer? I'll have the body transferred to Naval Station Norfolk…"

"You should contact the NCIS Office. I'm heading back."

He took a step forward and she took an automatic step backward, chastising herself for it. This man was the kind who would sense a weakness and exploit it. She could feel it, could see it in the way his dark gaze seemed to catch everything. She took a quick, hot breath.

"You're leaving? You don't work here in Norfolk?"

He pivoted around her and sauntered away, his walk naturally cocky. Kinley watched him, astounded by her disappointment, infuriated by her reaction to him, something deeply, intrinsically female in her admiring the way his slacks fit his backside. She shook off the thought, disgusted with herself, and went after him.

"No, I was on temporary assignment. The office was short staffed."

The fog had lifted and it was clear, the sky meeting the very blue of the ocean. The sound of the dock area was a constant din and the soft cadence of the cutter rocked against the protective rubber buoys with a hollow sound. The squawking of the seagulls, creaking of the ropes and hum of traffic rolling past on the street added to the background noise. The air was filled with the scent of salt and the ripe, briny aroma of seaweed.

He glanced back at her, and she wasn't sure why she fell into step beside him. Going through the doorway, she gritted her teeth as her disappointment intensified.

"Who should I contact, specifically?" she asked, following him down the gangway to the dock as he headed for the parking lot.

"Mike Steele. He's the SAC over there," Beau said.

When he reached a sleek cobalt-blue Mustang that screamed, *I'm fast*, he pressed the door release and grabbed the handle, pulling it open. She caught a glimpse of a black leather interior.

"Where exactly are you from, then?"

"They were shorthanded and requested assistance from us in DC." He closed the door and folded his arms over his chest. He looked indifferent and lazy leaning back against the car, but Kinley wasn't fooled.

"DC?" Oh man, was he a hotshot from major cases? "The Navy Yard?" She didn't like being caught off balance, and Beau Jerrott seemed to be a master at throwing her.

His gaze held hers fast. "Yes, the Navy Yard."

She wanted lead on this case and she wanted to be given her own team. This cutter mystery could propel her to where she wanted to go. It suited her that he was leaving, both professionally and personally.

He shifted his weight forward, invading her personal space once again, and she had to fight to keep from jumping back as her tension level rose into the red zone. She held her ground and tilted her chin up to look him in the eye.

"Ambition can bite you in the butt," he murmured.

"What?" she answered, breathless and hating it. Her

nerves gave a warning tremor as control of the situation seemed to slip a little farther out of her grasp.

"I see that competitive gleam in your eye. What do you need to prove and who do you need to prove it to?"

She gave a half laugh of impatience, shifting position in a way that put another inch of space between them. "I won't lie. This is a promotion-making case and I've…been working on that. So, yes, I'm ambitious."

"At least you know the chain that binds you," he drawled, shuffling his feet, inching his way into her space again. "That's a good thing. Just don't lose sight of the shore. Being a sailor, that's always in us. The shore."

"That's cryptic advice."

There was that grin again and those dimples. "I think you like a puzzle, lady," he said.

"Why are you here?"

"To give them my opinion," Beau said. "I'll do that and head out. My only regret is that I won't be helping Dixon get his justice. Good luck with the investigation."

Kinley drew a deep breath through her nostrils, trying in vain to stem the rising tide of attraction. "I could keep you posted about the investigation, if you wanted me to. Do you have a card?"

He arched a brow. "Sure, that would be good." His voice dropped an octave, back to that smoky tone.

Really, it was best he was going back to DC.

He fished out a card and handed it to her. But when she went to take it, he didn't let go. His blue eyes bore into her, suddenly intense, suddenly serious. "If they had no qualms about brutally killing six men, they will stop at nothing."

"With your petty officer in the middle of it?"

He turned back to the car and opened the door again,

slipping inside. "Looks that way, but this is your home turf. Bye, *Special* Agent Cooper."

He closed the door and started the car. Feeling oddly deflated, she headed back to the ship.

"Hey, Cooper." She turned around to find him still sitting in the parking lot, the window rolled down.

"What?" she said.

"You be careful."

"I can take care of myself, Agent Jerrott."

Damn.

He wasn't her protector. She didn't need one. So why was he compelled to tell her to be careful? Something about her made him want to unravel her control, make her want to break some rules. He was the man to do it. But only on a temporary basis. *Laissez les bons temps rouler.* Let the good times roll. Except, he would keep his distance and his perspective. He had never slept with a coworker before, even though, technically, Kinley wasn't his coworker. She was a wild card and she tested his resolve.

Special Agent Kinley Cooper was a very beautiful woman, but he wasn't headed for any kind of downfall. He was headed out of town and back to DC where he belonged. He'd already been in Norfolk for longer than he'd planned. His boss, Chris Vargas, wanted him back.

His cell rang as he pulled into the NCIS field office in Norfolk.

"Jerrott," he said as he got out of the car.

"Beau, it's Chris. Where are you now?"

He leaned on the roof of the car, the fall sun warm on the back of his neck. "I'm just getting to the field office to give them my take on the cutter they found with Dixon's body aboard."

"Good. You're staying."

"What? I thought you needed me back in DC?"

"We can manage without you, but SECNAV and the Commandant of the Coast Guard decided it's best to assign a two-agent team to the investigation and they're still shorthanded. You'll do all your work right from the field office on Naval Station Norfolk."

"Copy that. Who's the CGIS agent?" He looked over at a car that had just pulled into the spot next to his. The sun flashed on auburn hair and that gorgeous face rose into his line of vision just as Chris said, "Special Agent Kinley Cooper."

Beau groaned when she looked at him over the roof of her car with the same kind of look that was probably on his face right now.

"Problem?"

"Ah, no, she seems competent. I can handle her." He saw her mouth tighten and he smirked, loving her sass. Her green eyes narrowed at him and she snorted.

Chris laughed. "Well, good, then she'll keep you in line. I want regular reports."

He tilted his head, shoving back his hair, and she watched his every move. Uh-huh, she was just as interested in him as he was in her. "Yes, sir."

He flashed her one of his knockout grins and she looked at him like she was totally unimpressed. Trouble was what she looked like, and not the kind he usually dove into headfirst, either. He was in for a whole lot of hot and cold.

Hot case for them.

Cold shoulder from her.

Cold showers for him.

Chapter 3

Shortly after she closed her car door and they both headed for the NCIS office, another car pulled up. Beau turned to find SAC Stafford popping out of the car. He waved to them, pushed his door closed and came around the car.

Reaching them, they fell into step together. "Sir," Kinley said, giving Beau a sidelong look.

"I'm just here to give you your marching orders and to confer with SAC Steele." He gave Beau a nod. Once inside the office, SAC Steele came forward and shook hands with SAC Stafford.

He did a double take with Kinley. Beau didn't like it. Mike was married with two kids, yet the way he looked at her made Beau feel...damn proprietary when he had no reason to keep tabs on the redhead. In fact, she'd been cool toward him. She was going to be someone he worked with and that was it. He had to think about her like he did with his coworker Special Agent Amber

Dalton back in DC, who was like an annoying kid sister to him. Except he didn't have *those* thoughts about Amber or his sister.

Unlike him, Kinley offered her hand to Mike and he shook it with an appreciative smile crossing his face. "Sounds like you had a harrowing morning, Special Agent Cooper.

"Oh, please call me Kinley."

Beau bristled. Why hadn't she made the same offer to him? He took a deep breath. Why the hell was he acting like a spurned high schooler? He'd had girls all over him from the moment he could remember. The older he got the more he understood about how beautiful, soft and heartbreaking they could be. Okay, just once with the heartbreak, but that was more than enough. He wasn't prepared to go through losing a woman he loved like he had with Jennifer.

Sweet, *oh-please-call-me-Kinley* had heartbreaker written all over her, and he was worried that it would be in a way that was both unexpected and irresistible.

It was hard to find himself feeling a bit at a loss with a woman.

"I have the address of Petty Officer Dixon for you. His record was clean. Spotless, in fact. He was a good sailor and had never gotten into trouble. But go ahead and talk to his CO. He was stationed on..."

"The USS *Daniel Robinson*, Arleigh Burke–class destroyer, larger and more heavily armed than its predecessors," Kinley said.

"Yes, that's right. You know your ships," Mike said. "His family is actually in Norfolk." He handed Beau a scrap of paper and he went to pull out his phone and enter the address into his GPS.

"I know where that is," Kinley said softly, looking at

the paper. "Thank you for staying and lending a helping hand, again, Beau."

"Of course. I'm yours until you get some hands on deck."

"That's good, because both SECNAV and the Commandant of the Coast Guard want you to lead this investigation. With your SEAL background and your exemplary record, we're damn lucky to have you on this."

He heard the small gasp and saw her stiffen beside him, even as he was focusing on what Mike was saying. He glanced at Kinley, but she wasn't looking at him. Her eyes were suddenly carrying that bruised expression again, before it was suddenly replaced with anger.

Right. She wanted lead on this and, well, he'd effectively stolen her thunder, though he definitely was qualified for this investigation after having come off that special op for NCIS in Afghanistan. He still didn't like thinking about it.

He heard Kinley's boss ask to speak with her and they walked to the back of the room. He spoke to her quickly and at the end of it squeezed her shoulder. Her voice was quiet, but it was laced with anger. Stafford said something low and soothing sounding, but it didn't appease her. She brushed past him and slammed out of the office. Mike watched her go with that same male look in his eyes. And it torqued Beau off all over again.

Stafford grabbed his arm as he was heading out the door. "She expected to take lead. I tried to let her know about your qualifications, but there are extenuating circumstances I can't go into, and suffice it to say she's… uh…pissed."

"Yeah, with my great observational skills I got that."

"I could probably assign someone else—"

"No. She discovered all this. She has a right to be included in this case. I wouldn't want to take that away from her. I can handle it."

"I agree. She has earned her place here. It'll just take her a few minutes to calm down."

Beau didn't mind her anger. It showed that she cared enough to get mad. What he had to have was cooperation and that was more important than who led the damn team.

Outside she was pacing, the strong muscles in her thighs and calves rippling as she moved. She looked mad enough to shoot him. A really good reason never to date a woman with a gun. Her red brows were drawn together in a furious scowl. For the first time, he noticed the dark stain on her bra and her shorts. It looked like…blood.

She had been through quite a bit this morning. He approached her. She gave him a look that told him she hadn't quite gotten to a calmed-down place yet.

"Listen, Cooper…"

"No. I don't think so. Not right now. Just let me work it out."

She turned to leave and he followed close behind.

"I'll drive," she said flatly, then turned to him and gave him a steely-eyed glare. Nope, he wasn't going to get any kind of offer to call her Kinley and irrationally, he wanted her to ask him to. Most women it was easy to become familiar with. They never minded him calling them by their first names. Kinley wasn't only his Kryptonite; she was as hard as the fabled rock. "That is, if I have *your* permission."

He shrugged and moved to her car. She tucked in behind the wheel. "If you don't mind, I need to go home and change into more appropriate clothes."

"I don't mind," he said, keeping his voice neutral. She was pissed and he was in a position to step on her toes. It wasn't anything he couldn't handle. That thought brought with it a vision of his hands all over her. He brushed that aside. Professional situation. Professional behavior. There was something about her that made him wary. He couldn't quite put his finger on it.

She put the car in gear, but said nothing as she drove.

"Do you want to talk about it?"

"No."

She was about to see his persistent side.

"Why not? It's obvious that you're upset about me taking lead. Don't you think it would be best to clear the air?"

"There is zero I can do about it except fume."

"I didn't come here to step all over your case, if that helps."

"It doesn't."

"Cooper. I understand—"

"What? No you don't. Are you a woman trying to make it in a career that is predominantly male? You have to be smarter, faster and tougher than they are. And you can make zero mistakes. Unfortunately, I made a big blunder." She winced and swore softly under her breath.

"What kind of blunder?"

"None of your business. It doesn't affect my performance on this case." She ignored him completely after that, focusing instead on maneuvering them across the highway over the expanse of the Chesapeake Bay.

"Have you ever broken the news to a family?"

Her hands tightened on the steering wheel, and she took a quick breath. "No. I haven't. I can't imagine it's going to be the part of this job I like best."

When she pulled up to a small house across from

the beach, she got out and he followed her silent, curvy figure into her house.

"I would really like to take a quick shower. I've… got blood all over me."

"Of course. We're about to destroy Dixon's parents' world. Let them have a little bit more time."

She bit her lip, nodded and disappeared into the bathroom. He heard the shower come on and steered himself and his thoughts away from the delectable Kinley, naked, getting wet. Damn. That made him hard.

He sighed. Give him an uncomplicated woman like Daisy.

Her house was decorated in an eclectic style that was neat and beachy. Outside the sliding-glass door in the back was a small backyard with a barbeque and a nice patio. All she was missing was the white picket fence out front.

He went into her refrigerator and pulled out a bottle of water and unscrewed the top.

"I'm sure that you've been in a lot more muck and blood than I could have ever imagined."

He walked toward the sound of her voice. "That's for sure. I've been through swamps and mud, monsoon rains, dust-dry deserts and…" His voice just stopped, the water bottle halfway to his lips. His body froze. Whatever thought he was going to make just ended abruptly as if he'd suddenly dropped into a coma. His mouth went as dry as the desert he had just mentioned.

Her door was ajar just enough that he could see the full-length mirror on her closet door and it was… Damn…his brain just went to mush. There were no words to describe her naked body.

He slid his gaze over her. Her hair was down out of the ponytail and hung around her in a tumble of red clumps of silk, her lips moist. Her face was flushed with heat.

His throat tightened, his whole body tightened, as he watched a droplet of water trail down the dusky, soft-looking skin of her shoulder, over the enticing, plump, beautiful curve of her breast, down over her delicate rib cage, over her narrow hips and well-formed thigh.

He'd literally never been blindsided by a woman before, but she was so utterly gorgeous from the top of her red head to her red-painted toenails and he couldn't look away.

He knew he should turn his back and walk away. Stop looking.

But the message just got all jumbled up in his brain. That was something that also never happened to him.

Then those green eyes rose. She stilled and met his eyes in the mirror. She was raw Kryptonite, giving off an interstellar force of exponential power and frying his brain. She gasped and that sound shot through him like wildfire. Damn. It was like being caught in a tractor beam. He went weak. He swore his knees buckled. From the depths of those wide, dark-fringed eyes she returned his look, as if she couldn't look away, either.

He knew lust, and it was running hot through his veins, but there was something more. Something beyond the burning ache he felt for her. Something fiercer, with an edge of desperation he was trying to ignore and could barely comprehend.

She looked at him like he set her on fire, made her gasp. It was crazy. Crazy and hot and utterly sexual in a way he'd thought he would never know. Every encounter he'd ever had paled in comparison to just looking at her. The reality of it was so much more intense. The pure physical energy of her was a force to be reckoned with.

Joint Engagement

She was powerful, dangerous and unpredictably seductive.

It was as if he was touching her, breathing her in instead of just staring at her.

He'd felt it the moment he'd met her. Something…an
elemental vibe that coursed through him. It was easy
to think of her being beautiful because she was. Heart-
breakingly.

But that wasn't it. There was something inherent in
her. Something he wanted to…take…have.

He couldn't explain it. But he wanted it more than
he wanted that delectable body. It scared the living hell
right out of him.

When he expected her to look away, a soft casting
downward of her eyes, a lowering of her lashes, she
didn't. It made him want her more. She just stared at
him, caught up in him.

What did she see in him?

It was like a missing piece in this whole puzzle. He
was a lost cause. He'd slept around, didn't always remember names. Usually one night was all there was
even when he liked the girl. He'd been down that bumpy
road and he wasn't going down it again.

But she… Damn… What a cluster. She heated him
into more than lust. It was a yearning, a one-on-one
he'd never experienced before.

The sunlight cut into the room, just barely illuminated one of her legs. Standing there, shadows washed
across her, highlighting curves, she made his heart beat
hard.

In an instant, at first sight, she was special, and what
he wanted from her was a chance to see where it all
went. The sheer potential of the two of them meeting
somewhere he'd never been before.

Just a chance to lay himself up against her, to connect with her, mouth to mouth, body to body, to see if she could save him from all that running. Maybe just a bit, just enough to take the sharp edges off his dreams, to break the barriers that were as strong as Fort Knox. She was some kinda siege breaker.

He took two steps to the door and pulled it closed. Breathing hard, he wiped his hand across his mouth. What the hell was he thinking? This case had all the markings of something that could take a good bit of time to solve. He'd never felt this kind of attraction in his life.

He was hard-pressed to keep his ethics intact. It didn't matter if the girl had a cosmic hold on him. He wasn't going to do it. The barriers were as strong as he could make them. Pain was something he was used to. He'd been in blowing snow that froze fingers and toes and ran through the body like a hard, subzero knife; in cold water that would give someone hypothermia in seconds. He'd been shot, mortared, had shrapnel flying around him, and been beaten, knifed and, once, hit with a lead pipe. He'd gotten through Hell Week. He knew pain, but none of that was like what Jennifer had done to him. She'd shredded his heart, shredded it on purpose.

Instead of opening up about how she really felt, she'd sandbagged him for a long time, then literally packed up and took off without a word to him, leaving him emotionally stranded with an engagement ring in his pocket.

But Special Agent Kinley Cooper was a much bigger threat. She possessed Jennifer's go-for-the-jugular attitude. But she had a softer side to her that could undermine his ability to keep his distance, something he'd done ever since Jennifer had wrecked him.

He walked away from the door and back to the living room, sitting down on the couch. She had exercise magazines on the coffee table. *Yoga Art* and *Running*. When he heard the door open, he picked up a magazine.

"You really into yoga or are you just acting nonchalant?" Kinley asked.

Oh, she was going to hit it head-on. She could talk about this, but not about what was cheesing her off about him taking lead. "Do I look like the kind of guy that can bend himself into a pretzel? I'm sorry about that. I didn't mean to—"

"It wasn't your fault. I was the one who didn't close the door all the way." She tilted her head. Her hair was pulled back again, and she was dressed in a pair of slim white pants that came to her ankles and a red shirt that did nothing to stem the memory of how her breasts had looked.

"We have a professional relationship, so we'll just forget this ever happened. Right?"

Like hell. "Yes, absolutely." How could she say this like the connection they'd made hadn't been hot enough to melt metal?

She gave him a tight smile. "That's good, Agent Jerrott."

"Could you try to call me Beau?"

"I don't think so."

Okay, it shouldn't make him steam that she seemed totally unaffected. Had that all been one-sided in there? Hell, he needed to get a grip.

He stood and turned. She was at the fridge getting a bottle of water, and that was when he saw her take a deep breath, shiver oh so slightly. She rubbed the bottle on the back of her neck.

He grinned. It came from somewhere deep, deep inside him. A complete joy that he couldn't contain, even as he knew it was wrong to even contemplate that she felt the same way. She had been affected by that look they'd exchanged.

Then the smile faded from his face and that joy banked. His gut clenched in a way that brought that terror back. He read vulnerability there in the lines of her body, in the way she held herself. It tugged at his heart.

Shaken once again by this woman, he was caught off guard as she touched something raw inside him. "So," he said, turning his back to her, giving her a moment to compose herself. Or was he the one that needed the time? After a few seconds, he walked around the couch and approached her. She had straightened and put that neutral look back on her face, had the bottle unscrewed and was taking a sip. "You still mad at me?"

"Let's put it this way. I'm mad at the circumstances. I'm mad because I messed it up for myself. I want to clear this case. Discover exactly where that cutter came from, who murdered those men and what they were smuggling aboard that ship. That and that alone has to be our focus."

"Then we're on the same page. We're a team. You ready to go and get some answers?"

She nodded and walked around the counter as he made space for her to move in front of him. The scent of her was intoxicating as he followed her out the door.

Back in her car, she drove them over to the address they were given.

Parking in front of a nice residential home with pretty flowers lining the walk, they found a middle-aged woman on her knees on the concrete, planting what looked like her last batch of flowers. *Marigolds*, he thought.

Something about her reminded him of his own *mère*, who had been so grateful every time he came home from leave. His *père* was also a strong presence in his life, but his *mère* had taught him that while violence was maybe sometimes the answer, most of the time it wasn't. She helped him to understand himself at a young age and learn his strengths. Most everything he'd ever tried came easily to him. Schoolwork, sports, friendships and girls. Especially girls. Even the navy had been something that really hadn't challenged him.

It wasn't until he'd stepped onto that beach at Coronado that things got tough, then got tougher, then dropped them all into hell.

But there wasn't a day that didn't go by on the teams that he wasn't thankful for that training.

He'd been humiliated, called pretty boy, candy boy, obscenities shouted in his face every day. Very little sleep, scarcely any rest. When they hadn't been immersed in cold water, they'd been lugging gigantic logs. Tests that were designed to break a man down to the very fabric of his soul to see what he was really made of. It was then that he'd realized it wasn't about the physical or the body at all. It was all about his mind and determination. It was all mental. Because really, that fueled everything.

And he'd gotten basic, so damned basic.

But they hadn't broken him.

There was no ringing out for him.

The woman raised her head and stilled as soon as she saw them, her face wary and her eyes anxious.

"Mrs. Dixon?"

She nodded and came to her feet, pulling off the gardening gloves. "Can I help you?"

"I'm Special Agent Beau Jerrott, NCIS, and this is Special Agent Kinley Cooper, CGIS."

"NCIS…oh, God. Cameron? Has something happened?"

"Could we go inside?"

Full-blown worry on her face, she called out, "Matt!"

A man came to the screen door and there was no doubt that this was Cameron's father. The likeness was uncanny. When he saw his agitated wife coming up the stairs, he opened the door, alarm on his face when he turned to look at them.

Beau indicated that Kinley should precede him. She climbed the stairs with him close behind. Once they were seated in the living room, Beau leaned forward. "I'm sorry to have to break this news to you, but we found your son's body today."

Mrs. Dixon's wail of pain was muffled as she buried her face into her husband's throat. He just looked at Beau as if this wasn't real.

Beau didn't speak for a few minutes. He gave Cameron's parents a few minutes to absorb the shock of their son's death. He ached for the Dixons and their loss.

Finally, Matt Dixon said, "What happened?"

"He was shot to death and was found aboard a Coast Guard cutter drifting on the tide." Beau wished he didn't have to deliver this news, but there wasn't any way to soften the blow of hearing the details of their son's death.

"What?" he said, his face full of confusion. "Cameron was in the navy. I don't understand."

"That's what we're trying to figure out, Mr. Dixon. Cameron was in a Coast Guard uniform."

Mrs. Dixon turned her face toward them, leaning against her husband, wiping at her eyes with a tissue. She pulled herself together by sheer will and Beau got a glimpse into why Cameron had such a spotless record. She nodded at him and slipped her hand into her husband's. "How can we help?"

"When was the last time you talked to him?"

"About a week ago. He was going on leave to the Bahamas with some of his friends."

Beau exchanged a look with Kinley. She said, "We often sell off decommissioned cutters. It's possible this one was sold to the Bahamians. It's a good place to start."

Dread coursed through him. He nodded. "These friends…would you have their names?"

"Why?" When she saw the looks on their faces, she closed her eyes.

"There're six bodies in all," Beau said. "The other five were not military personnel." He couldn't imagine what they must be going through now. His heart ached for them.

"Oh, no, no, no," she said, losing speech for a moment, her husband rubbing at her back. "Mike Levin, Pete Samson and Buck… I mean David Walters. His nickname is Buck…" She trailed off, sobbing a bit. "Those guys were inseparable when they were boys." She broke down, clutching her midsection in even deeper grief. "Oh God. Mark's parents still live across the street and Pete's are a block over. Buck's parents died last year in a car accident and he and his brother, Tommy, and Tommy's wife, live next door. They inherited the house."

Beau had a sinking sensation that three of the bodies they'd found on that ship were possibly Cameron's friends.

She dabbed at her eyes and rested back against her husband. "Melissa, Tommy's wife should be home."

"How did he sound?"

"Happy," she said, her voice thickening. "They were supposed to fly back today and Cameron was visiting us late this afternoon. It's our fiftieth wedding anniversary today." Tears welled and slipped down her cheeks. "We were going to celebrate before he had to go back to his ship tomorrow when his leave was up."

"I'm so sorry," Kinley said, her heart in her eyes.

"He said he had a great surprise for us." Mrs. Dixon's face contorted in pain. "We got his surprise yesterday," she choked, then started crying again, burying her face into her husband's neck.

"What was it?" Beau asked.

Mr. Dixon, his eyes glistening, said, "An all-expenses-paid trip to Paris for our anniversary. My wife has always wanted to go." Then he broke down, clutching his grieving wife to him.

Chapter 4

After leaving the Dixons', Kinley still felt the keenness of their pain. Neither of them spoke as they walked next door, an ache in her throat. Mr. and Mrs. Dixon had identified three of the five men found dead with Cameron from the pictures on Beau's phone.

The Dixons' grief brought back the memory of her own and how horribly difficult it was to get over her father's death. The ache intensified.

The anniversary of his death had been one of the longest days of her life.

It was enough for her to deal with without having to deal with Beau and the way he had looked at her when she'd been completely naked in her bedroom. It was totally unexpected. She hadn't wanted that kind of connection to him. But there was something between them. A heavy attraction. How could she deny that? Her palms started sweating thinking about how he'd looked at her.

Under normal circumstances she would think he

was gorgeous. Drop-freaking-dead gorgeous. But these weren't normal circumstances. That hair, that accent and those eyes. The kind of man who could have any woman he wanted, and she suspected he did. There was also something very subtle and completely seductive about the way he moved, the way he talked and the way he looked at not only her but at anyone. With deep interest, as if whatever was being said was completely important to him.

This was work, and she'd already made a colossal mistake with Daniel and paid the price. The ending of their budding relationship, demerits for both him and her, and bitterness between the two of them.

"Sometimes I hate this job."

Kinley barely heard him, her attention focusing almost completely inward, everything else becoming vague and peripheral. A shudder of tension rattled through her, stronger than ever. She tried to steel herself against it and failed.

Failed.

This is an irresponsible and detrimental breach. Distractions get people killed, Agent Cooper.

She couldn't make the same mistake twice. She'd let down her guard and look what had happened. Daniel had been angry when she wouldn't make the concession and leave the CG so they could be together. He'd been a jerk. He'd betrayed her and her trust. He'd left her out to dry.

She really didn't want to feel a connection to Beau, but she couldn't seem to help it. She might have been able to manage if he hadn't seen her naked and done absolutely nothing about it, closing the door and keeping his distance and comments to himself. In fact, his restraint had only disarmed her more. He hadn't made one crass joke or given her any indication that only two hours ago, she'd been bared to his eyes.

God, she must be out of her mind with either her preoccupation with her father's anniversary or the fact that Beau had quite literally stolen lead on this case from her. She should be completely angry at him, but she wasn't. She was still frustrated and irritated, but could she blame Beau? Really, could she?

They reached the front door and Beau knocked. After a couple of minutes, a petite blonde woman opened the door.

"Can I help you?"

Beau flashed his badge, and Kinley did as well as he introduced them.

"What's this about?"

"Your brother-in-law."

"Is David okay?"

"I'm afraid not."

"Oh, God."

She called her husband as soon as Beau broke the news, then invited them in. Once she was seated on the couch, Kinley said, "Can you give us any information about his stay in the Bahamas?"

She wiped at her eyes. "He was having a great time. He and his friends had always been close. He was also ecstatic about something else, said he had landed this amazing job. I think he might have been a bit drunk when he called. He said it would be a piece of cake and a boat ride, and that he'd be home soon to help us out."

"So he was taking some kind of job? Did he mention what it was?"

"He said it was like Halloween. Dress up. He got interrupted when he was on the phone. Some angry guy was yelling and he had to hang up. He was a good kid. He really was. How could this have happened?"

"We think he got hooked up with some bad people. I'm not sure he was aware of who they really were if that is any consolation."

"Melissa?"

She rose from the couch and ran to the foyer to wrap her arms around her husband. He buried his face in her neck with a devastated look on his face.

"Looks like they played these guys with offers of money to pose as Coast Guard and it got them all killed," Beau said.

"Yes, so what was it they were smuggling into the country? We need to alert Homeland Security," she said.

Beau nodded. "And dig deeper."

They left a grieving Tommy and Melissa and interviewed the other victims' next of kin and got similar stories. Mark's mother indicated that it was some kind of Hollywood film and all they had to do was act as extras.

It was really hard to break the news to two more sets of parents. Kinley struggled to stay neutral, but it was so difficult when she knew what it was to lose a beloved family member. She had to get through this day as best she could. She was determined to find the scum who had murdered those kids, to make sure they paid. But the threat to the United States had to take precedence for now. They needed to identify the cutter and trace it to try to figure out what had happened. There was also the case of the last two unidentified men. That task they would have to leave up to the ME.

After they finished the last interview, Beau stood outside the house, partly in shadow. She couldn't help looking at him. She knew she should just stop. Stop analyzing him. Stop getting more involved with him. Never mind the looks and the magnetism. Just stop.

She held her silence, sensing that he was quietly seething. He stared out onto the residential street. "I went into the navy to protect—" he lifted his hand to encompass the street of pretty houses, small children playing outside, their laughter contagious "—all this."

His eyes glittered in the sunlight that cut across his face, his dark hair absorbing the light, the sun bathing his features in a golden glow—a high, wide forehead, dark arched brows, an aquiline nose that looked as if it might have been broken once or twice in his thirty-some years.

He looked like a battle-ready warrior, a man who pushed himself to his physical and mental limits. Free-fall parachuting at ten thousand feet, traveling by small rubber boat for a hundred miles, conducting a mission, then traveling thirty miles out to sea to rendezvous with a sub. The transformation from the teasing, affable, grinning devil he'd been earlier sent a shiver down her spine.

He had the hard look of a navy SEAL about him now.

"We're going to get these guys," he said in the kind of voice that indicated there would be no quarter. Full-out, hard-impact talk.

When they pulled up to the NCIS office on Naval Station Norfolk, she gave him a glance out of the corner of her eye. He looked deep in thought. As she parked the car and they both exited, he said, "So, Cameron was in the Bahamas with friends. You said you thought the cutter was decommissioned and sold to the Bahamians?"

"Yes, I can confirm it. It's a good clue and will narrow down my search."

Inside, Mike was in his office, but the outer office was empty.

"Here, take my desk," Beau said. "Well, the temporary one I was assigned." He sat down in the chair and booted it up, typing in his password.

"I'll talk to the ME over in Portsmouth. Be back shortly." Then he stood and headed to the ME's Office.

"Sounds good," she said, and before she realized what she was doing, she watched him walk out of the office. All the way out, until the door closed behind him. It wasn't until she heard the snick that she realized she was staring at him. Well, to be precise, his ass, something deeply, intrinsically female in her admiring the way his slacks fit his backside.

She shook herself as she accessed the database that housed the information regarding decommissioned vessels. She looked through the entries and her eyes snagged on the *Point Rival*, an eighty-two-foot Point-class cutter that had to be the ship that was lying at anchor on the docks. Another cutter, a High Endurance class named *Revere*. Both of the cutters had been recently sold to the Bahamians to make room for the new Legend-class National Security Cutter (NSC) *Henry*.

As she did the calculations on how long the ships would take to get to the Bahamas to discover when it could have been hijacked and sailed to the US, she thought this wasn't like her attraction to Daniel. Not even close. She'd been aware of him when he was in a room, but it was nothing like the presence of Beau. She swore she could feel the heat of him when he was next to her.

This was a disaster. The case that could make her boss and even the commandant sit up and take notice, and she was thinking about Beau inappropriately. That compressed her lungs and suddenly made her breathless all over again.

But it wouldn't be good to give Beau an edge anywhere, not in this investigation and not with her. She had a job to do and she wasn't going to screw it up again. Everything would be by the book on this and she would keep her hormones in line next time. So help her, God.

Even as she finished that thought, the image of dark eyes and a devil's smile filled her head. The memory of his eyes on her set off shivers that rippled from her neck downward, shocking her.

There wouldn't be a next time if she could help it. Could she even handle a man like Beau Jerrott, with all that raw sexuality? Could she be sure she could stay in control—of him or their relationship or herself?

No. She'd screwed up with Daniel and whatever feelings she'd had for him had gotten smashed and battered in the fallout. She wasn't sure what they'd been, even now. How much had been her overcompensating for her recent lack of a personal life, her loneliness?

Regardless of any of that, she'd lost credibility. She intended to get it back now that she'd been given a second chance.

When the door opened and closed, she didn't have to turn around to know it was Beau. She had just finished compiling her own information.

"How is it going?" he said in that husky, intimate way he had of talking. Trying to keep herself unaffected, she pushed a button and the *Point Rival* flashed up on the wide-screen monitor on the wall between the desk she was sitting at and the one Beau settled behind.

"This is the *Point Rival*. We decommissioned it recently and it departed yesterday on its way to be delivered to the Bahamians." She pulled up the second picture. "This is the *Revere*. It was also decommissioned and headed for the Bahamas. We sold both to make way for the new state-of-the-art Legend-class National Security Cutter *Henry*. The *Point Rival* never made port. I've already contacted the officials in the Bahamas. The *Revere* is already docked, but it's a much faster vessel and outdistanced the slower *Point Rival*."

"That's the ship we have docked here, the ones with the men's bodies?"

"Yes, you can't completely sand off the call numbers. I have a crew working on it right now. I'm sure it's the *Point Rival*."

"What do you think happened?"

"I don't usually make assumptions."

"Guess. Project. You have to have some kind of theory."

"I don't like guessing."

"You just made assumptions about the Point Rival."

"Ah, but they were researched and quantifiable facts about the ship. It was a calculated deduction. I don't have any facts on what could have transpired between those men and what happened on that ship. That would be pure conjecture."

He gave her a hint of a charming smile. "Ah, *chérie*, you need to loosen up a bit." His smile spread and her heart skipped a beat. "C'mon, give me your best hypothesis. I won't tell anyone you made a guess," he leaned forward and whispered.

Her chest expanded at how completely attractive he was. The memory of his hot, burning eyes sent a heat flash over her skin. "I have a feeling that you know exactly how to cajole what you want out of women."

"I might know a thing or two," he said with another

one of those devastating grins. "But, I'm pretty interested in getting you to loosen up a bit."

"I'm probably not going to loosen up, but I can make a small concession here. I think they were attacked on the open sea."

His mouth tightened. "How many crew are we talking about?"

"There were ten Bahamian crew members. An officer and two enlisted CG." She tried to focus on what she was saying, to stay professional. "They had a small window. If it had been me, I would have done it at about the halfway point. It would get them back here in about fifteen hours. The fog was a plus for them. If my calculations are correct—"

"I bet your calculations are always correct."

That comment made her feel better than it should. After what had happened with Daniel, she doublechecked everything. "If they are, they either didn't have a very good navigator or ran into some rough seas. Instead of coming to shore in the dead of night, they came in after dawn. They lucked out with the fog." He was doing it again. Looking at her like *that*. As if every word she said was gold he could deposit into the bank. "I have the coordinates of where it would have been in the time span it took for the *Point Rival* to come back to Norfolk." She pulled up the map and Beau rose to get a closer look, standing way too close to her. He smelled spicy and delicious. As he studied the screen and the route that had been logged for the cutter, she couldn't help but send her eyes over his face while he was distracted.

He had the most tantalizingly kissable lips, so full and enticing. A frisson of heat rolled through her when he absently wet his bottom lip. Her eyes followed his tongue. His bangs were a heavy mess, curling across his forehead. The rest of his hair waved over his ears, coming to a point on the nape of his neck. It was definitely just shy of regulation. But it looked so soft, touchable and she wanted to run her fingers through his hair, feel his heat.

Abruptly he turned to face her. "Most likely they killed..." He trailed off when he met her eyes and must have seen the desire there. She quickly looked away, but not fast enough. He'd caught her staring. Damn. He continued, "Killed the Defense Force members and your CG escorts, transported Dixon and his friends on board, rolled into Kroebuck Beach and ditched the boat."

She blinked. "I'm afraid they are most likely dead. There was another reason that I did the calculations to try to pinpoint where the *Point Rival* was when it might have been hijacked. It's an excellent place to start looking for any survivors. I immediately contacted SAC Stafford the moment I discovered that the ship was most likely the *Point Rival*. Search and Rescue has already been dispatched based on my coordinates."

"Bodies were probably tossed overboard."

She nodded. To cover her embarrassment, she said, "They must have had a dinghy, and that's what I heard as it pulled away. But I couldn't see anything in the fog. I also alerted Homeland and they have been combing over the beach where the cutter almost ran aground."

They had most likely transferred Cameron and his friends from a boat they probably boarded in the Bahamas.

His eyes caressed her, a tight look coming over his face. He looked away. "That sounds feasible. Good call. I'm sorry to hear about your crew members."

"I didn't know them, but it's always such a terrible

loss to lose CG in the line of duty." Heaviness weighed her down just thinking about the families who would be notified when Search and Rescue had a chance to scour the ocean. But hope was always a tricky thing.

The outside door slammed and she jumped. One of the agents came into the room and waved, settling in at his desk.

When she looked back, Beau was studying the map again. How did he do that? Seduce without even trying?

He was a beautiful man, but if he'd been conceited or shallow, it would have been easier to discount him. It was something in his eyes, a tortured quality that drew her. She blew out a breath. He slanted a glance at her and she said, "What did the ME say?"

He smiled. "The most I got out of him was that there was a banging chicken place about a block from him."

"Really?"

His smile deepened, the magnetism pulling harder. "Yeah, he said forensic science cannot be rushed. Thanked me for making his job easier with the identification of Cameron and his friends, but he wasn't going to give me any information until he'd autopsied all the bodies and run the DNA. He did say with the IDs that he could focus on the unidentified victims and that should cut his time."

"I guess your considerable charm doesn't affect men."

He shook his head, shrugging. "When I'm on a mission, I use everything at my disposal, Cooper."

Kinley didn't respond as she brought up the photos of the two dead men. One had a weasely face, even in death.

The other man was black, and as she stared at the picture, he looked vaguely familiar. Still staring at the picture, she picked up the phone to make some inquiries.

Hours later, Kinley rubbed the back of her neck and blearily looked at the time in the corner of her computer monitor: 3:00 a.m. She'd spent her time following a couple of hunches and putting out feelers. She'd have to wait until the morning to see if they panned out. Should she update Beau? No. If nothing came of them, there wouldn't be any need to fill him in. She looked over at Beau's desk. His head was down and he was fast asleep, his breathing even. She'd heard that SEALs could sleep anywhere, caught short winks and were up and ready to go.

She turned off her computer and, leaning over Beau, she shut his down, too. She looked down at him in slumber and had the overpowering urge to slip her hand into his hair.

Instead, she gently touched his shoulder. He came wide-awake and took a deep breath, then let it out slowly.

"What time is it?"

"Three a.m."

"Damn, I gave up my hotel room." He rose and rubbed the back of his neck.

Before she could stop the words, she said, "Why don't you just crash at my place?"

"You sure?" he said, rubbing at his eyes.

"Yes, c'mon. Let's get to bed…uh…some sleep," she amended quickly.

He just flashed her a sleepy grin and indicated she should go first. She turned and walked toward the door. It was a quick drive to her house and she was now having second thoughts. When she'd offered, she hadn't been thinking. It wasn't a good idea to keep the tantalizing Beau anywhere near her in a personal situation. But he'd worked so hard today and the time and trouble of checking into a hotel seemed stupid when she had a perfectly good guest room.

She drove home while Beau followed in his sleek muscle car. Once inside, she showed him the guest room.

"This is nice of you. Thank you, Cooper."

She nodded and retreated to her room. After undressing and slipping on a silk nightie, she got into bed. She reached into the bottom drawer of her nightstand. Inside was a wooden box. She set it on her lap, clenching and unclenching her hands. Her chest filling. With trembling hands she lifted the lid. Her eyes grew moist. She reached for the picture of her father with his arm around her shoulder. They were laughing hysterically. It was the result of a joke she'd told, and his girlfriend had caught the moment on film. She brushed her fingers over his face, squeezing her eyes closed.

She set the photo down and reached for the watch. It was a dive watch in perfect condition. She got it serviced every year. She'd do that as soon as this investigation was over. The next thing she removed was his Navy Cross, and as she opened the case, pride infused her. She had no doubt he'd died protecting her to his last breath.

God, how she missed him. How she loved him. And he had loved her unconditionally. His anniversary was over. It had passed, her father's death rolling over into another year.

Her heart contracted and she covered her face.

She set everything back into the box and replaced it. She settled down onto her pillows and sighed. Tears leaked out of her eyes as she drifted into sleep, into her nightmare.

The fog was so thick and that jittery feeling came over her. She looked around, searching for something so very important, but the sense of loss ran through her over and over, wearing on her, tearing at her conscience, ripping at her heart. The sound of gunshots was the worst of it. The sounds all around her. Her pulse jumped, and her breath came in short, shallow, unsatisfying gasps. Adrenaline and frustration pumped through her in equal amounts.

Then she was running as if through water. Horrible feelings piling up on top of one another. Rage, panic, helplessness, fear, hatred. Hearing the end of her world in those eerie pops. She came up against a hard body and *he* was just there. Beau. She looked up into his face. He was looking out into the fog, his body primed for battle.

And for the first time since the death of her father she felt…safe.

"It's okay, *chérie*. I've got you."

Kinley started awake. She was sitting up in bed and Beau was there on the edge, holding her in his arms. She was crying, the tears hot and wet against her cheeks. The air heaved in and out of her lungs in tremendous, hot, ragged gasps. Her nightgown was plastered to her skin with cold sweat.

She wasn't in that fog. She was in her bedroom and a man she barely knew was holding her. He was so warm, so comforting, and she was so, so lonely, the grief felt as fresh as it had that day. The stiffness left her in a rush and she collapsed against him.

Kinley pressed her face into his strong neck. This was the worst time of the year for her. She was usually able to weather the day as long as she kept her emotions at bay, but breaking the news to the families had made the grief she'd never really dealt with build, until she was suffering this…this emotional breakdown.

She pulled in on herself, trying to get control of the tears, worried that she was showing Beau just how weak she was. All she heard was her pulse roaring in her ears.

This was all rooted in a past she refused to let go of, was perhaps incapable of letting go of. It always hurt. *Hurt so bad*, a small voice inside her said. The voice of a young girl who had only her father to rely on for love and comfort. The father who looked out for her, who protected her, who sacrificed his life for her.

Kinley bit her lip against the pain, squeezed her eyes shut against it. She trembled, afraid if she even breathed, the dam would burst and she would lose it. Break down into a mass of weakness, guilt and pain.

He murmured to her in French. Even though she didn't know what he was saying, the tone of his voice released her tears and she wrapped her arms around his neck. She shouldn't be doing this, but she needed an anchor in this storm. It felt too good to be held, to let someone be strong.

He sent his hand into her hair, displacing the heavy mass and cupping his big palm against her scalp.

Her emotions frightened her because there was always a chance they would get out of control. The numbness allowed her to run roughshod over them.

But with Beau, she didn't want the numbness. She was quite aware she'd held on to it with Daniel, and that it was easy to let go when things had gone south. She was also aware that she'd done that with the two previous boyfriends before Daniel.

So, why couldn't she do it with Beau? She wanted to

feel him in every way possible. Let go and give in to the sizzling attraction that was something…extraordinary. Something wholly dangerous. She craved the closeness, the heat, wanted it to fill that terrible void inside. She trembled with the promise of how…*more*…he would be.

Beau looked at her with eyes as deep and dark as midnight and she found something in them she wanted to have. But that wasn't possible. They worked together and she couldn't make the same mistake twice. *He wouldn't be a mistake.*

The seductive quality of him swamped her senses and she knew she was vulnerable. He melted her and opened her up. It would have been easy if she didn't feel anything for him and he was simply comforting her. But her awareness of him was thick and heavy in the air.

And that was the problem. She should let go of him and weather this storm as she always did.

Alone.

But she couldn't seem to make herself let him go. Suddenly, alone seemed so, so…lonely.

Chapter 5

Beau held her in the dark room, her sobs tearing at him. He had no idea what had upset her. He had woken up at the soft cries and made his way to her room to find her thrashing in her sleep.

Nightmares could catch even the most battle-hardened warrior unaware. He'd had his fair share of them, and this had been a terrible day full of blood, grief and stress.

Normally, he would think there was no way in hell he wanted to get caught up in this. He usually chose uncomplicated women who just wanted to have a good time. He'd had complicated and it had damn near done him in. Kinley Cooper was definitely complicated in ways that would tie him into really tight knots. But unlike the past, he was unable to turn away from her. In fact, it killed him that she was unraveling.

He damned her for being so brave, damned himself for caring. No good could come of it for either of them. But even as he was convincing himself of that fact, his feet had been moving unerringly toward her small, huddled shape.

He tightened his arms around her, and let her cry all over him, melting his jaded heart as easily as ice cream left out in the sun.

"It's been a rough day, huh, Cooper?" he murmured, his lips brushing her fragrant, soft hair, her faint perfume filling his head. She was so dainty, so delicate in his arms, but he knew what that slight body held. He'd seen the steel in her and he couldn't freaking help being a champion for a tough cookie…damn…for *this* tough cookie.

"Yes, very," she said, her voice soft in the darkness, making his heart contract at the broken quality to it.

Dammit. He rocked her against him, the movement soothing him, too. He didn't mind bending the rules to get something done that needed getting done. Hell, he wasn't exactly Mr. By-the-book. He worked with her on an investigation, but that was temporary, and they weren't even in the same agency.

Still, it was that something…that *thing* that was flowing between them that kept him skirting the razor's edge.

He hadn't felt what he was experiencing with Kinley with anyone.

He was willing to give her the time she needed to get her bearings.

It took some time.

"I'm sorry," she whispered, "I'll be okay in a minute. I promise. This is the worst day of the year for me."

It took way longer than a minute. A very long time, in which she just snuggled against his naked chest, all curves and heat, her face pressed into the hollow of his neck, her warm, wet tears sliding down his throat in a slow, heartbreaking trickle. Her breath hot against his bare skin, her arms wrapped around him in a death grip, he drew from his training to stay cool. He could stay cool as a cucumber, even when his skin was on fire.

But she moved one of her hands then, flattening her palm on the back of his neck, rubbing her way over the swell of muscle to his shoulder. He gritted his teeth. He was trying to keep a tight rein on his purely male, purely gut-deep reaction. She was turning him on, but she wasn't really trying to. This was purely an "any port in a storm" case, and the difference in their reactions was not lost on him. In addition, he needed to deal with it now and realize this kind of disquiet in her presence wasn't going to miraculously disappear.

No. In fact, it was only going to get worse as he got to know her. He was a pretty good judge of character. He'd had to be as a member of SEAL Team 10. Split-second decisions were his bread and butter and kept not only him but his teammates alive, allowing them to complete their missions.

His directive was to comfort her, not get lost in the feel of her skin, the scent of the kind of body that would give any man hard, hot fevered dreams. It would have been that much easier if he hadn't seen her naked. But he wanted to explore that body and the tantalizing spirit of the woman who inhabited it.

He came back to the directive with a jolting mental punch. He would have been able to follow through, would have held her all night without doing anything but murmuring to her and keeping his hands to himself...

But Kinley raised her head, still holding fast, still fused to him, and dropped her head back, dragging her hair over the skin of his shoulder in an aching, seductive tease. She locked on to him like a dangerous heat-seeking missile. Unwavering, her eyes captured his and his mission went south, everything went south, a tortured, unexpected, complete ambush.

He froze with the threat of danger. His heart started hammering against the wall of his chest. SEALs knew how to do things the easy way, quick in and quick out, devastating results in their wake. But he wasn't thinking quickly here at all. He wanted in, *into her*, slow and deep. Instead of avoiding her gaze, he hit it straight on and went the hard path, allowing his gaze to slowly caress her face, allowing his awareness of her closeness to duck past his barriers, allowing the arousal to jack him up to the friggin' max.

His hands tightened around her upper arms where they had slipped. Hell, he didn't need this, he told himself, not for one second did he need this. He needed his head in the investigation, but there only seemed to be enough blood in his body to fill one head and it wasn't the one he thought with.

What was it about her? She was beautiful, but he'd been with many, many beautiful women. She was in his arms, all warm and lovely with those laser-green eyes and a mouth that had been his undoing from the moment he'd laid eyes on her, and he couldn't figure it out.

It didn't help that he knew she wanted to kiss him. That thought had been clearly telegraphed to him with the way she'd looked at him back at NCIS. Okay, that look had said more than kiss him. That look was more about devouring him. He was all for it until she'd looked away in embarrassment after being caught staring at him. He never minded the staring. It was tantalizing to have women want him from just running their eyes

over him. It suited him that they kept it all surface and
about how God had put his face together. He'd unabash-
edly used his looks to get what he wanted, a temporary
fix. He'd used them in missions to disarm and distract.
He'd even gotten those kinds of looks from teenagers
and grandmothers, and that amused him. But nothing
about the way Kinley had looked at him amused him.

And she was looking at him that way now, a tumbled,
mixed-up look filled with wanting.

It was hot enough to fry his synapses and his brain
started shutting down, all his energy focusing on her.
He should keep this…keep this…

Whatever stellar and completely rational thought
he was trying to hold on to got lost somewhere in the
sheer heat of her gaze.

Her lips parted and he was so tempted, was going
down in flames. Then he felt it beneath his hands, the
shiver that went through her. He was a man who enjoyed
women, and shivers were usually so, so good, but not
this one. This shiver was all about her emotional state.
His gaze instantly narrowed. Tears welled in her eyes
and in the next second she was crumbling all over again.

"I can't believe I'm here again and this is all screwed
up. So screwed up." Her voice was barely a whisper, her
words a little muddled and filled with remorse, regret
and a tantalizing husky need.

"What is this about, sugar?" He was very careful
to curb his Southern inclination to call a professional
woman by an endearing name on the job, but with Kinley it simply slipped out in his genuine concern for her.

Her eyes softened even further and she dropped her
head. "Really, you want to know?"

"I think this is more than a nightmare. It's really
none of my business. If you want me to leave, just

say the word, *chérie*." Great, now he was calling her *sweetheart*.

"Oh, God." She sniffed and he was completely shredded. He pulled her against him again, but she struggled out of his arms, clutching her stomach, and stumbled out of the bed, retreating to the window. She threw it open and breathed deep gulps of the night air.

But she collapsed over the sill and he could have held out and given her the space she thought she wanted, but the anguish, the tears spilling onto her cheeks, gave her a slightly bruised and helpless, damsel-in-distress look, a look that affected him at a visceral level.

He couldn't take it. He just couldn't. He took two long strides to her and dragged her against the length of him and, it was so not a good idea as he clenched his teeth at the feel of the silk of her skin and skimpy nightie.

He felt her surrender as she gave in, her sudden bravado lost to her as quickly as it had come.

He took a breath because, damn, he needed a breather. "Tell me what's making you cry and I'll hunt it down and kill it with my bare hands."

A watery huff, half laughter and half despair, gusted against his neck. "I'm afraid that not even a navy SEAL can take care of this."

"Try me."

"When I was sixteen, my father was murdered."

He leaned away from her. "That sounds exactly like something I can handle."

Her brows furrowed, her straight little eyebrows bunching toward each other. "They were terrorists and they melted away into the fog. It was a long time ago, but yesterday was the anniversary of his death. The heavy fog yesterday morning set me off and I've been on edge since. Then…then finding Cameron and those other men, the blood and violence, it brought it all back."

"I know how that can happen. Sometimes it'll just be a smell or a color and I remember something that happened when I was on a mission."

"I have to admit, I haven't ever been in combat." She looked up at him and he smoothed his thumb under her eye to wick away the moisture, her skin so soft. "I've been involved in confrontations with go-fast boats and drug smugglers, but not like what you've seen."

He'd never been this close to a woman he wanted before without initiating sex. She was pressed against him like a hot lamination. "We try to avoid combat as much as possible. It's usually covert, grab-and-go, or recon."

Her face was earnest. "But you've seen combat, haven't you?"

"I've seen my share."

She nodded.

"Was there any attempt to catch the bastards who killed your father?"

"I'm not sure. I was only sixteen. The guy who talked to me, the one in the suit, said that I didn't have to worry. They would take care of it. No one told me anything else."

"And your mom?"

"She died from cancer when I was one. I don't remember her at all. It's always been my dad."

"That must have been tough. What happened after he died?"

"I lived with family. At eighteen I went out on my own and joined the Coast Guard. I haven't looked back."

His thumb slipped down her face, chasing a tear that

hit the rim of her top lip. Without thinking, he rubbed over it and she made a soft sound in her throat.

"Tell me to let you go," he said, his voice balanced on a keen edge and soaked with desire. "I can be your shoulder, Cooper, but…I'm thinking things that are probably not a good idea. Have been thinking these things since I laid eyes on you."

Her hand shifted to the arm attached to the hand that was cupping her face. She smoothed her palm up his arm and covered his hand. "You do things to me that have never been done before, but we work together so I was trying to keep it professional, and I have history. Not fair to you. We…"

A nicer guy would have helped her to fill in the blanks.

Beau was not a nice guy.

He brought up his other hand, bracketing her face between his palms, delving into all that tantalizing red hair. The next time she said, "We…" in her softly confused voice, her gaze imploring him to understand, he leaned down and kissed her, opened his mouth over hers and gave in to that hard, utterly decisive need to feel her heat. He felt like he'd just jumped from a plane and was free-falling.

Her unbound breasts were cushioned against his chest, her soft skin beneath his fingers, her mouth opening for him, letting him inside—and the sound of instantaneous surrender she made in the back of her throat went through him with all the galvanizing punch of g-force acceleration. He felt the heat of her mouth all the way to his groin, turning him on, stirring him up, when he had no business getting stirred by her at all.

But she was sweet, the taste of her damnably erotic, totally mind-blowing and completely forbidden.

He opened his mouth wider and adjusted angles, so he could have more of her—more contact, more of her tongue in his mouth—because it drove him crazy in the most exquisite way. She melted against him, opening herself even more to the kiss. It was such a tease of what he really wanted: more *her*.

He was in so much trouble. He was all about just one time, and he never engaged his heart, ever, not since Jennifer. But in the short span of time that he'd known Kinley, she'd burrowed her way in under his defenses. Yeah, it was always about that damn bullet you didn't see. The one that slammed into you like a battering ram and took you down. For a second, he thought about pulling away—and then he thought to hell with it. She fed something he didn't know was hungry.

All this because of her. Was he crazy or what?

Probably, he admitted, because he wanted to kiss her anyway, despite his past, her history, their professional relationship getting all shot to hell.

And the last place he wanted to be was in bed with a coworker, but they weren't really coworkers. This was a temporary assignment and then he'd be back in DC.

It was exactly where he wanted to end up tonight, though. In bed with her. It was all temporary, including the sex. He'd made love with lots of women, keeping it loose and easy. He tended to be particular about his lovers. He liked women, loved them at their best and was fascinated by them at their worst, but he didn't need to sleep with everyone he met.

He just needed to sleep with this one, Kinley Cooper. He needed to be with her.

It was attraction, wrapped around raw need. He didn't want to allow any thoughts about how she could save him, save him in a thousand different ways. It was a fear-induced adrenaline boost that he quickly blocked out.

And he still wanted her, even with those obstacles.

So they would do it as many times as they wanted. Sex. With her.

Hell, she'd practically fallen into his arms, so why not? It was the perfect situation. Straightforward, simple, with no complicated extraneous objectives in mind, nothing to get all screwed up—especially his head. He wasn't going to let his head get into this at all.

"Beau." His name was a plea, a hushed, desperate demand for help. His insides compressed from a solid mass to instant mush.

He cupped the back of her head. He'd just realized something and it pissed him off. "Give me permission." He closed his eyes. "Give it to me." The demand was a harsh rasp of his voice.

"For what?"

"To call you by your first name. I want it."

She gasped and clutched at him, shivering. The good kind of shiver, the one that had everything to do with desire, the uncontrollable, turned-on kind.

"Yes." Her voice wisped out of her.

"Kinley." He growled low in his throat at the victory. "Do we need protection?" he asked, taking her mouth again, her hips cradling his, her hand sliding up the back of his neck, playing with the hair at the nape, pulling him closer. He loved the hot sweetness of it, the way she softened against him.

She couldn't answer because he slid his tongue into her mouth and felt the sharp need of desire take hold, the taste of her, the honey of her tongue sliding against his, teasing him.

Her other hand jolted him like a surge of electricity when she touched his waist just above the elastic of his skivvies.

His hands slipped down the length of her back, a groan escaping as he cupped her butt and pressed her fiercely against his throbbing erection. Now, right damn now, he let himself remember what she'd looked like this morning when he'd met her eyes in that mirror. The high, full breasts, the delicate rib cage and flat, enticing belly, the juncture of her thighs that was currently pressed against him and those long, shapely legs. His mouth got demanding then, hard. His breathing harsh, he mindlessly turned her away from the window, toward the bed, the breeze drifting across his heated skin.

When he reached it, she was already folding down to the mattress, clutching him, but he stopped her by catching her lower back and holding her suspended.

Her green eyes were heavy with need and swollen from crying. He'd never seen anything so damned beautiful. The wispy nothing she wore was a tangy lemony color. The material left nothing to the imagination.

He reached up with his free hand and sent his fingers over one of her nipples, the bud tightening.

He bent his head as her hand slipped over his biceps, holding on. He made a humming sound of deep pleasure as his mouth closed over that hard little knot. The filmy material rasped against his tongue and her.

His chest heaved. With one simple pull, his hands looking so huge, he stripped her. She closed her eyes, her mouth partly open from panting, making a soft sound in the back of her throat. She was so lush and full, and hearing her groan and seeing her nipples harden on a pair of the most exquisite breasts he'd ever laid eyes on sent a flood of heat to his groin.

He lowered her down as he braced his knee on the mattress, wanting nothing more than to get closer to her.

She was sweet, such a visceral addiction, all heat, the taste and feel and scent of her imprinted on every cell in his body, driving him goddamn crazy. She rose up with a hand against the middle of his chest. Before he could figure out what she was about, her fingers grasped the waistband of his shorts and she pushed him back up, his foot dropping to the floor.

She was level with his lower chest and stomach. She looked up at him, those green eyes looking bruised and so lost. He wanted to ignore it. But he couldn't. That she found him gorgeous. She didn't have to say it. It was all there in the way her eyes went over his face.

She ran her hands up over him. "Damn, yeah, baby, I want you to manhandle me. I do, but…" He was shaking so hard—never deny him a willing and consenting woman. But Kinley had been hurting and she was reacting to the pain of her father's death and the terrible things that had happened today.

As she took a breath, she dragged her fingernails down his chest all the way to the top of his briefs.

He sucked in a heated breath and expelled a heated groan, then lost his voice completely.

Curling her fingers into the waistband, she dragged them down and released his hot hard-on as he groaned.

He loved a woman who knew what she wanted, especially if she wanted him. When she took a breath, he felt it against his impossibly rigid erection.

"Oh, Beau…" Her words trailed off, punctuated with the slow glide of her fingers up his shaft and then down, setting off explosions of sensation and pleasure that made his knees buckle for a moment. It was incredible.

With the iron will he'd honed in the Navy and the

tough mental mindset he'd developed during his time on the teams, he grasped her wrists and finally found his voice. "No, *chérie*," he whispered.

He pushed her back, unable to let her go. He settled down onto the mattress and pulled her into his arms, smoothing back her hair.

Her gaze locked on his just like it had in the mirror when they were devouring each other. He stretched out over her, covering her, his body aching to have her. He kissed her, then tightened his arms around her. "I'm not going to take advantage of you."

"A man with a conscience," she said softly, desire in her voice and she looked at him with those same bruised, lost eyes, so lonely. His head came down, and he covered her mouth with his, filling himself with the taste and scent and softness of her.

He kissed her with something that was akin to comfort. Something that he wasn't aware he still had in him. And it felt so good, better than he thought it would with an aching erection and a sweet, naked woman in his arms. Damn. When he raised his head, she buried her face in his neck. All he wanted to do was hold her and fall asleep.

Chapter 6

Kinley woke slowly, at first reveling in the hard warmth wrapped around her. She snuggled closer, burying her nose into the tantalizing scent of something wholly delicious, spicy and...male.

Very, very male, ripped and hard.

Her eyes slid open languidly. They should have popped open, and even as part of her brain was calm, the other side was going, *What have you done?* But when her eyes collided with Special Agent Beau Jerrott and slammed into a brick wall of *wow*, her breath caught and held...and held. Oh, dammit. Beau. Oh...God... Beau. He definitely put the "special" in special agent. He was only inches from her face. His lashes thick above his cheeks. His oh-so-kissable mouth slightly parted in sleep, his enticing hair thoroughly mussed and looking even sexier than usual.

Memories filtered back to her from the previous night. How sweet he'd been, how comforting in the way he'd held her. Her heart hitched at that. But she should be careful. He'd been so kind…she only had one explanation. Her defenses had been so low and she'd been hungry for the touch of someone, to feel the warmth and comfort that could so easily be found in the physical. Her heart melted at his restraint. She was going to find it difficult to stay guarded against him. But she decided that she needed that barrier.

His mouth, his skin, the feel of him in her hands were also potent memories. And she'd fallen into an even more terrible trap then she had with Daniel. With Beau it was different. There was no other way to describe it. She should be freaking out. She should be moving away and trying to bring this crazy situation to a place where she could manage it, but looking at him was fine for right now.

Her eyes went over him, down the length of his naked body, and discovered the sheet bunched around his nice-looking feet. Under his clothes, the man was as put together as he looked while dressed. She tilted her head when she caught ink out of the corner of her eye. Rising up on her elbow, it was not lost on her that she was 100 percent naked, as well. But she wasn't self-conscious about her body. If it was any indication from the way Beau looked at her, she didn't really need to worry.

The tattoo was around his thick biceps, rounded even in sleep. It was a chain—more accurately, links in a chain. Wanting to get closer to see what the small lettering said, she brushed her breasts over his arm and peered closer. He shifted in his sleep and she glanced back at him, caught up in the way his face changed. He made a soft humming noise.

When he seemed to settle, she turned back to the tattoo, trying to get closer.

"It's a chain. The lettering is initials of the people in my life who've made a difference."

She froze at his husky, drowsy voice. When she looked at him, his eyes were half-lidded and sigh worthy.

Without taking his eyes off her or even broadcasting his intention, he shifted and brought her against his chest so that she could get a better look. Her skin vibrated from the feel of him. His sleeping presence had been potent, but when Beau was awake his charisma was palatable.

One hand slipped into her hair as he nonchalantly ran it through his fingers.

She closed her eyes. Oh, damn, he was just so cool and collected. She had to wonder if he did this often. Woke up with strangers. That made her barrier harden just a bit.

"The first link holds my *grand-père*'s name, the second my *mère*'s and *père*'s initials. The third my first-grade English teacher who introduced me to books and opened up my world. The fourth is my navy recruiter for giving me the world, and the one after that is my drill sergeant from my BUD/S training, who made me understand the world better."

Her voice rasped out, "The last one is empty."

"I haven't found the person to fill that link yet," he said softly.

"That's a really cool tattoo."

He shifted so that he could see her better. "How are you doing?"

"You mean after I blubbered all over you last night,

or that I'm freaking out just a bit because we almost had sex?"

"Um, I'll go with, 'Who needed a shoulder to cry on?' Alex, for a thousand?"

Kinley snorted. "You trying to charm me, Beau?"

"Maybe. Is it working?"

"Maybe."

He sobered and his hand was in her hair again. "Really, how are you?"

"Better. I'm sorry…"

He slipped his thumb over her mouth. "No need to apologize. We're not robots or machines. We're human, *chérie*. It's totally okay to let your feelings show. Yesterday was a tough day for you. I have to admit, I got choked up once or twice after finding out that Cameron and his friends were all primed to make a nice amount of money only to lose their lives instead. I want to find these bastards and make sure they pay for what they did, especially if they are out to harm more US citizens. On top of that, your father's death is profound. So, no apologies."

Without thinking, she brought her hand up and brushed her fingers against his rough cheek. He kept catching her off guard with these kinds of statements. It was genuine and heartfelt. Men didn't serve their countries by putting their lives in danger every day out of the blue. There was a core of steel there, something admirable and honorable. Beau was a navy SEAL. They never really stopped serving. NCIS was a service to the navy and Marine Corps.

He smiled slowly. "Kinley," he whispered, and she remembered that she'd given him permission to call her by her first name. The memory of his fierce, demanding tone sent tingles through her.

"Now let's talk about the whole getting-naked-and-almost-doing-it thing."

She finally gave in and slipped her hand into his hair. Damn, it was so soft. "You think this is a time to joke?"

He shrugged. "I'm not going to pretend I'm not attracted to you. I'm also not going to pretend that it wouldn't have been crazy amazing with you last night."

"But."

"What makes you think there's a but?"

"I have buts and doubts and I promised myself I wouldn't do this again. It wasn't a good move for my career."

A shadow passed across his face and his jaw hardened. Somehow she had hit a nerve. "Okay, so you're right. There is a *but*. I do this often, usually one night only."

She took the hit and reinforced her barriers. Kinley didn't want to hear this but she was glad that he was saying it. It put everything in perspective. She pushed away from him. "Sounds like I dodged the bullet, then. I wouldn't have liked to be just another notch, Beau."

"Damn," he said and caught her arm. "But…"

She stopped halfway out of bed. "Another one?"

He rose and pressed his hard, hot chest against her back, his mouth going to the place where her shoulder met her throat. "It's not like that, Kinley. I don't notch. I enjoy sex with women. But I doubt that one night with you would cut it."

Every shred of common sense, every rational thought screamed at her to put everything in perspective and walk away, run away if need be and never look back. But that would be like trying to put the genie back in the bottle. What had almost happened last night seemed… almost…inevitable. She could only hope that he was able to maintain that formidable control. Because she was losing some of her perspective. "Beau," she said, her voice going insubstantial at the way his mouth sent shivers down her spine.

He moved up her throat, setting off explosions of sensation to go with the new set of shivers he was causing. "Tell me to let you go. Tell me you're not feeling the same way."

Kinley closed her eyes. "I can't tell you I don't feel this attraction, but you saved me…us last night from making a mistake."

"We both know relationships don't work. Physical needs are met."

That hit a nerve in her. She had never been able to find one that fulfilled her. It was true. Scott, her boyfriend before Daniel, had wanted something Kinley wasn't sure she could give. She'd been hollow since her father's death, her safety snatched away. Try as she might, she'd never gotten it back.

She'd been overprotected from the world and the trauma she'd suffered that day had changed her deep inside. It had taken away her innocence and made reality real and ugly.

After her father was gone, it was about protecting herself, because there wasn't one person who cared enough to alleviate her pain or give her comfort.

Until Beau had offered her that comfort last night. Wrapped her up in his arms and eased the pain. But, and this was a very big but, she wasn't about to give up any more of herself until she was sure she wouldn't be rejected or twisted up inside at the loss. She couldn't fool herself into thinking she wasn't tangled up with Beau.

She'd thought she might feel something with Daniel, that she might let go of her self-protection. She'd hoped that the numbness would go away and that she could let herself go. Trust. But it hadn't worked. Scott had wanted too much and Daniel had ended up not being the man she'd thought he was. So what Beau had said was true.

Or was it? He did something to her. Something she couldn't quite fight. The way he'd looked at her yesterday was still searing and intense in her mind. She couldn't quite close it down, as if he'd found some chink in her armor.

"That's pretty jaded. What was her name?" she asked, leaning back against him.

He took a careful breath and shook his head. "You want to hear my sad story?"

"If you want to tell me."

"Nothing to tell."

How did he do it? He made her feel like no man had ever made her feel. But she didn't trust it and his response reinforced it. Too afraid of buying into this feeling, then finding out it was just nothing but an illusion.

His breath was hot and heavy against her skin. "She's in the past, best leave her there," he murmured, dragging her and dropping her back against his arm. He leaned into her space, one hand sliding down her belly and back up again. Then he looked down. "A heart," he said, gazing at her piercing. "Sexy."

Kinley's heart kicked into overdrive as he came closer, though fear wasn't the dominant emotion. It should have been, but it wasn't.

That strange sense of desire and anticipation crept along her nerves. He wanted her, she could see the promise in his eyes and felt something wild and reckless and completely foreign to her rise up in answer, pushing her to close the distance, to take a chance. His eyes dared her, his mouth lured—masculine, sexy, lips parted in invitation. What fear she felt was of herself, of this attraction that was drawing on her and miraculously giving something back.

How to read him? It was impossible. Was he the womanizer that he claimed to be? Or was he just a bruised and battered soul like her? Hurt somewhere in his past in a way that made him shun love by never allowing it, like she shunned it by never letting it matter?

Thinking around him, when he was leaning over her like this, was impossible. It was only possible to feel.

He went to kiss her, but before his mouth touched hers, her cell chimed. She fumbled over and grabbed it. "Hello."

"Kinley, it's Kirk. I know it's early and you were up into the wee hours of the morning, but I wanted to let you know that we got hits on your hunches."

Her stomach jumping, she glanced over her shoulder at Beau, then reached down and snagged her nightie. It wasn't exactly a decent garment, but at least she wouldn't be naked. "The black man is National Defense Force? I thought I had recognized him."

"His name is Umprey Thompson and yes. He was one of the members who was here to escort the decommissioned *Point Rival* to the Bahamas."

"It's confirmed? It's the *Point Rival*?"

"Yes, confirmed. Search and Rescue have been notified. We're going by your coordinates, but we don't hold out much hope that the crew is alive. If they eliminated these guys, we suspect they eliminated the original crew. Took them down from the inside."

"And was my hunch on the other victim correct?"

"Spot-on. Got a hit off Automated Fingerprint Identification System on one Dudley Martin. He's got quite the rap sheet here in the US, mostly drug offenses. He's also wanted in the Bahamas—for trafficking. With the drug connection and the hijacking of the *Rival*, the commandant is steamed. He wants you and Jerrott to head to the Bahamas and continue the investigation there. I'll keep you posted on any developments here. He wants any leads followed to the furthest extent. We need to know what we're dealing with here. I've already briefed the director of NCIS. I'm sure Jerrott will be getting a call, as well."

Right on cue, Beau's cell rang and he answered it.

Ah, damn. This wasn't the way she'd wanted the lead on the case to discover her hunches had panned out. She was so careful now about what she revealed to whom until she was sure about the information. "No hits on the blood we found at the scene yet?"

"No, the ME is working on it. I've already updated him on these developments."

"I have another hunch about that, too."

"Go on. You're on a roll."

She glanced at Beau and he was frowning. He gave her a steely-eyed glance, then focused back on his own conversation. Okay, that was decidedly a we're-going-to-have-an-uncomfortable-discussion look for sure. "Don't waste time checking AFIS. Go right for Interpol."

"International database, huh? All right. I'll pass that along."

"Thank you, sir," she said.

"Kinley, you're doing fine. That was some damn good work."

"Thank you, sir."

The reassurance went a long way toward calming her doubts.

"Dorrie, you have those reservations?" he asked, his

voice muffled. Dorrie was their assistant. "I'll let you speak with Dorrie. Keep me posted, and Cooper?"

"Yes, sir?"

"Be careful," Kirk said, his voice laced with concern.

There was a pause, then Dorrie said, "Hello, Kinley. I have you and Special Agent Jerrott booked out of Norfolk International for 10:00 a.m. Does that work for you?"

"Yes, Dorrie, that's fine. Thank you."

"Sending the e-reservation to your phone now. There will be a car waiting for you at the Nassau airport. I'm sending that, as well. The DEA works out of the American Embassy in Nassau and is expecting you. And, Kinley," Dorrie said, her voice dropping to a whisper. "I wanted to give you a heads-up. The agent you're to meet is Daniel Wescott. I'm sorry, Kinley."

"Damn," she said, closing her eyes. She wasn't prepared to see Daniel ever again, but she was a professional and he was the contact, so she would suck it up and get the job done, no matter her personal feelings. Her phone dinged and she said, "Just got it. Thanks."

She disconnected the call.

Beau was leaning back against the pillows still on the phone.

"No, Chris, she didn't, but we were up late last night." He cut her a look and she gave him a noncommittal expression, her gut churning.

"Yes. It was good work. I'll get the details from her. I'll check in when we land."

He disconnected the call and stared at her, definite steel there. Oh, man. He was pissed. She was starting to think of him as an ally, but now with this look he was giving her, she was sure she had fractured what little trust they were building in their relationship. Tenuous as it was.

"I'm going to assume that you didn't deliberately leave me out of the loop to make me look like a complete idiot."

She took a breath. "They were hunches. I didn't tell you because that's all they were, just hunches. I've learned that until I have solid information I shouldn't share." The terrible incident she had been involved in with Daniel came back at her like a wrecking ball. She didn't like second-guessing herself, but that was all she could seem to do now.

"So, it was by-the-book deliberate?" Energy. It emanated off of him in waves without him even trying. "That makes me feel so much better. I don't like being caught flat-footed with my boss." His voice was low, calm, smooth. Only the tight muscles in his jaw, the gleam in his eyes, gave away his agitation with her at the moment.

Her eyes didn't know where to look. It was so distracting to argue with him when he was completely naked and looking...well, looking like he did. She willed her rapidly beating heart to slow down.

He sat up, chest muscles contracting, six-pack abs rippling. His eyes were a stormy blue.

What kind of quagmire had she just immersed herself in? She never really knew whether she should just be honest, and if she voiced her doubts, would he discount them like Daniel had?

"Could you, um—" she reached down and picked up his boxer briefs "—get dressed?" Oh, damn, her need to check and recheck everything was coming back to bite her on the butt. She'd just wanted to make sure she had her facts straight. Right? That was it, because of what had happened with Daniel. She was even more sensitive to that now. Damn, had she been undermining Beau's authority? She didn't want to do that. He was the lead and she respected that, but she was angry. Had been so angry when they'd first given lead to him. Was he now going to question everything she said? Had she lost his trust? Even though they had just met and in her need and stupidity she'd almost slept with him, she still had to find some common ground to work with him.

"Do I have to watch my back and cover my ass?" he said, the intensity of his gaze impossible to look away from at such close range.

She started, shaking her head. "I didn't do it deliberately." She bit her lip. "I wait until I have results before I share anything."

"You're sure about that or are you leaving me out in the cold?"

"Yes. I…wanted to make sure before I said anything. It's important to check things over before you present ideas."

"We're a team. Everything you have to say, I want to know even if it sounds like the dumbest thing in the world. Women are recruited by agencies because they bring a different perspective and look at solving problems differently. They contribute unique and important perspectives, experiences and skills. In many cases, women possess different analytical skills, approach problems differently and have different talents and abilities than men. These different skills, approaches and talents often spell the difference between success and failure on a case or investigation."

He rose up from the bed with powerful movements and all she wanted to do was push him right back onto it. The sun was just rising, lighting the room. He snatched the underwear out of her hand and slipped them on. It didn't help. He was still too potent, but that was true even when he was fully dressed. God, it might help if he'd get a haircut. His hair was so damned sexy, and coupled with those penetrating eyes… Oh. He was talking to her.

"What did you say?"

He set his hands on his hips and gave her an irritated look.

"Sorry," she murmured.

He sighed and a slight smile broke out on his face, but it didn't diffuse the friction they seemed to generate just by being in the same room. "It would help if you'd keep your eyes on mine."

"Really, you think that would help?"

"You testing me, *chérie*?"

"I think it's the other way around."

He stepped up to her, flashing an irresistible half grin, an intimate sparkle in his eyes. "You think so?"

She shivered at his closeness. "We need to get things back on an impersonal level. I appreciate what you did last night. It was…what I needed, but we should keep this relationship professional. Things could get so muddled up and complicated."

"Just to clarify things. I agree that our relationship should be professional, but after being this close to you and going against my desire for you…" He shook his head. "That's going to be tough. *Technically*, we're not really partners." he said, softly.

"That's true, but it's better if we try to get back our objectivity."

"You sure about that?"

No, she wasn't, but this was a terrible lapse on her part. It was safer. She wanted the man, especially after feeling his naked body against hers. She wanted him desperately. "During this investigation, we need to keep straight what is important. Fulfilling the mission."

He sighed and went to go past her, the scent of him strong as he stopped too close to her. She had to keep her hands clenched to keep from touching him.

"Good point, Kinley. Just remember to keep me in the loop on…everything. Yes?"

She nodded, his closeness making her breathing shallow.

"Own your ideas. Don't worry about consequences until you have to deal with them."

"That's hard for me," she said as he stared at her, his eyes going to her mouth briefly.

"Never said it would be easy, but you have the courage in you. I see that." His eyes dipped and roved over her mouth again, the half grin taking on a special warmth, the sparkle in his eyes softening into a steady gaze that was penetrating, intoxicating and very sensual.

This wasn't going to be easy at all.

Chapter 7

The plane set down on New Providence, the island upon which the capital city of Nassau was located. Beau was finding it difficult to keep his mind on their next steps. Waking up with Kinley had been unexpected. Mind-blowing, but unexpected. With the attraction still burning between them, he wasn't used to sleeping with a woman he wanted and not sleeping with her. She was a sensual ache he couldn't seem to shake, even with his formidable will.

There would be a time when they weren't working this case together and he was anticipating getting her completely naked again with a totally different outcome.

"The DEA agents are going to meet us at the hotel."

The DEA and the Coast Guard worked with Operation Bahamas, Turks and Caicos (OPBAT), a combined Coast Guard, DEA and Government of Bahamas partnership to combat drug smuggling to and from the Bahamas, working out of the American Embassy.

She nodded. She was a bundle of contradictions. She questioned herself plenty, but when it came to breaking the news to the families, she'd been a rock. He'd been like that before the SEALs, questioning himself, looking for pitfalls and falling into one anyway with Jennifer. His trust had been shattered along with his illusions of love. What he'd thought was real love.

He really was over her. That wasn't a factor, nor was he pining for her. He'd just learned a valuable lesson the day he'd come home and found his world had caved in. He hadn't forgotten that lesson. He'd spent his time avoiding commitment.

After she'd left and he'd been ground into dust by the drill sergeants and rebuilt into rock-hard granite, his confidence knew no bounds. His belief that the world was a dangerous place hadn't shifted much. He'd seen it firsthand. But he didn't fear it any longer. His training and his abilities had made that world just a bit more manageable. What had changed was his outlook toward it.

She nodded and led the way into the car-rental place. As soon as their car was ready, they both reached for the keys. When his fingers brushed over her skin, he felt the connection straight to his toes, his gut twisting into knots. Damn, why did he have this constant reaction to her?

He'd come close to breaking one of his cardinal rules and looking at her. He suspected he might break a few more.

"Do you want to drive?" he asked.

At the touch of his hand, she pulled away as if burned. Yeah, that's how it felt every time she touched him. "Not if you do," she replied. "You're the boss."

He wanted to shake her up, get that I-want-you look

off her face so they both could breathe. "Well, they drive on the opposite side of the road here. Can be confusing."

"You'd better drive, then."

When they pulled up and parked at the hotel, he noticed that she seemed to get more anxious. He'd been to the Bahamas as a SEAL on maneuvers. With its seven hundred islands and two thousand cays, it was over one hundred thousand square miles of gorgeous tropical paradise. A nation built by pirates and rumrunners and a strong British contingent. Nassau alone had three forts.

As they came through the lobby doors, two men rose. One was Beau's age, sandy hair, an overconfident air about him. The other guy was older with white hair and a mustache. At first glance they looked like a couple of drug dealers. The sandy-haired guy was dressed in a sleeveless white button-down shirt and dark slacks, and the older guy had his hair in a ponytail and was dressed in a very loud tropical shirt and white shorts.

The sandy-haired guy took one look at Kinley and stopped. A wary look mixed with hope appeared on his face. He knew Kinley—well.

Beau frowned, an unsettling feeling coming over him. He didn't like the way the guy was looking at her. Beau was used to hanging with a woman for a short period of time. There was usually no follow-up, no matter how much he liked her. He avoided commitment like the plague. Why was it all of a sudden he wanted to grab the guy's collar and say in his most back-the-hell-up voice, *She's mine!*

"Kinley," the guy said, giving Beau a cursory glance. "I didn't know it was you they were sending. What a pleasant surprise."

"Hello." Her tone was flat and that gave him a lot

of satisfaction. "Daniel Wescott, this is Special Agent Beau Jerrott, NCIS."

The guy finally looked at him, and then his face changed as he took in Beau's expression. Beau didn't extend his hand and neither did Daniel.

"This is Ken Stewart, my partner."

"We thought we'd give you a chance to go up to your room and drop your bags and we'd take you out to dinner and compare notes," Ken said, looking between Beau and Daniel. As a seasoned agent, it was no surprise the older guy was cluing in on their tension.

"Sounds good," Beau said.

"Kinley, could I speak to you for a moment, alone?" Daniel said.

She glanced at him and her mouth thinned. "Maybe later. We should get going." They headed for the front desk and signed in.

On the elevator, she was quiet and Beau wondered if she'd heard a thing he'd said this morning. "Who is this guy to you?"

"Someone I used to know."

"As in dated?"

"It's personal, so I don't believe I need to answer that."

The elevator opened and she headed out to her room. Before she could open the door he said, "It does matter. He's now part of the investigation and I think this morning I said I don't like being left out of the loop."

"Are you asking this as lead investigator in this case or as the man who wants to sleep with me?"

Damn if she didn't keep catching him off guard.

"As lead on this case," he lied.

"Yes, I dated him. It was a disaster."

"DEA? Is this the guy you worked with on the task force?"

She gritted her teeth. "Yes. Okay? Can I go now?"

"Kinley. Is this going to be a problem?"

She studied his face, shifting anxiously. "I don't know, Beau. Is it?"

"On my part? Is that what you're asking?"

"I can only guess you're pushing this because you think *this* is personal and it will affect my professional performance. It won't. Suffice it to say that he and I are no longer…together. Is that enough?"

"I want the details."

"We don't have time for that now. Stop being jealous."

He backed up out of her personal space. "I'm not jealous," he said. She gave him a skeptical look and disappeared into her room, closing the door.

He headed to his room and undid the clasp of the garment bag and hung it in the closet. The suits would identify them immediately as cops. He decided it was best to go casual, but for now, he just loosened his tie, undoing the top button. As this was a tropical island, his heavier-weight suits weren't cutting it.

He took off his suit jacket and shrugged out of the shoulder holster. Setting it on the bed, he pulled the tie completely off and unbuttoned his sweat-soaked shirt. He went into the bathroom and washed his face and the back of his neck, pushing his damp hair out of his eyes. Damn, he needed a haircut. Chris was going to get on his ass when he got back to DC.

He tried not to examine the unsettling feeling that continued to plague him. He had every intention of getting the details out of Kinley. It had nothing to do with him being jealous. He just wanted Kinley to be forthcoming so he wasn't caught off guard in this situation. It was about the information, not about his feelings in the matter. He didn't like going into situations blindly. Collecting data was second nature to him. Knowledge was power. That's all it was.

He ran a towel over his hair and smoothed it with his fingers. Heading back into the room, he rummaged around in his garment bag and came up with a blue T-shirt that went with the gray suit he was wearing. Pulling it over his head, he resituated the holster and slipped back into the jacket. A little *Miami Vice*, but it would do until he could get something more appropriate.

Exiting the room he found Kinley just coming out of hers. She was dressed in the same outfit as before, but he noticed that she kept her weapon in a holster in the small of her back.

When he came abreast of her, her delicate scent ambushed him. Feeling proprietary, he wanted to slide his hand down to the small of her back and usher her into the elevator.

But he was out to prove that he could resist her and stay completely professional in public, even though that isn't what he wanted in private.

Back in the lobby, Daniel and his partner waited. They rose when they stepped out of the elevator.

"We can drive," Daniel said.

As soon as Kinley moved forward, Daniel cut Beau off by stepping into his path. When they reached the car, Daniel opened the front door for her.

Beau seethed, not understanding why this guy was getting to him. He didn't chase women. He didn't worry about who else they might be involved in. He and Ken were relegated to the backseat as Kinley took shotgun.

Pulling out into traffic, Daniel struck up a conversation with Kinley in low tones and Beau could barely hear them.

Ken said, "You were a navy SEAL, right?"

He turned to him, surprised. "You know me?"

"You gave us support, oh, about three years ago. Colombia. Pulled three agents out of a Colombian stronghold. Hair was a bit less pretty boy and you were in full-body armor, but I'm pretty sure it was you."

"I don't normally talk about missions," Beau said. Classified meant classified in his book.

"Yeah, I hear that. But since we were both there and one of the guys you pulled out of there was me, I guess I can finally say thanks."

Beau nodded and met Kinley's eyes as she turned to look at him.

"I saw you take down three guys. All without any of them knowing you were even there. Man, never saw anything like it. Right in the open, as confident and as slick as hell. Knew it was SEALs the minute the first guy dropped. Knew my ass was getting rescued."

Beau didn't say anything. He met Daniel's sourpuss face in the mirror, as Kinley's focus was now totally on the conversation in the backseat.

"I remember that mission," Beau said, bending his rule just a little to get Daniel's goat. "In and out in one minute forty-five. Black Hawk standing by and you guys were out of there. No casualties. It was a win."

"Yeah, except for the damn cartel. Heard you guys took down José later on."

Beau searched his memory, then it came to him. Tall, dark, Colombian José Carberra spraying machine-gun fire out into an open lawn where he thought Beau and his team were hidden. Unfortunately for him, he didn't check behind him. By the time he was alerted, they had already scaled over the wall and breached the compound.

"Heard José wasn't in the surrendering mood. Can't say I felt too bad about that. Bastard tortured me and killed my partner outright. Guess I can thank you for that, too."

"Doing my job."

"Like hell. I'm sure that's your canned response. I'm here today because of you."

"You're welcome."

Daniel slowed down for a quaint, white horse–drawn carriage. Beau was used to those as they traversed the city streets of the French Quarter in New Orleans, where he'd been sent fresh from NCIS training.

As pink and light blue colonial-style buildings and architecture flew by, Ken said, "So you gave up the teams for a NCIS badge."

"That's right."

"What do you remember most about Hell Week?"

This guy was a SEAL lover, one who enjoyed meeting and talking to SEALs. He understood why. He'd been saved by Beau's team. "Sand," he said.

"Sand?"

"Yeah. We ran everywhere, tired, wet and cold. There was sand in my shoes, crotch and ears, even between my buttocks. That junk itches, especially when you're constantly wet from seawater. They didn't let us sleep. When we were allowed to lie down, a few short minutes later the instructors ran in beating trash-can lids with clubs, blowing whistles, throwing M-80s, cherry-bomb-size explosives."

"Damn. DEA training is a bit less intensive," he said with a chuckle.

"We found pure coke on the hijacked cutter," Kinley said after a few moments of silence.

"That cocaine could be part of a big shipment we heard got transported out of Cuba headed for the Bahamas," Ken said.

"How much of a threat is Cuba in drug trafficking?" Beau asked.

"Mexican drug traffickers control much of the movement of drugs. So they are the go-to guys," Ken said.

"Maybe this was a smaller operation, a way to bypass the Mexicans? Keep the profits to themselves?" Daniel said.

"It's possible," Ken replied.

"This seems too involved and elaborate for a drug run to me," Kinley said. "There is a definite presence of drugs on the cutter, but at this point we don't know how much. What I don't get is why the whole hijacking and CG impersonation bit. Most drug runners just launch go-fast boats and try to outrun us. This was a staged and deliberate subterfuge. I say something else is at work here."

"You always did have a unique perspective at looking at situations, Kinley," Daniel said.

Kinley stiffened at the regret in Daniel's tone, and Beau found himself jealous all over again with the way Daniel seemed to be trying to make amends for something from their past.

They pulled up to a pink rectangular building with what looked like a hand-lettered sign saying McKenzie's.

"Are the reports of the Cubans cracking down on drugs exaggerated?" Kinley asked.

Ken responded as Daniel parked. "Even with the indication that drugs are being stamped out in Cuba, we're not buying it. A number of major drug trafficking figures from Colombia, Mexico and Peru were reported to be holding meetings or living in Cuba. Given the repressive nature of the society, it is unlikely that these visits went unnoticed or were unapproved by the Cuban government."

"It's more a pipeline, then," Beau said.

"Correct, with the exception of the *Las Espadas Cruzadas* cartel. We estimate two tons of cocaine per year was flowing through Cuba to other destinations. That's what pissed José off three years ago when we seized a shipment of more than ten tons of cocaine in Cartagena, Colombia, just days before it left for Cuba. From Cuba, the cargo was supposed to be reshipped to Spain. Large shipments like this are never made without the 'pipeline' already having been tested. The company shipping this cocaine had previously made four other container shipments to Cuba that went on to Spain."

As they exited the car, Ken said, "This is a great place to eat. One of our favorites. Right, Wescott?"

"Yeah, it's great." Daniel replied. "Conch is a Bahamian staple, brought in fresh each day and really good. You should try the conch salad made with mangos and pineapple. Totally different taste for seafood."

They entered the stall-like building with four columns painted the same pink as that stomach relief medicine. As they entered, he could see the harbor and the long span of the bridge over to Paradise Island.

They ordered from a young girl, Beau getting the salad. He didn't want to be jealous, tried to keep himself neutral, but he just didn't like the way Daniel crowded Kinley. He wanted to shove the guy away from her.

When they each got their dishes and headed for the table, Beau inserted himself by pretending to bump

Daniel. "Sorry about that, buddy." But it put him in the perfect position to sit next to her. Since it was a booth-like setup with a narrow wooden table between them, Daniel and Ken had to sit across from them. Daniel wasn't happy about the arrangement. Too bad.

"So, we tracked down Umprey Thompson's widow. She lives here. The Defense Force is willing to back off until you have a crack at her. She hasn't been told about her husband." Ken said.

The subject of Paradise Island came up and Ken launched into all the fun stuff to do there. Once lunch was over and they headed back to the car, Beau pulled up a picture on his phone. "Was this guy on your radar?" he said as he settled in the back seat. Kinley got in next to him.

"Yeah, we know him. Dudley Martin. American. He's a two-bit drug-dealing scum," Ken said with a frown. "Bad news if he's involved."

"Local authorities have been searching for him to question him. We've been looking for him, too. He looks dead," Daniel said.

"He is. We found him on that drifting cutter," Beau said.

Ken shook his head. "Predatory bastard. He probably lured those poor damn tourists with a lot of cash to pose as CG. Too bad your petty officer wasn't savvier in port."

Beau nodded and growled. "He was just a kid, looking to hook his parents up for their anniversary with a trip to Paris."

"Ah, that's tough. Glad the bastard's dead," Ken said.

Daniel pulled into traffic and said, "Looks like Dudley's lifestyle finally did him in. A lot of palms were greased to keep him out of lockup. He was the front guy for the *Las Espadas Cruzadas* cartel. In English, that's—"

"Two Crossed Swords," Beau said.

Daniel nodded. "They operate out of Cuba and are connected with Kaamil 'The Assassin' el Ajeer."

Beau sat up straighter. He'd been on that hunt when he was still on the teams, but they'd never found him. "The leader of Sons of the Republic. The CIA has been trying to take that bastard down for some time. Elusive as all get out.

"Yeah, and he loves the Caribbean."

"Sure. The white sand beaches, the turquoise water and tons of coke." Beau nodded.

"It has long been a paradise for smugglers who take advantage of the many islands, crowded waters and weak law enforcement.

"That is a fact and why we formed Operation Bahamas, Turks and Caicos. We estimate that as much as twenty percent of the cocaine that reaches the United States moves through the Caribbean, although that figure has varied over time."

"Do you have Mrs. Thompson's address?"

"Sure. Ken?" Daniel asked.

Ken pulled out a notebook and ripped off a piece of paper. "Here you go."

Beau accepted the paper and tucked it into his suit jacket.

"So any insights on what Martin might be doing on that cutter?"

"Martin is a known associate of a fugitive we're currently seeking. That's why we want to talk to him."

"What's his name?"

"Diego Montoya. He's the logistics guy for the *Las Espadas*. He was supposed to testify for us, but pulled

a fast one and disappeared. We believe Martin was involved in helping him to escape."

"Montoya and Martin were tight?"

"Very. Diego trusted him with his life. Spent some
time together in lockup. It's rumored that Martin protected him on the inside and he was repaid in kind."

"Let Kinley and I check out Mrs. Thompson and see
what she knows."

"Sounds like a plan," Daniel agreed.

Thirty minutes later Beau and Kinley pulled up
to a faded mint-green house that looked recently re-
paired and restored. At the door they knocked and a
black woman answered. She was dressed in a simple
white dress and a colorful scarf used as a belt around
her waist. With her cloud of dark, kinky hair her light,
amber eyes and chocolate skin, she was quite striking.
A little girl with the same color eyes hung on her skirts
dressed in a light blue shirt and khaki shorts. When the
woman saw them, her face went blank and impassive.
"Can I help you?" she said, the soft, husky tone of her
voice wary, apprehension in every line of her body.

Beau showed her his badge and Kinley followed suit.
"We're from NCIS and CGIS."

"CG? As in Coast Guard?"

Kinley nodded.

Mrs. Thompson's eyes started to fill with tears. "Umprey is dead, isn't he?"

"Yes, I'm sorry, but he is," Kinley said softly.

Mrs. Thompson backed up and tears spilled from
her eyes. She called, "Momma!" A woman bustled out
of the kitchen and Mrs. Thompson picked up the small
girl and spoke rapidly. "Please take her to the park."

The mother eyed them as she left, her lips thinning

with a hostile look. Apparently Americans were not very welcome in this house.

"Please." She swallowed hard. "Come in."

They sat in a small sitting room and Mrs. Thompson grabbed a tissue from the box on the table and blotted her eyes. "How?" she asked, her voice clogged with tears.

"He was found on the cutter he was transporting back to the Bahamas."

"I knew this was a bad idea. That weaselly white man was nothing but trouble."

"Is this the man?"

She looked at his phone with a look of disgust on her face. "He is the one. He looks dead. Tell me he is dead."

"He is."

Her face contorted into anger and sorrow. "He double-crossed my husband, then."

"Can you tell us what you know?"

Mrs. Thompson looked out the window and shifted. "This is very dangerous for me and for my child. There have already been drug men here looking for the white man. They say that I should call them when my husband comes home."

"Do you know what drug men?"

"Something with 'Swords' in the name, but I don't know the full name. They each had a tattoo on their neck." She pointed to the right side of her neck, just below her jaw. "Two crossed swords."

Beau nodded and leaned forward. "There were four Americans, one of them a navy petty officer found on the ship. Do you know anything about them?"

She closed her eyes and covered them. "I told him this would not end well. What they forced him to do. They threatened us and left him no choice."

"What did he agree to?"

"That white man, Martin, he was to recruit four men to pose as Coast Guard to trick anyone who might spy the ship. Offer them a lot of money. The uniforms were black market. I know because I got them for him. They forced me to."

"Do you know why?"

"They were transporting someone into the country…"

Suddenly gunfire cracked across the quiet street. Mrs. Thompson's windows shattered. Beau dived forward and pulled his weapon.

"Get down!" Kinley shouted, lunging for Mrs. Thompson and dragging her out of her seat with a fierce tug and pushing her facedown into the floor.

"Stay here," Beau ordered.

Kinley pulled her weapon from the small of her back and nodded, pressing her hand into the middle of Mrs. Thompson's back.

He stayed low, heading to the back. As he reached the kitchen, two men with submachine guns came through the back door. He shot each twice in the forehead before they could even react. Bastards thought they would have an easy task, killing two defenseless women and a small child. Once outside, he listened and heard someone approaching. Reaching into his pocket, he pulled out his KA-BAR knife and flipped it open. As soon as another gun-toting goon came around the corner of the house, he caught him around the neck and with one slice silenced him. Letting the body drop, he made his way around the house just as two more men were going through the front door.

"Kinley!" he shouted.

Two more men materialized in the street and shot

at him, and there was no way for him to get back into the house. He heard automatic gunfire, then return fire from a handgun. One just like his.

He squeezed off a couple of rounds and dropped one of the guys. The other backed up, returning fire, but Beau was already behind cover.

Staying low, he ran for the front door, his heart pumping. As he breached the front door, Kinley was obscured behind the couch. All he could see were her feet sticking out. His heart climbed into his throat.

He rushed forward, calling her name in an agonized voice. As he rounded the couch, he stopped dead.

Kinley was on all fours, her hands pressed against a huge bloodstain on Mrs. Thompson's chest. The red a grim contrast to the stark white dress. The woman's eyes were open and staring up at the ceiling.

She turned to look at him with a stricken look on her face. He could see she was trembling. The two men who had come into the house were lying on the floor not far from her. They'd never expected Kinley to take them out. Her weapon was in easy reach.

Beau knelt down.

"Call an ambulance," Kinley said, concern thick in her voice.

Beau felt for a pulse, but it was too late for Mrs. Thompson.

"She's dead," Beau said.

"No," she said softly, looking shellshocked. "Oh, no. Beau! The park! Her mother and daughter!"

"On it." After a fast run to the park, Beau found Mrs. Thompson's mother and daughter safe.

Back at the house the local authorities were pulling up. He showed his badge and turned the grandmother and daughter over to them for safekeeping. Back in the house, Beau went to one of the downed tangos.

Kinley said, "I called Daniel."

Beau nodded. He turned the guy's head and exposed the right side of his neck. Two crossed swords were tattooed just behind his lobe and level with his jaw.

They answered the local authority's questions that were asked, showed their badges and were released.

He carried Kinley's weapon as she went into Mrs. Thompson's bathroom to wash off the blood. Beau stood behind her. As she wiped her hands, she met his eyes in the mirror. "You did good. Don't start second-guessing yourself now."

She accepted her weapon and tucked it back into the small of her back. "Two Swords," she said.

"Yup. Looks like they wanted her dead and unable to give us any information."

"So it was someone they were transporting into the country."

Kinley's phone rang and she answered. "Yes, sir. This is conclusive? All right. Thank you." She listened intently, then her eyes widened. "The commandant? But wouldn't this be handled by the Atlantic area commander, sir?" She listened some more. "Oh, I see. All right. We're heading there now."

She rubbed her hands over her face. "They want us to head over to OPBAT at the embassy for a briefing. We got a hit off Interpol. The DNA matches Diego Montoya, and the commandant and director want to talk to us. Mrs. Thompson died for nothing."

"That's significant that the commandant is involved?"

"Yes, normally he doesn't handle these kinds of matters, but he's royally pissed at the boldness of Montoya and he personally wants to make sure that man is apprehended."

During the ride over to the embassy, Kinley sat mute in the front seat. He could see how she rubbed at her hands. He reached over and covered them after the fourth time. "Are you okay?"

"Yes. I'm fine." She clasped his hand though, tight. "That's the first time I've ever…killed anyone."

"They were clean kills, and you realize they were going to kill you?"

"Yes, I know that. It's just…not what I expected. I've shot at targets for forever, and I've been on drug busts where I've had to pull my weapon, but so far I've never killed anyone."

"Well, if you ever get used to it, that's when you have to worry."

She turned to look at him. "Have you gotten used to it?"

He squeezed her hands and shook his head. "I have a professional detachment. They're tangos in my head. Always the enemy. I did my job in combat. Not something I've gotten used to, but I have no regrets, Kinley, and you shouldn't, either."

She nodded.

Back at the embassy, in their conference room, they all sat down in front of a wide-screen.

"Go ahead," Daniel said.

The screen flashed on. One side was taken up by the commandant of the Coast Guard, and the other was filled with the director of NCIS, with Chris standing close behind him.

"Agent Jerrott," the director said. "We want you and Agent Cooper to remain in the Bahamas to track down any information you have on Diego Montoya in cooperation with the DEA."

"Yes, sir."

"Keep us posted on any leads you uncover. We will keep Homeland informed."

The screen winked off. Beau turned to Daniel and Ken. "Let's go hunting, boys."

"Who're we hunting?" Daniel said.

"Anyone who has two swords tattooed right here on their neck."

Chapter 8

Kinley was dead tired after running down government and DEA informants. They were no closer to nabbing a cartel member.

She rubbed the back of her neck as she rolled away from the computer Daniel had allowed her to use.

Rising, she walked to their break room and put some coins into the snack machine. She wasn't really hungry. From her vantage point she spied Beau at the computer. His cheek rested against his hand as his eyes scanned the screen. His broad, long-fingered hand. He leaned back and stretched all those muscles then ran his hands through his hair, and it settled haphazardly against his cheeks and forehead. Her gaze riveted to his moves, she accepted the shudder of pleasure that rolled down her spine at the image of those strong hands caressing her flesh.

Nope, she wasn't hungry for food, and her hunger shouldn't be this intense for a man she'd just met.

This candy bar was a desperate attempt to quell the anxiety growing inside her. Anxiety that had little to do with solving the job at hand, and a lot to do with the fact that, despite her attempts to not think about him in the way she was thinking about him, her desire hadn't eased at all.

Working side by side with him and watching his quick mind in action certainly hadn't helped matters at all. Wasn't it enough he had a body that wouldn't quit? He had to have a tantalizing mind, as well? She stole another glance at him and shivered, taking a much-needed breath. As she turned around, she almost ran right into Daniel.

"Hey, sorry," he said as he steadied her. "Can I have a word with you?"

She looked down at the candy bar, twisting the wrapper in her hand. The last thing she wanted to do was talk to Daniel. She hadn't missed the way he'd looked at her, a starving man who remembered how she'd filled him up. But, in her experience, the illusion was unfounded and he'd acted in a way that made it difficult to look at him and not feel contempt. "About what?"

"Did you get my emails?"

So many emails the minute he'd gotten his promotion. She'd noted the date. But she'd just hit the delete button whenever one came into her mailbox. She'd also blocked his number. How he didn't get the hint was beyond her. "I got your emails."

He gave her a pained expression. "Did you read them?"

"No," she said, her voice going flatter, her chin rising. "I didn't."

He looked away and was silent a moment. Finally, he said, "I wanted to apologize. I'm really sorry about what happened. I don't have an excuse except that I was wounded, sick with what happened. On medication. My mind was fuzzy."

Her thinking paused for just a short moment. Doubt settled in. All that was true. He *had* been wounded and on medication. But, he hadn't set the record straight when he could have. She didn't want him to make her think about what had happened between them. It made her examine what she was doing with Beau much too closely. Whenever she thought too hard about Beau, she got really scared.

She went to go around him, but he grabbed her arm just a bit too tightly. She stopped. "Look, I know I messed up big-time. But I haven't been able to stop thinking about you." He drew her closer, but Kinley jerked away from him.

"What do you want?" she snapped.

His face softened, his eyes going tender. "Another chance. A chance to make it up to you. We had something good."

She tried to remember what it was like with him, but Beau…kept getting in the way. The way his sexy, soft hair felt against her palms and fingers, the feel of his muscles beneath her touch, the way he tasted and sounded when he kissed her. The way he'd held her against him while she cried her eyes out. Where had Daniel been when she'd been heartbroken and scared? Letting her take all the blame. "We did, and you destroyed it. You betrayed me. You let me take all the blame and we both know it wasn't my call."

"I know," he said softly with remorse. "It was my call."

She closed her eyes. "A man died, Daniel, because of my hunch, the hunch that was discounted. I begged you to call for backup. Now, because of that I second-guess everything. *Everything*. You took something from me and I can't get it back. I thought I could trust you, but I couldn't. I can't."

"I know," he said, his voice sounding crushed. "I won't ever forget that my actions got a man killed. Never, but I've got to put that in my past. I think we can get past that."

She tried to camouflage the unsteadiness in her voice. "I don't think so."

"Don't make any decisions right now," he pleaded. "Think about it." His earnest expression made her chest ache. She'd spent so many years constructing a safe, stable world. Daniel had been key in teaching Kinley how easily—and swiftly—that safety and stability could be altered. She didn't need the reminder.

"I can't…"

He met her gaze, his eyes bleak. "I know you can't make me any promises. Just think about it."

Before she could tell him that there was no way she was giving him anything but a letdown, Beau spoke.

"Kinley." His voice made her jumpy. It sounded so clipped. She turned to find him at the door. "You about ready to go?"

"Yes." She looked at Daniel and he reluctantly let her go.

When she got to Beau, he turned and headed for the street. She followed with the candy bar still in her hand, but dropped it in the trash on her way out the door. It wasn't what she was hungry for, she thought. She couldn't stop herself as she ran her eyes over his broad back. Once she was seated in the passenger side, Beau took off. He didn't say anything as he drove. He clenched and unclenched his hands on the wheel, his face tight.

This time she covered his hand on the wheel, wondering at the many things that could be plaguing him. "Are you all right?"

"Just tired," he said in that same clipped tone. Ah, dammit, had she done something wrong when they were looking for a member from the Crossed Swords? Had he found some kind of flaw from when she'd taken down those guys while trying to save Mrs. Thompson's life? Maybe he'd changed his mind about her. Doubts assailed her as she watched his angry face, her insides jittering. It would be better, much better for both of them if he would just lose interest.

But, if she was being honest with herself, that thought made her feel a *little* bit out of control.

She tried her best to appear unaffected and coolly in control as she sailed across the lobby. Beau reached past her and pressed the elevator button. When he stepped in after her, it felt a bit tight, as if he was suddenly taking up way too much space, using up way too much of her precious oxygen. And yet he was standing a normal distance from her, not so much as looking at her. None of that seemed to help with the way she reacted to him on a purely physical level. She'd never been so aware of a man before.

Was he really someone she could truly trust? Was there anyone she could really trust?

Then there was the way he'd held her. Even more than his physicality there was his compassion. She'd felt it so keenly and he'd been so patient, so gentle and kind. That more than anything she couldn't seem to get past.

Case in point. He'd been affected by Mrs. Thompson's death, whether it was knowing that the little girl they'd seen briefly was going to grow up without a mother and father or the fact that six goons had been dispatched to murder two defenseless women and a child. All she knew was the way his jaw had hardened and the regret in his eyes when he saw that Mrs. Thompson was dead.

Maybe he was blaming her.

Even as she thought that, she dismissed it. He had been the one to tell her not to second-guess herself and she shouldn't be doing that now. She glanced at him and all her thoughts just seemed to freeze. Beau was the full deal. Tough, deadly warrior, compassionate man, intelligent, and all residing in a physical body that was hard to resist.

There was plenty to make a woman's mouth water from looking at him, but how many of those women had experienced the real Beau? He seemed affable, but she thought it hid a guarded man. She knew about hiding everything that was uncertain in her. She recognized it. He might seem easygoing, but there was a coil of danger that shivered across her skin.

Beau remained silent as they ascended. But it wasn't his silence that made her nerves jangle, it was how taut he was, and she was sure it didn't have anything to do with fatigue. That silence of his was making her analyze things she didn't want to think about. As soon as the doors opened, she sailed out and walked briskly to her room. She was struggling with her own hang-ups. Was she using her whole professionalism spiel unfairly to help her to keep her distance from Beau? They weren't partners. They wouldn't be seeing each other after this mission was over. She was starting to get the really bad feeling that she was closing herself off emotionally because Beau was someone who was pushing her out of her comfort zone. Even with Daniel, Kinley hadn't had to go very deep to realize that it was nothing more than a temporary thing for her. She needed that to keep herself safe. To not get in too deep.

Except now, it wasn't working. She was going to be disappointed if he didn't want to… Oh, damn, she was such a ninny.

She slipped her key card into the door and when the green light pulsed, she pushed it open. As she turned toward him to say good-night, he crowded her inside.

He pushed her up against the wall. In the light from the hall, before the door closed, she glimpsed his dark blue eyes, his hair a tousled mess and a hint of beard stubble shadowing his incredibly handsome face. But instead of looking like a man who was going to kiss her, he looked like a man who was going into battle. The intensity in his eyes reaching right inside her, squeezing her heart.

Then the door slammed and they were cocooned in the semidarkness, ambient light trickling though the window.

"Are you going to give that bastard another chance?" he said harshly.

She'd been completely wrong about his anger. It wasn't directed at her and it wasn't anger. It was his reaction to Daniel touching her, getting close to her. He was completely jealous.

He could deny it all he wanted.

The easygoing, charming Beau hid this side to him. Not so easygoing. Not a surprise. He was a SEAL. The toughest of the tough. But she heard the need for reassurance in his voice.

There was a light and a dark side to him and the combination was doubly dangerous. "Are you?" he whispered. His hand slid to the back of her neck, and he tilted her head. Before she could say anything, his mouth was on hers. Hard, demanding. Hot, so hot, moist, a seductive tease that made every bone in her body melt.

She couldn't compare Daniel to Beau and use the same tired reason that she'd used with him. If she was being honest with herself, the reason she needed the distance with Beau was because she wanted him and he was more of a threat to her control, her fear of getting too close. What happened with Daniel and the death of his partner had shattered her confidence. But Beau was already so different. He listened, was supportive and took her seriously.

And her tingling mouth had been waiting for this. It had been sensual torture. She'd expected a warrior's kiss, bold and aggressive, attempting to conquer through sheer will and force. It was because he'd looked so fierce and determined.

But it wasn't what that felt like. It was an onslaught, all right, an all-out blitz. But he kissed her with an almost desperate need and it couldn't be more seductive. The fact that he wasn't as confident as she expected touched that unstable and unsure part of her and made her ache for him just that much more.

He took her emotions and twisted them around more than any man she'd ever met. He kept surprising her. And the way he twisted her, left gaps in her armor for him to slip through and affect her... Wholly, intensely, without intent or design—just pure reaction at a base level that maybe he wasn't even aware of. This wasn't a seduction by him; it was a seduction of him. That was much more difficult to resist than a confident man taking what he wanted, making it all about him and his pleasure. With Beau that just wasn't the case. There wasn't anything more alluring or a bigger turn-on than a man she was crazily attracted to who wanted her and made no secret of it.

She pressed back, kissing him just as fiercely, letting the life of him, his sheer sexy presence, filter through her, seep into her, absorbing him through her pores.

He slipped his hands under her arms, curling them around her back, and lifted her effortlessly into him, growling softly against her lips when she wrapped her legs around his waist, the sound rumbling through his chest.

Her hands coiled around the heated muscles of his biceps, traveling up to his broad, flexing shoulders and around his neck, anchoring herself.

He was breathing harshly. His hot, velvety tongue slipped into her mouth as he drove his hips into hers, and he made a soft sound this time as his erection ground against the core of her.

He supported her bottom as he pushed them away from the wall and moved to the bed. She held onto him like a limpet. He stopped at the edge of the bed and let her slide down his body. Pushing her jacket off her shoulders, it dropped to the floor behind her. He cupped her cheeks, pushing the hair off her face, his palms smooth.

She stared up at him, into eyes that held her so solidly, so completely. Body shaking, lips trembling, she held his passionate gaze, held on to it tightly.

She slipped her hands beneath his jacket and lifted it away, shoving it until he shrugged out of it. Reaching for his shoulder rig, he unbuckled, turned and set it on the chair near the bed. Kinley reached back for her weapon and unclipped it from the small of her back and moved around to slide it onto the nightstand table.

She couldn't lose herself in this man. She had to hold something back. It was self-preservation. Temporary meant short-term. Could she let herself trust him, even though she was losing her resolve?

She closed her eyes. Was she going to take this step? She was driven by her own goals, but she couldn't seem to get past one all-consuming feeling—she felt safe with him.

With Daniel it had been about sex. About alleviating some of her loneliness with the physical closeness.

But that wasn't the case with Beau. She wanted to wrap herself around him, there was no doubt about that, but it was a deeper connection with him that she sought. She squeezed her eyes closed, the fear welling up in her.

"If you don't want to do this, Kinley, sugar, tell me."

Tenderness slammed into her, hard, coming from such a closed and tight place it almost hurt. He was making it difficult to keep her guard up.

And was the fear that this wasn't quite a temporary feeling more of a reason to keep him at arms' length?

He remained motionless and she let go of a little bit of her stupid fear, let go a little bit of her artificial walls. The experience of him would be the reward. It was time that she stopped denying her needs out of fear.

"Do you want me, *chérie*?"

The tone of his voice melted her completely. He wasn't demanding or pushing her. It was a simple question. She had a simple answer.

"Yes, please. I want…you."

He made a soft, surrendering sound in his throat, pressing against her from behind, his chest heavy against her back, his hard-on up against her buttocks. She leaned back against him as he pulled the button-down shirt out of her slacks, his hands slipping beneath.

His hands smoothed over her rib cage, up over her lace-covered breasts then back down. When he came up again, he went under the lace cups, his palms rasping over her nipples.

She gasped, and arched as he moved. He made quick work of her buttons and her shirt was off. Her bra was nothing but a memory as it dropped from his hands to the rug.

He stripped her of her pants and undies in one smooth move, spun her until she was up against his fully clothed body. She reached for the hem of his T-shirt and dragged it up to get her hands on his bare skin. He made a soft sound as her mouth connected with his chest. He discarded the shirt in the pile at their feet.

Her mouth found his flat nipple and she sucked him with strong pulls, her hand going to the hard heat beneath the zipper of his dress pants, squeezing and fondling him.

He swore in the semidarkness. "Take them off."

Her mouth still tasting his hot skin, she undid his belt one-handed and unhooked and unzipped, the loosened pants falling off his hips. Grasping her around the waist, he bent down, dragging her belly against his open mouth. He licked her all the way to her breasts, sucking a hard nipple into his mouth. She cried out at the feel of his hot, greedy mouth.

Slipping her hands between his briefs and his hard ass, she rolled them off so that they flowed down his body.

She pushed him back and he folded down against the mattress. Kneeling, she came between his legs and licked his erection. He moaned deep when she slipped her mouth over the head of him, sucking gently. He twisted against the mattress as she worked him over.

Rearing up, he grasped her under the arms and pulled

her across his hot, muscled body. Reaching for protection, he rolled it over himself with practiced ease. Flipping her onto her back, he straddled her. Using his knee to open her legs, he fit himself between her thighs.

"Beau," she whispered. "Oh, please."

He grunted when he took her, slipping inside to delve deep. She wrapped her legs around his hips and he pulled out and thrust again. She clutched at him as his strokes got short and quick, then slow and deep.

She exploded, the pleasure detonating in concussive waves of intense pleasure. After a few more thrusts, he stiffened above her and groaned, pumping hard.

For a few minutes they lay together, him still buried deep inside her, her legs wrapped around him. As her breathing slowed, Beau withdrew, jerking a little as he slipped out of her.

He dragged her against him, his arms going around her tightly. For a few more minutes they clung to each other. He slipped out of bed and disposed of the condom.

Sliding back in, he rolled to his back and she settled against his chest.

"Tell me about him," he demanded on a growl.

Kinley sighed. "Why? Because you're jealous?" She said it with something akin to marvel in her tone. As if it was just completely improbable.

He rolled on top of her, supporting his upper chest with his forearms. His groin settled against her groin and hips. "I'm not jealous."

"Yes, you are."

"I want to know what I'm up against." He dipped his head and nuzzled the curve of her jaw, his stubble rasping against her skin.

"You're not up against anything." It shouldn't have charmed her as much as it did.

"Tell me about him. What happened between the two of you?" He smoothed damp strands of hair off her face.

This time it wasn't a demand. It was a request and she couldn't resist that look and those thickly lashed, midnight-blue eyes. Against her better judgment, she said, "I was the only woman on the task force. There were two DEA agents, and an FBI agent. With the exception of Daniel, they were all over forty and one of them even called me little lady."

He rolled his eyes. "They didn't take you seriously."

"No. That's an understatement." She traced her fingertips over his face. "You probably haven't noticed, but women who attempt to fit into jobs that are traditionally held by men have to be faster, smarter, with infinite patience."

"I work with a woman, Kinley, and I love it. She kicks my ass regularly. She's so damned smart and intuitive."

"Who is this woman?"

He chuckled. "Who's jealous now?"

"I'm not jealous," she insisted. She would just ignore the way her gut tightened and a sense of protective need came over her.

"Special Agent Amber Dalton. She's a pistol and she has a boyfriend. Some navy swabbie. I think of her like a sister. But enough about Amber. I was asking about Daniel."

She still wanted to know more about Amber, but that would have to wait. "I couldn't figure out how so many go-fast boats were getting in and out so quickly."

He gave her a wry look. "You were the one who had

a hunch about the mothership concept?" When she nodded, he said, "I'm impressed."

She flushed under his praise. "Yes. I told Daniel's partner. He was the one that called me little lady. I suggested that it was probably a freight ship and guessed the manifest would show that it came from South America."

"You found one in the harbor?"

"Not exactly. I knew they wouldn't want to seem suspicious, so I figured it had to be one that had already off-loaded. We used helicopters to find it and it was sitting just off the coast. We went out there, just the three of us, to check it out. Daniel's partner decided he was going to go aboard. I was against it and insisted we call for backup."

"He discounted you again."

"He did and so did Daniel."

That was why she was so apprehensive about seeing him again. He'd set off those feelings all over again and she didn't want to dredge them up. It was really why she couldn't ever see herself with him.

Time had diminished their time together into fragments of memories, memories that she'd deliberately pushed away into some dark corner of her mind. Once she locked feelings away, she didn't think about the past. And she didn't want to think about it now.

"You were sleeping with him?"

"I created such a wonderful fantasy in my mind, and I'd been so sure that being with Daniel would be what I had been searching for. I really believed that something special and beautiful would happen." She buried her face in his neck to avoid his eyes, feeling completely ridiculous. That she was opening up to him like this was unexpected and shocking.

She didn't want to dredge up the disillusionment, the panic, the humiliation. She did not want to remember how she'd felt after all her romantic expectations had been shattered and she'd been confronted with the cold light of reality.

He cupped the back of her head and kissed the top of it. "It was his call?"

She nodded. "He said it would be a quick look-see. They boarded and the smugglers came back." He massaged her scalp, running his fingers through her hair, and it was so soothing. "I went overboard, into the water before they saw me, but I had enough time to radio in. Daniel was wounded and his partner was killed before backup got there."

"I remember reading the story. You took down the smugglers and confiscated seven tons of cocaine."

She felt hollow. "And I was brought up on disciplinary charges. Daniel said nothing and I took the full blame. I got reprimanded and chewed out for not following procedure."

"Why didn't you say anything?"

"I thought we had something. But when he didn't back me up, I realized that I was alone. By then, it was too late. He'd already let me take the fall. I was distraught and felt so betrayed. He left and took his promotion. I haven't spoken to him since."

He sent his hands through her hair again. "What a freaking coward. He was worried about losing his promotion."

"Yes. I was such a fool. I don't intend to be that kind of fool again."

His head dipped down and he kissed her mouth, lingered over her lips. It was more a comforting kiss and her heart softened. This smart, fierce warrior was sweet, too?

"Are you this wonderful to all your conquests?"

"You're not a conquest," he said, his head rising and his eyes pinning her. "There is no subjugation here. There is nothing but participation."

She reached up and cupped his face, running her palm over his stubble with languid sweeps, the rough texture stimulating. "Okay, I concede that. But you didn't answer my question."

"I'm not with them long enough to have the option. But with you, Kinley, I don't feel sweet." She gasped when she felt him harden.

He reached for protection again and said, "Not sweet at all."

Chapter 9

The snick of the lock woke Beau immediately. His eyes flashed open. Without hesitation he rolled and took Kinley with him down to the floor. He instinctually covered her body with his as automatic gunfire slammed into the headboard above them.

Beau reached for his pants and snagged the KA-BAR he always carried with him. He had no doubts as to who was trying to kill them. Had to be the *Las Espadas*. It wouldn't take much to find out where they were staying and grease some palms to get their room keys.

His heart pounding, adrenaline drop loading into his system, he tried not to worry about Kinley. She knew how to handle herself.

Buck naked, he dove for his weapon on the chair. The window above him exploded with a shattering sound followed by a whoosh as the vacuum on the room broke. Wind and shards of glass sliced the air.

With a somersault, he grabbed his weapon and came to his feet behind the two men firing at the bed. Beau took no chances and went for head shots. The two goons dropped. But another one came through the door and knocked his gun out of his hand. It went spinning across the carpet. A knife sliced at his face, but he was already spinning away and it only nicked him on the jaw. They must be working in teams of two and when they didn't find Beau in his room, they came here.

With a quick flip of Beau's wrist, the KA-BAR's blade was ready and deadly. Moving fast, he held the knife in a reverse-edged grip. He slashed at his opponent, who avoided the maneuver but wasn't fast enough to avoid Beau's follow-up fist, which smashed into his face. As he stumbled backward, another man entered the room. Between one heartbeat and the next, Beau flipped the knife up, caught it and flung it. It buried to the hilt in the man's throat, just as Kinley put a round in his chest and head. When she turned the gun on the only man left, Beau said, "No!"

"But you're unarmed." Her voice was filled with concern.

He shook his head. The knife-wielder came at him again with a slash. Beau caught his wrist, pulling the knife away from his body. With a lightning-quick, snapping blow, he hit the man's nose with the heel of his hand, dazing him. Stepping into the man's body, Beau used one hand to grab his wrist. Tucking his assailant's arm under his, Beau grabbed him by the throat with his free hand. With punishing power, he lifted the guy and took him down to the rug. With two blows the man was out.

His blood rushing, he was across the room. Taking her shoulders, he said, "Are you okay?"

She nodded as sirens wailed in the night. Either hotel guests or the staff must have called the police. Beau walked around the bed and pulled on his briefs and pants. As she hurriedly got dressed, she asked, "How are we going to explain this?"

"We were discussing the case when we were attacked," he said.

She nodded. "Beau, you're bleeding."

"It'll be fine. Give me your gun," he said. "We don't want any weapons in our hands when the cops get here." He placed both guns on the bed.

They both grabbed their badges as the first Bahamian officer shouted, "Police!"

Beau and Kinley raised their hands with their badges prominently displayed as the police rushed into the room.

Fifteen minutes later, Daniel and Ken entered the room. Ken shook his head, taking in the carnage. "Looks like they picked on the wrong guy." He chuckled.

Daniel took in the bullet spray peppering the mattress and headboard, the blown-out window. Then he looked at Kinley and his lips thinned. "Are you all right?" he asked, his eyes flickering to Beau.

He'd guessed, but Beau didn't give a damn.

She stepped away as Daniel reached out and moved closer to Beau. "Yes, I'm fine."

Daniel looked disappointed, then went to one of the bodies and crouched down.

"Las Espadas Cruzadas," Beau said. "One of them is alive and on his way to the hospital. Shall we?"

Daniel rose and nodded. "Let's go see what this bastard knows."

At the hospital, the prisoner had been cleaned up,

his nose set and bandaged. When the cartel goon saw Beau, he shouted death threats at him.

Beau wanted to smash his face again. In Spanish, he asked, "Why did you come after us?"

"Orders," he said, giving Beau a nasty look. His eyes went to Kinley, caressed her face and moved slowly down her body.

"Ojos aquí," Beau ordered. He wanted the cartel goon's eyes on his own and off Kinley.

"Vamos a violar a tu mujer antes de matarte."

We will rape and kill your woman before we kill you. Beau grabbed him by his hospital gown and dragged him close. "You're not going to live to see the next few minutes, if you don't answer my question."

It was obvious the guy understood him. It was in his eyes.

"Who ordered you to come after us?"

He stayed mute.

Beau hit him in his freshly bandaged nose. He howled and covered it.

In heavily accented English, he growled, "We were to kill the women and child and anyone one else who saw us," he said, his voice muffled.

"Is this about Diego Montoya?"

The man's eyes widened and he spat. "That *pendejo!*"

"What do you know about him?" Beau's voice was low and hard-edged.

"He's a dead man walking."

"Like you?"

"What is that supposed to mean?"

"Only we're putting the word out on the street that you're cooperating with us. So, you might as well."

His eyes widened and he hesitated only for a second. "I'll need protection!" he said, fear alive in his eyes.

"What do you know about Montoya?"

He blew out a breath looking like a trapped rat. Beau had zero sympathy. "He changed his appearance and we're looking for information on who did the surgery. They want to know what he looks like now."

"Here?"

"No, in Cuba."

"The doctor's name?"

"I don't know. I swear."

No matter how Beau came at the guy, he didn't have the information they needed. Both he and Kinley reported back to their respective supervisors. They checked out of the hotel they were in and into another one. Two DEA agents watched over them while they slept. Well, he tried to sleep. Lying on his back, he missed the soft warmth of her snuggled up to him. Who the hell would have thought he'd enjoy a snuggler?

Dammit, he didn't know what was wrong with him. It was as if his technique for keeping himself distant had suddenly eluded him.

He shifted restlessly, thinking what might have happened if he hadn't been in her room when those goons had broken in. He was a seasoned warrior, used to sleeping with one eye open, tuned to his surroundings and any change in them.

He wasn't downplaying Kinley's abilities, but she'd never been in combat. Combat was complete and utter chaos and the only things that'd kept him alive were his teammates and his training and skill.

He shifted again to his side and pushed the heavy hair off his face. Damn, he'd been sleeping alone for a long time, so why in hell couldn't he just shut down?

He wanted Kinley with him...to keep her safe. Dammit, he hadn't wanted to fall into that trap. Simple investigation hadn't made him worry about her. But they'd been in two firefights since they'd landed on this island. *Las Espadas* had quite a presence here. Made him wonder why Daniel the bastard wasn't aware. Or were they out in force because of the possible sightings of Montoya?

Montoya. What a piece of work, a lowlife and a very wanted man. Montoya had originally been a pilot flying drugs and he'd happened to get the DEA on his tail, but had managed to not only elude them, but to get the drugs where they needed to go.

The leader of *Las Espadas*, Pedro Martinez, wanted to reward his ingenuity. He hired Montoya as a kind of air-traffic controller, negotiating directly with the Mexican cartels, then guiding their cocaine flight from Cuba to secret runways in barren stretches of Mexico. Knowing he was being monitored, he'd sing a snippet of a song as directions to pilots.

He'd become a gatekeeper to Martinez, fielding his phone calls and accompanying him on foreign trips. He was the one who opened the conduit of money from "The Assassin" into the cartel's coffers.

So, the doctor in Cuba could have been compromised. But they wouldn't know that until Beau went hunting for him.

He was determined to keep Kinley out of any more firefights. He had to give her credit. She had reacted quickly and even taken down targets without hesitation. She was such a bundle of uptight nerves, that had surprised him. But in a battle, she threw down and threw down hard.

Daniel, the bastard, had been a fool to treat her like he had.

He had never discounted a woman. He might have

had a long string of them, but he always chose the kind that knew the score and didn't mind playing with him for a night. His reaction to the way Daniel was trying to get a second chance with her was something that Beau didn't understand. But all he could think about when Daniel had cornered her in the snack area was that he wanted to break his face, even though Kinley was more than capable of taking care of herself.

He sat up and ran his hands through his hair again, swearing softly. Sweat broke out on his brow. Struggling for breath, he knew he might have made a mistake here and he wasn't used to admitting that. He felt his short leash getting shorter. If Daniel touched her again, he wasn't sure what he would do. He flexed his hands, weapons in their own right.

All he could think was *mine*. She was his. It might be temporary, but for now, right this freaking second in time, she was with him.

He also realized that they were going to Cuba. He'd already suggested to Chris that he take this mission solo. Mostly because he was trained for this kind of covert op and he would be able to get the job done quickly. In and out, smooth as butter. She could stay in the Bahamas. He gritted his teeth at the thought of leaving her here anywhere near Daniel. But Cuba would be dangerous.

Solo. Yeah, that's what he'd been doing for a number of years. Taking the warmth women had to offer in brief spurts, meeting the needs of his body, but never engaging his heart. It had been simple…until now. From the moment he'd met the fiery redhead, he'd been… intrigued. Besotted.

He rose out of bed and slipped on a pair of shorts. Knocking softly on the adjoining room door, he waited.

The feelings that were growing for her were impossible. Especially when she wasn't interested in a relationship that could jeopardize her career. The only factor that played a role here was if she was as involved in her career as Jennifer was. He was long over his ex, but not the ingrained fear of trusting the wrong person again and getting his heart broken. Yes, Kinley was different than Jennifer in so many ways. Her coloring, her outlook on life, her confidence.

Trouble. God, he was in trouble here.

She answered the door in one of those nothings that women wore to sleep. This one was hot pink.

"What's wrong?" she asked when she saw his face.

"Nothing." When she snuggled into his arms, he maneuvered them both back into her bed. Just where he'd wanted her.

Her eyes a sleepy green, she said, "You should be sleeping."

"Couldn't," he said, then dipped his head and pressed his mouth to hers. The clamoring in him settled down immediately. He kissed her for a few more minutes. "How are you doing?"

She shrugged. "It's been a crazy week so far."

"Yeah, that is for sure."

"I'm glad you're on our side."

He smiled.

"Can you show that knife trick to me sometime?"

"Sure. It'll make you more of a badass."

She laughed softly. "Right. That fits."

Without saying a word, he settled against her. With her soft, steady breathing, the intoxicating scent of her filling him up, he sank against her and fell right to sleep.

He woke up at her restless movement as she groaned softly, and kicked off her sheet. He looked down the length of her body. A damp sheen of sweat covered her skin, from the backs of her calves, in the tender hollows behind her knees, up her thighs and over the incredible curves of her butt. Was there a woman on this planet as put together as Kinley Cooper?

She made a soft sound in the room and he straightened. Was that a whimper? Suddenly she thrashed and he knew a nightmare when he saw one.

"*Chérie*. Wake up."

Her eyes fluttered open and she stared up at him. "You were having a nightmare."

"It was a bad one," she shivered, wrapping her arms around his neck. Settling against him she closed her eyes.

He held her close, knowing what she was going through. This had been quite a case so far. She made a contented sound and he let himself drift until he fell asleep again.

The warmth of him was a surprise when she woke up but hadn't opened her eyes yet. His arm was around her waist and his face buried in her hair. She could feel the heaviness of his breath against her neck. She sighed. That was all she could do. The scent of him wrapped around her, a scent that told her he was all male, hot and spicy.

She looked at the clock. Breakfast was going to be here in a few minutes. He shouldn't even be in her room, but she couldn't dredge up enough energy to protest with his heavy muscles against her back.

She tried to slip away from him, but he tightened his arm around her waist, and dragged her under him.

"Where you goin', *chérie*?"

His accent was thick, his voice husky in the morning.

"Breakfast will be here any minute," she said looking up into his arresting face.

"Mmm." He nuzzled her. "I think I found my breakfast."

"Beau, no," she said weakly. "We have a briefing in an hour."

There was a knock on the door and he sighed.

She slipped out of bed and grabbed her robe as he rose and watched her walk away from him. He disappeared through the adjoining door when she opened the door. Both male agents turned, their gazes going over her.

Kinley smiled at the woman who rolled in the tray and ignored the male interest. When the girl raised her head, she stopped in midroll as Beau, dressed in a T-shirt and jeans came back through the door, it was quite obvious that the way the man looked knocked the poor girl for a loop.

He was deliciously tousled, his hair mussed, beard stubble making him look even more appealing and quite dangerous. That girl was too young to have any defense against him.

"I'll take that for you," he said with a smile.

She came back to herself and relinquished the cart. He took the warmer off one of the dishes and wrinkled up his nose. Then the other. He looked up at her. "Ah, shoot, sugar, I like the Big Easy, but I don't like eggs over easy. Do you think I could get 'em scrambled with just a bit of pepper?"

"Of course, sir, right away."

She picked up the dish and, blushing heavily, exited the room.

As soon as the door closed, Kinley arched a brow at him.

His lips curved. "What?" he said innocently, holding her gaze. The combination of that twinkle in his eyes and his laughter was downright lethal.

"You know what."

"Are you saying that you think I have experience in cajoling members of the opposite sex?"

"Oh, I don't think I could stretch my imagination that much," she said.

He laughed and picked up a blueberry off one of the plates and popped it into his mouth.

When Kinley entered the meeting room back at the embassy, she settled into one of the chairs and Beau took a seat next to her. As soon as Daniel and Ken entered, the wide-screen came to life, revealing both the director and the commandant flashing on the screen.

"Agent Jerrott, your request to go into Cuba to track down a possible picture of Diego Montoya is granted, but your request to do this solo is denied. SA Cooper and Wescott will accompany you. Agent Westcott has a contact who may have information on the identity of the doctor. You and Cooper will pose as a wealthy married couple."

Kinley stiffened beside him and turned to glare at him. He didn't look at her. He had been trying to cut her out of going to Cuba? Why? Didn't he trust her to pull her own weight? Did he think she was incompetent? Couldn't handle herself under pressure or undercover? Disappointment in him flooded her system and on its heels, anger. Hadn't she just spilled her guts to him about being discounted? Hadn't he heard a word she'd said?

"Sir, with all due respect, I've logged hours of undercover work, covert ops—"

The commandant said, "I have reviewed your file, Agent Jerrott. But this operation is better served with subterfuge than brute force. You will not engage the *Las Espadas*. You will locate the surgeon with the ruse that Agent Cooper wants plastic surgery, get a picture of Montoya and then get out. You have three days. In your mission packet you will find the map of where you need to be for extraction. Don't waste time. Good luck."

Chris said, "You'll acquire weapons once you're inside."

"Yes, sir," he said.

Kinley left the conference room and was directed to a room that had clothing laid out. So many different outfits, expensive jewelry, suitcases and a set of... wedding rings.

"Kinley," Beau said.

She couldn't look at him right now. "It would be better if you gave me a few minutes," she said. What she couldn't quite handle was her doubts. What if he was right? What if she messed up? There were so many things that could go wrong.

"Chérie," he said, his voice closer, which meant so was he. She had to look up, but she really needed more space and more time. She was raw inside. Dealing with Beau up close in her personal space was more than she could take on at the moment.

"Don't call me that. Not right now." She took a steadying breath, and looked up.

"Let me explain."

"What is there to explain? You don't trust my abilities. After what I said to you..." She stepped back, picking up an outfit, thinking it might be too big for her.

He took a step closer and she tensed. She tried not to show it, but that much was really beyond her at the moment. The stabilized world she'd thought she'd constructed for herself had just been proven to have very shaky foundations. And she didn't know what to do about that. What she did know was Beau Jerrott was the last person she'd ever reveal that to. He'd already gotten too much of her, had a way of looking at her, into her, like he saw far past her defenses, to some other place she was unaccustomed to people reaching. And that was without her being stupid enough to hand it over to him.

"No offense to your commandant, I don't do brute-force missions. SEALs are all about stealth." He said it quietly, but somehow the softer tone wasn't the least bit comforting. In fact, it only served to unnerve her further. He saw too much, too easily.

"You want me to stay here. Admit it. You don't think I can handle this mission." She put her hand out when he took another step. "I was a fool to ever think anyone in the good-ol'-boys' club would ever take me seriously. Just because we're sleeping together doesn't give you the right to make decisions for me. I've been taking care of myself for a long time."

It was hardly a blink, and if she hadn't been expressly looking for it, she'd never have noticed it, but there had been a flicker. She pounced on it without thinking twice. She was being eaten up inside thinking that he didn't trust her.

"If you have concerns of any kind, why not just voice them? Don't go behind my back and—"

His eyes went hard and flinty, and she had to resist the urge to shiver. "I didn't go behind your back." Gone was that soft Southern drawl. In its place was a flat, steely voice that showed the other side of Beau. The warrior side. "I didn't even mention you."

"Right. You don't have to. It's firmly in your head.

I'm a risk. Thanks, Beau. Thanks a lot." She went to push past him, wanting nothing more than to end this conversation. She'd been badly rattled by the whole thing and this confrontation only made it worse.

He took her arm gently but firmly as she brushed by and turned her around to face him. "I'm not going to lie to you. Do I want you safely here? Damn right."

She winced at that.

"You'll be out of your element, Kinley. I don't… I couldn't handle you getting hurt."

"Admirable," she said, trying to maintain the steely facade, thinking her heart might melt out of her chest any second. "Is this about my abilities or my safety?"

"A little of both."

Sex with a fellow agent could lead to this and it was her lapse to deal with. Men were overprotective of women—it was second nature. With Daniel, she'd been thrown to the wolves. But what was happening here with Beau? Was it his feelings for her that were making him hesitate, or the fact that she was going to be in a situation she hadn't been fully trained to handle warring with the need to protect a woman he was intimate with?

His response changed things. "You need to put your feelings aside, Beau."

He gave her a startled look.

"What feelings?" he growled.

"We've been intimate. You want to protect me. It's part of the reason you want me to stay here. I can hold my own. I'm not as well trained as you are, but I can adapt and perform my duties. I know my way around a case, so stop with the macho bull."

His jaw flexed as if he was gritting his teeth. "I like and respect you, Kinley. You can—"

"What? Trust you?" she demanded, embracing the righteous anger that filled her, along with the fear of failure, that it could all unravel at once. She tried to yank free, but he didn't let her. "You should have told me your concerns. How can I trust that you're not holding something back?"

"I don't hold things back. Not to spare anyone's feelings. Not when the stakes are high."

His gaze locked to hers, so intent, so focused. So trustworthy and steady. Still, she wavered. She was so tired of the fear of not trusting herself. Maybe that was more the issue here.

"You think I can handle this?" she said flatly. He wasn't the only one who could do steely.

"If I said I'm not sure, would that piss you off?"

She felt the blood drain from her face. So it was true. He did harbor doubts. The blood came rushing back, flushing her cheeks until they felt hot, as she realized that he had a right to his own opinion. It was up to her to prove him wrong. He took both of her arms then, pulled her closer. "But, then again, I've seen you hold your own, act when you needed to, and you did a damn fine job. It's purely instinctual that I want to protect something I feel is…precious."

"You'd better not be charming me."

"I would, if it would help, sugar."

"Don't call me sugar. It's distracting," she said, without meaning to, which only caused his gaze to intensify.

"I can't help it. You melt in my mouth."

She didn't know what to say to that except, *Oh, God.* Standing this close, looking into his eyes, she saw no sign of deception, no wavering. He was either charming her, or he was telling her the absolute truth. She wished the stakes on knowing which it was weren't so high.

"What exactly are you worried about? Let's get this out in the open so that I'm aware what you consider a liability."

"It's mostly combat that worries me and the undercover aspect," Beau admitted.

"We're thoroughly trained in the Coast Guard. Military training, Beau. I was trained hard, maybe not as hard as a SEAL, but I will not slow you down. We may be tasked with protecting the coast, but make no mistake, we're no pushovers. You need to let go of your elitist attitude here. The Coast Guard is part of the military. You should give me the respect I deserve for that."

He rubbed at his forehead. "Damn, Kinley, you're right. Sometimes I lose track of the fact that any other branch of the military may not be trained as thoroughly as the SEALs, but that doesn't mean they can't do what needs to be done. They prove that every day by doing their duty. Maybe I was reacting to the fact that I want you to be safe, instead of giving you the due your time on the job and the abilities that you've already shown me that you are quite competent. But you will give me this. When we go into Cuba, we're on our own. It's a totally different situation than taking down go-fast boats from the deck of a cutter with canon and mortar fire at your fingertips."

"Granted," she said.

"Daniel is seasoned. He's been undercover and in some hairy situations where he had to rely on his own abilities. I'm talking about experience here, not training. Is that clear?"

"Okay, I will give you that as well. I will follow your lead, but I am resourceful and think quickly on my feet. I will not be a liability."

"I guess you can't prove anything by sitting in the

Bahamas and not being challenged in a job you've vowed to uphold in any capacity the US requires. Your boss and the commandant have faith in you. But, the strength of the attraction between us isn't something to be easily dismissed. I think we can both hold our own. You can be a firebrand when you want to."

She fought the urge to smile then. How did he do that? He had concerns about her…and he was making her smile. "Firebrand? If you start calling me Red, I'm going to slug you."

"That might be worth it. You think you're tough enough to take me?"

"I'm soft enough to make you."

The corners of his mouth curved. "You are. I think nothing gets by you, not even me. Especially not me. You pull no punches and take no bull."

"I won't let you down."

"I know you won't and maybe you have a point with me skewing my feelings towards being a bit over-protective. I'm aware you can hold your own. You already have."

And that was just it. Looking at him, so steady, so strong-willed, so profoundly sure of himself, she could only hope that his trust in her wasn't unfounded.

Because she wanted to do right by him on the job. It was important to her.

She needed that.

The depth of need she'd developed for him so swiftly was more terrifying than failing. That was reason enough to step back.

If only she had the strength.

An hour later they had donned their married-Canadian-couple personas and were headed for their private plane. Mr. and Mrs. Ryan Nadeau. Her name was Simone.

"Whoa, almost forgot," he said.

He reached into his pocket and pulled out the set of rings. He slipped the ridiculous diamond and band onto her finger, then shoved the gold band onto his.

She swallowed hard at the way it felt to be connected to him, and it had nothing to do with the rings.

And everything to do with her heart.

Chapter 10

Beau indicated Kinley should precede him up the steps, his fingers still tingling from sliding the rings on their fingers. The way she'd looked at him as he did it made his heart thump against his chest. Playacting. He was only playacting being married to her.

Daniel was behind him with a very sour look on his face.

Playacting or not, she was something in that high-class getup she'd chosen. The DEA undercover gurus had tried to pick something out for her, but Kinley had done a damn fine job on her own. He paused on the stairs and Daniel slammed into him, but his gaze was riveted to the tan sandal with the blocked heel. The shoe was elegant, expensive, leather and handmade, and it encased a sweetly feminine foot whose arched lines extended up a delicate ankle, a silken calf to the hem of a cream-colored dress with black diamond patterns on it. It was wrapped around a set of the most dangerous curves he'd ever seen and tied right under the bodice molded to her body. His fingers itched to see if that one flimsy string would bring the whole cool, collected facade crashing down with the fabric. Before she'd gotten on the plane he noticed the gold necklace nestled in the hint of her delectable cleavage. She looked nothing like the no-nonsense special agent.

No, with her richly colored hair swept up under the elegant, broad-brimmed, rakishly angled white Panama hat and a pair of sleek sunglasses, she looked like she was born to a privileged and pampered lifestyle. Silken auburn strands drifted down, caught in the slight breeze blowing across the tarmac and brushing the nape of her neck, telling him that he was in way more trouble than he had bargained for.

Damn.

Kryptonite.

Hitting him where it hurt. All those cyclone curves and auburn hair.

"Could we, Jerrott?" Daniel groused.

Beau watched as that sweet backside wiggled into the plane. Beau turned and gave him a wide grin, and hopped the stairs into the plane two at a time, then ducked inside, nodding to the pilot as he did.

The older man just smiled and tipped his fingers to his forehead. "Ready when you are."

"We're ready if Wescott would stop dawdling."

"Me?" he sputtered, then narrowed his eyes when Beau smirked.

The pilot chuckled and closed the cockpit door as Beau made his way into the main section of the small private jet.

Kinley was seated in the central area, where there was a large round table surrounded by four cushy leather chairs. There were also seats along either side of the plane, situated next to the windows.

"Jeez, the DEA gets some nice toys," Beau said.

"Confiscated from some drug lord," Daniel said, settling into a seat next to Kinley.

Beau smiled at Kinley. She had both her arms and legs crossed, and didn't look particularly happy with him. Of course, he was supposed to be the so-cool-frost-gathered-around-him Ryan Nadeau, the obscenely wealthy independent software developer.

Daniel rose to close the outside door and Beau leaned down.

"You are transformed," she murmured. "I could almost believe that you are as big a bastard as your profile says you are. The way you got out of the limo and left me to my own devices was well played."

Her eyes went over him and he felt the force of her green gaze. He knew how to play the part of a bastard.

He grinned and leaned down, his voice a wisp of sound. "That queen-of-the-realm tone you're using really turns me on."

She tried to maintain her frosty expression, but he saw her fight the smile. He extended his hand to her. "We need to buckle in for takeoff."

She took his offered hand. She was such a mix of uptight and cute, he never knew what to expect from her. He drew her up, but resisted the temptation to pull her directly into his arms. Wescott was a complete wet blanket.

He led her to a window seat and waited until she got comfortable, but rather than taking the seat next to her, he sat next to the window on the opposite side of the plane. She looked surprised, and perhaps even a little disappointed. He smiled to himself and buckled up.

When Wescott came back, he paused, looking surprised also that Beau wasn't sitting next to her. He wasn't worried about Daniel. Kinley wasn't interested in him, but that didn't seem to stop the frisson of heat that made his hand fist.

He was making it a point to not crowd her. It was important that she understood he knew she could handle Daniel.

The pilot came over the speaker with instructions for takeoff. As the plane accelerated, then lifted into the sky, Beau glanced over at Kinley. Her hands were in her lap doing a twisting little dance. He was sure it wasn't fear of flying because she'd been completely relaxed on their way to the Bahamas from Norfolk. So she had to be worrying about the mission.

She turned and met his eyes and he smiled at her, realizing that she wanted him close. He regretted that he couldn't hold her hand.

Despite the intimacy they shared, he had no idea who she really was. She was sharp, smart and, when it came time to step up and do what was needed, fearless. He wanted to know her better outside of work. Outside of the danger and the need to maintain in public a professional relationship. But he was starting to think that maybe…he could find out.

He was completely floored with his next thought. As hot as she looked and as hot as she made him, he wanted to hold her hand. Oh, he wanted her. Kind of hard to deny that one, given the ongoing rock-hard state of his body. But now he wasn't interested in getting naked with her simply to get naked. He didn't just want her casually. Which was ridiculous, considering that's how he'd operated on a regular basis. But, sitting here, reassuring her with his eyes, he wasn't sure he'd ever had

Special Agent Kinley Cooper casually. Not even from the first. That was a freaking first for him. Or at least, it had been a long time—okay—since…Jennifer. She had broken his heart. He hadn't forgotten what that was like.

But Kinley… If he let himself get too deep, he was afraid she would wreck him. Carve out his heart. Hollow him out.

"Daniel, why don't you fill us in on your contact and how this is going to play out," Beau said to distract himself from that train of thought.

"My contact is very elusive. I have never met him. He uses burner phones and gives me tips as he gets them. He has been one hundred percent accurate every time. He will get the information we need. He also gave me the name of a gun dealer in Havana who can help us out with weapons. The meet is set up for tonight at the La Casa del Luna. He will supply us with the doctor's name."

"Risks?" Beau asked.

"Minimal in my opinion. Like I said, he's been totally spot-on. He offered to help because he lost a family member to the cartel. He wants them taken down."

"A dance club. Not loving that," Kinley murmured.

Daniel shrugged. "He chose the place. We have to go along with it. I'm not worried. We should be in and out with the information and on our way by about ten-thirty."

When Daniel got up to go to the bathroom thirty minutes later, Beau unbuckled his seat belt and slid over next to her. Yeah, apparently he was a stupid sumbitch. She started and turned to look at him. He curled his hands over hers. "There's no need to be nervous. I have your back."

"Yeah," she whispered. "That's part of what makes

me nervous. You'll want my front and everything else in between."

He laughed out loud just as Daniel came out of the bathroom. Beau met his testy look, but he wasn't budging. He'd had her for most of the flight.

When the captain came over the speaker to let them know they were descending into Havana, Kinley's hands tightened in his. He squeezed them as they waited until the plane touched down and the captain gave the all clear before they rose to depart.

"Get the car and luggage," Beau said to Daniel, who nodded, walked to open the hatch and disappeared through.

Kinley took a deep breath near him. "We'll have to buy clothes. They only had so many on hand that fit us."

"No worries. I'm sure you're an amazing shopper."

"Why, because I'm a woman?"

"Maybe, and it's part of the mission, which you'll take very seriously. So, you ready?" he asked.

"Yes. I'm ready."

"And prepared?"

"Like you were ever a Boy Scout."

"I was, as a matter of fact." She snorted. "Scout's honor." He moved in behind her, herding her toward the door. He leaned in close to her ear. "I won all my derbies. It's all about the wood."

She tried to huff, but it came out as more of a laugh. "Oh, man," she muttered, giving him a rolled-eye look over her shoulder before she ducked, stepped out of the plane and onto the metal steps.

He followed her, using her descent in heels as an excuse to touch her elbow in a steadying gesture. Given she could probably do cartwheels in those things, it was completely unnecessary. Pathetic, even.

Wanting something with her was starting to get to him. He was walking a dangerous path with not only his own emotions, but with hers, too. The unknown here was how important her career was to her. What her priorities were where it came to him.

He lost that train of thought as her whole persona changed as she hit the tarmac and headed toward the terminal. Her whole aura went from Kinley to Simone in a heartbeat. He made a similar transformation, changing the affable look on his face to that of a serious CEO and busy businessman.

They sailed through customs and were soon searching for Daniel at the curb. When he pulled up in the Mercedes and came around to open the door for them, Beau took Kinley's arm again, on the pretense of helping her into the car. It was late afternoon, but the fatigue was pulling at him. He hadn't slept much last night, what with the attack.

She settled into the seat like she'd been born into luxury and he settled next to her, closer than he should sit, but hell, they were supposed to be married.

Why did that thought make his heart jump each time?

"After shopping, I need a shower and some food. You?" Kinley asked.

"That sounds great. When are you supposed to meet the guy with the guns, Daniel? I'm not too keen about doing anything, including meeting your contact, without some firepower," Beau said.

"Agreed," Daniel said. "He's not far from here. It shouldn't take any more than half an hour."

"And your contact?" Kinley asked.

"Not until ten-thirty at La Casa del Luna."

"Kinley's right. Dance club. Not a great choice. Too many people," Beau growled.

"He's a little bit on edge because of the crap going down with Montoya. The *Las Espadas* are hunting for him hard."

Beau still didn't like it.

"After we freshen up, Kinley and I can go get the guns while you scope out the floor plan and do some recon. Will that make you feel better?"

It was on the tip of his tongue that no freaking way was he going to let her out of his sight. She turned to look at him and she saw it right there in his eyes.

She looked a bit hurt and completely mutinous. He realized they would have to do the job, whatever that entailed.

"Beau—"

"I'm sorry. I just—" He shook his head. "Yes, you go with Daniel to pick up the weapons."

Trust. He'd meant what he'd said, but she was clearly calling him on it. "Get me something nice, shiny and deadly," he said. The idea of being separated from her didn't sit well with him, but not so much because of the trust issue. It was a knee-jerk reaction to something that was totally unreasonable and personal. They were undercover; she for the first time in a city that would not be that friendly if something went south. Until he had a better handle on who the players were and what the danger level was, he didn't really want to let Kinley out of his sight. But Daniel was a seasoned agent and for that matter so was Kinley.

Daniel eased the Mercedes through traffic and pulled over in front of a neocolonial structure with graceful arches. He stopped at the curb, and several bellmen immediately moved in their direction.

He smiled at Kinley as his door was opened. He could see the fatigue etched on her face quite clearly now, and he was sure he didn't look any better. For a woman who came to average height, she could move fast. He caught up to her and put his hand on her lower back as the bellmen held the lobby door for them.

Kinley smiled when she saw the shops. "Go ahead and go up, the two of you. I'll get this task done and be right up." She was already focused on the job.

He was all set to go in after her, or hover outside, just to keep an eye on her, but realized that trust was about more than believing her capable. It was also trusting her to take care of herself. She wasn't exactly fragile or helpless. Which was a big part of why he was so drawn to her. But it didn't make him feel any less conflicted. He wasn't used to feeling so proprietary or worrying so much about anyone.

But just because she'd clearly done a good job taking care of herself up to this point didn't mean bad things couldn't happen. He swore under his breath. He'd worked with partners before, even a female partner. Amber was as tough as they came and Kinley was cut from the same tough-cookie cloth. But there was an emotional element tied in here which was tying him up in knots and confusing the crap out of him.

It was the part that wasn't rational or reasonable, more like a primal directive to protect and defend. He snorted at himself. Caveman mentality.

He stared after her as she disappeared among the racks of clothing, thinking about that, which led him to also think about what would likely happen if they went up to their hotel room at the same time. And finally, resigned, he sighed and turned toward the registration desk. "Yeah, good call."

Thirty minutes later he stepped out of the shower, his muscles loosened up from the hot water. He should feel good, but he didn't. Probably the latent anxiety he'd tried to ignore, quite unsuccessfully, waiting for Kinley to show up. She hadn't come into the bathroom, but that could be because she was aware of what would happen if she got anywhere near him while he was naked. More distraction they didn't need right now. And he was already feeling far more distracted having been through the emotional roller coaster of the past half hour than he'd like to be.

Falling for her was hell on him.

Whoa, slow that damn train down, he thought immediately. *Just a slip of the mind. Crazy slippery mind.*

Then he stepped into the master suite and found Kinley stretched out on the bed, fast asleep. And thought falling for her was also one of the best feelings in the whole world. The relief was far greater than it probably should have been, but he was human. She was here in one piece. That was all that mattered.

His body, however, was even happier, if its reaction to seeing her all flushed and relaxed was any indication. In fact, it felt quite rejuvenated. Perhaps a cold shower would have been a better idea. Yeah, if he had been functioning on more than one brain cell, it would have occurred to him.

He hated to wake her, but they had a timeline here and were slowing it down. Besides, she looked too good in that bed and he couldn't jump her bones. She would rather have the short time they were allotted to clean up. Again, he was struck by how little he really knew her. And by how badly he wanted to correct that. It would take a lifetime to know everything about her, but this was about a temporary assignment. He was going back to DC and she was going to probably get a promotion out of this.

He rubbed the towel over his hair, then tripped over a long row of bags lined up against the side of the bed as he rounded it. That was some major shopping in the twenty minutes he'd been in the shower. She'd obviously made a nice dent in the DEA credit cards issued in their names.

His eyes caressed every inch of her. A bundle of surprises, a sharp mind. Special agent and shopaholic. She stretched. Stretching was good. Another part of his body thought it was good, too. His emotions were far too turbulent to deal with that temptation at the moment. His eyes roamed over the bags. Getting dressed was a good idea. Not the idea he wanted to contemplate, but it was safer.

Kinley woke up to find Beau leaning over the bags with nothing but a white towel around his waist. He rose to his full height as their eyes met. He looked so hot all mussed, disheveled. He made scruffy look so damn sexy. She worked at fighting off the waves of lust inspired by just looking at him.

There was a distinct reason she couldn't keep her hands, her eyes, her mouth off him. The way he'd looked when he was talking to that customs officer after he got just a tiny bit rough with her. He'd been dressed all in white. A white polo that fit him like a second skin, delineating every muscle in his torso, hugging his broad shoulders, the material stretching around his biceps, showing just the bottom of his sexy chain tattoo. The white, casually elegant pants had encased his long legs, the cuffs rolled up to show strong ankles above a pair of white deck shoes.

Women had been passing by him, unable to take their eyes off him as he made it clear without even raising his voice to the guard that his wife wouldn't be treated with anything but kid gloves. His jaw had been hard and stubbled with beard, all the lines of his body showing the barely leashed power and grace of every big, bad boy who'd ever been at the top of the food chain. The thing that made her heart skip a beat…he hadn't been pretending or playacting. He was downright serious.

He reached for something in one of the bags and the towel came unraveled, and just that easily she unraveled right along with it. It slipped off his waist, baring his hip, the globe of his butt revealing a tat inked right at the top of his thigh. *All in.* He caught at the terry before it fell fully off him. She hadn't seen him in the light of day and the scars and healed wounds on him only made her heart tighten even more.

How she wanted him to let it fall.

She sat up knowing that they didn't have time for this. Unable to help herself, she scooted across the mattress on her knees until she reached him. There was a rounded scar on his shoulder, a long, easily recognizable knife slash, long healed along his rib cage.

"Don't do it," he said, whisper soft. "You do it and it's over. I'm not going to be responsible for my actions because, *chérie*, you make me freaking crazy. I'm about to say to hell with clothes and climb up into bed, right into your waiting arms, and into your warm and willing body."

She ran her hands through her hair instead of touching him. "Later, then," she said, giving him one more look and crawling to the other side of the bed.

"Yeah, work. Focus on that and take deep breaths," he said, holding the towel at his waist, covering up that tantalizing tattoo she wanted to know more about. But he was right. It was time to focus on the mission they were here for.

He picked through the first bag as she unbuckled the beautiful tan sandals and slipped out of them one by one. Barefoot she stood.

"How did you know my size?"

"I guessed. I think I came close, but if something doesn't fit, we can exchange it. I told the salesgirl I couldn't possibly be bothered with remembering your delectable measurements. I just took advantage of them."

"Nice," he said, giving her a sidelong look, his wet hair framing his face.

"I said it with a lot of affection."

"Cute." He held boxers and T-shirts. "This is all good, but I think I'm going to need a bit more to be presentable."

"Ha-ha." She snorted. "You are definitely cute. I kinda like you the way you're dressed, but I guess I'd have to fight off the female masses if you went out like that. I'll have to fight them off, anyway."

He rolled his eyes. "I only have eyes for my wife, even if she can't be bothered with my measurements."

"I'm only interested in bothering with one particular measurement."

He dropped his chin and chuckled, a pained sound. "You're killing me, *ma belle*."

She grinned. "There are shirts and pants hanging in the closet." He grinned back at her, the twinkle in his eyes potent. Even with a sea of bed between them, there was still a shiver of danger racing all over her skin. Grabbing a bag, her nerves jittering as his eyes tracked her to the bathroom, she paused when he said, "Kinley."

She turned toward him and he rounded the bed. Her pulse surged when he tucked the towel end tightly against his waist. Reaching her, he leaned against the doorjamb. Even in the expansive room, she felt… crowded.

"I've been wondering all damn day about that little string keeping you together. One tug…?"

She gave him a provocative smile.

He reached out and fingered the string under her breast and her heart rate raced. Her brows rose on a dare.

He leaned toward her and she drew in a deep breath. He smelled so fresh and clean. A drop of water from his wet hair dropped right between her breasts. She shivered.

"Mmm," he said, "You make it so hard…to focus."

He pulled the string and the dress loosened around her. As it parted, he brushed the back of his fingers against her cheek. "So hard."

She curled her hand around his nape, delving into his thick, wet hair, and pulled his mouth down to hers for a quick kiss. "You're a SEAL, you have the willpower."

"Hooyah," he replied softly against her mouth, pressing his mouth to hers. His kiss wasn't quick.

He let her go. "Is your curiosity satisfied?" she asked.

"For now," he said with promise as he stepped back. She wasted no more time scooting into the bathroom and closing the door.

She took her time in the shower, her stomach rumbling. Turning off the water and stepping out, she vigorously rubbed her hair dry and faced the mirror to take on the arduous task of transforming herself into a

rich party girl. She agreed with Beau. She didn't like
the idea that they were meeting at a dance club. There
were too many things that could go wrong.

But even though she didn't exactly trust Daniel personally, he was very good at what he did professionally.

She gripped the sink, her insides going a little hay-
wire. She trusted Beau, both personally and professionally. Completely. With her heart and with her life. She
knew he still had questions about her—in his position,
he'd be a fool not to—but the fact that he'd given her
any latitude with choosing guns had been gratifying, to
say the least. He'd wanted to balk, and that had given
her a momentary pang, but despite whatever misgiv-
ings he was still harboring, he'd stood by his promise
and sanctioned it.

After her hair was dry, she did an elaborate reverse
braid to the side. Pulling out the short, red-ribbed
stretchy skirt with a form-fitting matching white top,
she sighed. So not her style. The tight tank had built-
in support and didn't require a bra, and panties under
the skirt would show lines. Slipping into the red lace
thong that cost way too much for so little material, she
felt extremely…underdressed.

She took a breath before she opened the bathroom
door and stepped outside. He was talking on the phone,
but she could smell something delectable coming from
the dining room in this obscenely priced suite.

He stopped talking and stared. She moved into the
room and drifted past him. He shook his head and
started talking again.

"No, I was…distracted for a minute, Chris. Continue."

He was talking to his boss. Probably briefing him.
She should check in with Kirk, but she was too hun-

gry right now. She settled into a chair and sent her eyes over Beau.

He was dressed in a gorgeous high-end blue silk shirt. The minute she'd seen it, she knew it would suit him. The rich colors accented his black hair and dark skin. The blue brought out the midnight in his eyes.

He'd paired it with a pair of cropped black linen pants and a pair of black canvas deck shoes.

He disconnected the call and sat down. Dishing up some of the salad he'd ordered, he said quietly, "Where exactly are you going to…ah…stash a weapon?"

"Thigh holster."

He coughed a little as if something had gone down wrong. She patted his back. Before he could reply, there was a knock on the door and Beau rose and opened it for Daniel.

"You ready to go?" he asked, his eyes taking her in just like Beau's had. Daniel's gaze used to do something to her insides, but now Beau elicited tsunami-like waves that swamped everything else.

"Yes, I'll be right there."

Daniel knew it. She wasn't sure if he was resigned to it. It was true that she wasn't sure where she was going with Beau now that things had gotten more complicated. But now was not the time to get her head messed up about that. She needed to be on her game.

"I'll get the car." He disappeared out the door and closed it behind him.

"Don't let your guard down for a moment. Regardless of the fact that Daniel is supposed to watch your back."

"Meaning you don't think I can handle picking up a few guns?"

"No, it's not that. I know better than anyone that you

can handle yourself. It's just…I don't want anything to happen to you."

The way he said it, the look on his face, made her heart squeeze. She tried to ignore that and focus on business, even though she knew that wasn't at all what he meant. "But you just said you know I could take care—"

"I didn't say it was logical, or rational. It's… I'm a caveman." He smiled. "And, trust me, it's not something I'm proud of, either."

"Then don't," she said, even as her insides were melting a little. No one had ever cared enough to be that concerned about her, not since her father. "I will manage."

He reached across the table and covered her hand, looking away. "I can't guarantee anything. After living through enough battles in my time on the teams, I err on the side of caution. We were a team, but we lost guys just as fast as a blink of an eye. Couldn't be foreseen." He looked at her. "We make a good team." His smile returned, but there was something tender, almost vulnerable in it. "I like us together on and off the playing field."

She couldn't manage to look away, couldn't seem to find whatever it was she had left that would keep her head strictly on business. "We do. We so do," she said, relieved to be honest with him. "This is not a conversation for now, though."

"You go, but watch your gorgeous backside."

She got up and slipped on a pair of slinky red sandals with a flat heel. She never knew when she would have to run. "I will."

She went to slip out the door, but Beau caught her arm and spun her against him. "*Ma belle*, I'm partial to SIG Sauer or a HK45C. With the HK, two hits—one hitting the tango and the tango hitting the ground."

His mouth dropped to hers, the kiss hard and quick.

"I'll bring you something good back," she said, shivers running down her spine.

Chapter 11

He scoped out La Casa del Luna. He did his damn recon job, the whole time thinking about Kinley going to a gun buy in body-hugging spandex and if he had to guess, she wasn't wearing panties under that skirt. Jesus. A *thigh* holster. What did she think this was? Spy games?

He sat across the street watching the club. It was on a busy street downtown. There was nothing out of the ordinary going on over there that any other run-of-the-mill club wouldn't be doing right before a huge dance party was going to raise the roof. It was thirty minutes before it opened and another thirty before they were to meet Daniel's contact.

Damn, he didn't like it. There were too many exits. He rose, not crossing until he could duck into the alley just past the entrance. He made his way down the narrow littered walkway, which smelled of spicy rice and beans. The alley dumped out into an area that butted up against abandoned ramshackle apartments and a shabby warehouse just beyond it that looked like it was ready to come down. It was probably slated for demolition.

He crossed back over and went behind the club, but found nothing out of the ordinary. It would be hard to find someplace to make a stand. Not that he wanted a street shoot-out. If they were caught by the Cuban police they would lock all three of them up for being in possession of illegal firearms and they could kiss Diego Montoya and his possible terrorist connection goodbye.

That bastard, el Ajeer, was planning something and he was either being backed by the *Las Espadas* or he was backing them. Many terrorists turned to drugs as a way to fund their war of fear. But he was elusive and careful.

That's why they couldn't afford for anything to go wrong. Not a damn thing.

He came around the other side of the club and was satisfied that he knew all points of egress, and was already formulating contingency plans in preparation for any worst-case scenarios.

The place was opening up and Beau spied Daniel and Kinley walking toward the club. He crossed the street to greet them.

"How did it go?" he asked.

"Smooth," Daniel said.

"He was too jumpy for me," Kinley said.

"He's in a jumpy business."

"He was sweating."

"It's frigging hot out, Kinley."

Uh-oh, they'd been arguing, and he figured she must have told him there was no chance for them. That made him want to smile, but he was more interested in what Kinley was saying.

"It wasn't that kind of sweating," she said through gritted teeth.

"You're overreacting."

Daniel walked away from her and into the club. She leaned toward Beau and slipped the clipped holster against the small of his back and an extra clip into his pants pocket. "I got you the HK."

"Nice." A weapon he was very familiar with. "You okay?"

"Daniel's pissed at me. I told him that the gun dealer was acting hinky, but all he wanted to talk about was us."

"You and me?"

"No. Him and me."

"And?"

"Oh, God, not you, too. This isn't a damn soap opera."

"Kinley…"

"You already know what I told him," she whispered. "And he didn't take it well. We'll talk about this later. I think we should keep sharp, Beau. I got a bad feeling about all of this."

"All right."

They walked into the club and the music inside was in full swing. A lively beat, very Spanish and stirring as all Latin music was. The place was filling fast.

Daniel was at the bar downing what looked like a beer. "Stay close," Beau murmured in her ear so she could hear him. He approached Daniel, who gave Beau a disgruntled look.

Damn. He sat down on a stool and said, "Get your act together, Wescott. This isn't the time or the place."

Daniel's shoulders stiffened then relaxed. He cut a look to Kinley and closed his eyes. "Noted," he growled.

Daniel finished the rest of his drink, but Beau was relieved when he turned around on the bar stool so he could scan the dance floor.

"There he is," Daniel said. "Hang back. Kinley, come with me."

He took her hand and spun her out to the dance floor, making his way across to a tall, dark-haired man. Every cell in Beau's body was primed.

Keeping Daniel and Kinley in his sights, he quickly scanned the area and froze. He saw the tattoo before the contact pulled out a gun and shoved it into Daniel's stomach, just as the guy with the tattoo came up behind Kinley, grabbed her and dragged her toward the back.

There was so much noise and it was so dim that no one even noticed. Beau was already moving, but he was hampered by the dancers, crashing into the wall of bodies. He was immediately aware that they'd been compromised but also knew that *Las Espadas* were not aware that there was a third operative, namely him.

Reaching a hand to his waist, he unsnapped the guard holding the 45C in place. By the time he got to the back door, Daniel, Kinley and the two men were nowhere to be found. Suddenly, unexpectedly, a group of people spilled out of the doorway and headed to a small opening in the fence just beyond the patio, the noise of their ascent masked by music. He tensed and left his weapon where it was, down and right against his leg. There were a group of them and Beau felt impatient as they started funneling through the gap in the fence, impeding his progress.

All of them looked too young to be up and out this late at night. As he followed them, he noticed that some of their clothes looked painted on and all of them had painted faces. They were tipsy and laughing.

He was jangling with the need to just push them aside and bulldoze his way through the fence, but he didn't want to cause a scene and draw attention to himself. He surveyed the hole as one of the girls caught a sleeve on the chain link. A guy with blue glitter in his hair helped her get free. Beau's blood pumped hard through him.

The next guy got caught on the same piece of fencing and they all started to laugh.

He heard the guy say it might be too dangerous for them to dance if they couldn't navigate through a damn fence. Beau thought that if they didn't get their butts through the fence, he was going through them like a wrecking ball. That is where the men had to have taken Kinley and Daniel.

As soon as the group went through, he turned sideways and slipped through the fence. Running on pure instinct and adrenaline, Beau started toward the ten-story ramshackle apartments. It'd be a good place to take them for questioning. He heard music coming out of the place as he got closer. What the hell?

This was another club, only it was one that was piggybacking on the Luna. The music was punk. Definitely not as melodious and spicy. He heard a scream and recognized Kinley's voice. It was cut off suddenly. He didn't hesitate this time. He pushed his way through and headed down a darkened stairwell, following the hard beat of the music down into pandemonium.

He kept close to the wall all the way down the stairs. On the landing, he strode past a group of kids shucking their clothes, revealing body art beneath. Looked like some kind of painted-on latex. This must be some kind of new craze.

At the top of the last flight of stairs, he saw the body-painted kids lit up as they hit the black light of the pitch-black club below. There were bright cobras in orange and black, and butterfly masks in a myriad of pinks and blues, and some sugar skulls. There was even a full-body skellie, along with Aztec designs, devils, moons, and some celestial stars motifs. As he descended into the dark, he found himself faced with a jam-packed, whirling mass of neon art. Hundreds of kids with brilliant hair, some multiple colors, others with glitter. The crush of so many bodies made it hard to move. All of them clueless. A tank could roll through here and they would still be dancing.

He surveyed the room, his gaze running over the crowd. There was too much movement, too much shifting, screwing with his attempt to make sense of all that fluctuating humanity. It was impossible to discern faces among all those people and the dark was hampering his ability to find Kinley and Daniel. They were as invisible as he was.

They could be right in front of him and because they weren't neon, he would never see them.

They could be anywhere…but he spied a light way in the back of the room. Must be some kind of security light. It illuminated what looked like a stairwell.

He plunged into the crowd after them. They might be invisible, but so was he. They wouldn't know what hit them.

He kept his eyes on the stairwell as he worked his way through the crush, reaching back and pulling the HK from his holster, keeping it close to his leg, thumbing off the safety and chambering a round.

No one saw the deadly firepower in his hand as he shoved his way through the brightly lit writhing bodies.

As he reached the edge of the crowd and the stairwell, his heart stuttered when he saw the light illuminated an exit. Did they go out this way?

Kinley. The anguished cry echoed in his head. He had to find her and Daniel. Cold fury took over.

Which way had they taken her?

He looked up the stairs and back at the door. He had a split second to make a decision that could mean life or death for them all.

They wouldn't kill them, not right off, he told himself. The cartel was probably searching for information about Montoya just like they were, but he was sure they wouldn't be gentle with her in any way.

He took off running, taking the stairs two and three at a time. At the first landing, there was a hallway and several doors, some open, others just hanging by the hinges. He checked every apartment, all gutted and trashed, except for the last one that had some dilapidated sofa in it and an intact coffee table where kids were doing drugs.

He swore under his breath, finished checking the other doors and went back to the stairs—knowing he had nine more floors to go and that every minute she was out of his sight put her deeper in danger.

He had no choice but to endure from one minute to the next.

He might have been discharged. But once a SEAL, always a SEAL. SEALs never gave up and he was a frogman to the core, a SEAL with mayhem in mind. Murder and mayhem. He was trained in the art of stealth and killing. He had a warrior's soul. All in, all the time, and he wasn't losing her. No goddamn way was he losing her. The men who had taken Kinley were going to die.

* * *

Kinley's cheek stung where one of the men had slapped her in the club to get her moving. He shoved her in the middle of the back and Daniel looked mutinous for a moment, but she shook her head.

She still had her gun in the holster concealed beneath her skirt. The one thing about men would always remain true. They constantly underestimated a woman.

She stumbled, going down to one knee, reaching for her weapon.

The guy that looked Middle Eastern grabbed her by the hair and hauled her up. She elbowed him in the ribs and turned, but the contact grabbed her wrist and twisted. She tried to counter, ducking a punch and stepping down hard with the heel of her shoe. Daniel realized what was happening and lunged at the Middle Eastern thug. They tussled, both of them fighting frantically for their lives. A shot rang out. It was loud in the hallway. For a minute Kinley couldn't breathe.

The Middle Eastern man grabbed her around the middle and hauled her back against his body. Immobilized by the goon, the contact easily ripped the gun out of her grip. Then the man who held her tightly spoke, his accent not Spanish, the language unmistakably Arabic.

She was in the fog again; those men speaking to each other, the gunfire making her run like a scared rabbit, getting turned around. The freezing fog wrapping around her like a blanket. The everyday, familiar sights of the street lay mysterious, hiding, looming out at her in the whitened haze at the last minute like images from some half-forgotten dream. Her lungs stung from the cold, wet air. The fog and fear became one, settling coldly, chilling deep to the bone.

It was the same dialect. She was sure of it. Panic,

stark and razor sharp, skittered across every nerve ending she had.

Beau would be coming for them. She had no doubt. None. All she and Daniel had to do was survive.

Music coming up from below, subdued but still discordant, made the building hum around her, telling her she was still near that underground club they'd dragged them through until she'd started to struggle and that goon had hit her.

Beau couldn't be far behind, a few minutes at most.

Daniel rammed the man holding her, jarring her loose. She scrambled to her feet and took off running down the hallway. She got all of ten feet before she was hit from behind.

The contact landed on her, taking her down, and she cried out.

"Leave her alone," Daniel shouted and there were the sounds of a struggle. Then he had her by the hair again and when he jerked her up, she saw Daniel lying in the hallway, the blood stain growing, his eyes stricken and his lungs pumping for oxygen. The thug stood over him with a knife.

Kinley realized they were as good as dead unless Beau got here soon. They were now helpless, Daniel in critical condition.

The man screamed at the contact in Arabic, Kinley had no idea what he was saying, but the contact went pale, very, very pale.

Then she caught it, the name—el Ajeer.

Nausea coursed through her, and she had to fight being sick.

She'd never forget that day, or the man who had murdered her father, trashed their town house and taken his trident. That meant this man who was holding her wasn't just a member of *Las Espadas*, he was part of el Ajeer's Sons of the Republic. She had no illusions about what they were capable of. Drug lords were predictable and brutal, but el Ajeer's men were butchers and cold-blooded killers with very little respect for Americans and even less for women.

Oh, God! The man responsible for her father's murder was in Cuba?

Was he coming *here*?

The Middle Eastern roughly pulled Daniel up and he stumbled against the man. She tried to go to him, but the contact tightened his hold in her hair.

They dragged her out of the hallway and slammed her into a chair inside one of the trashed apartments. She didn't know what floor she was on.

She did know she was losing the feeling in her arms. They'd jerked them behind the back of the chair and tied her with a plastic flex cuff. They'd also tied her around the waist and secured both her ankles to the legs of the chair. Like the rest of the building, the apartment had been ransacked, with its few shabby contents in pieces and the walls broken through.

Tall and with mean eyes, the contact had propped Daniel against the wall. The bloodstain had spread and dripped, and it was pooling beneath his hip. She was shaking as she met his eyes, and she saw that he knew he wasn't going to make it.

"I'm sorry."

"Hang in there," she said firmly.

The goon who had been carrying her paced about. If he meant to scare her, it was working. She was gasping too hard and too fast, and she made a conscious effort to slow her breathing before she passed out. Her mouth had dried up from the fear, a distinctly metallic taste on her tongue.

Beau would find her. He was coming. She knew it. All she had to do was stall. Hopefully it would be quickly enough to save Daniel. He looked gray, his eyes glassy, sweat running off him in rivulets.

She'd never been in this situation, this helpless. She couldn't move, and no amount of pleading was going to get her out of this, not with the thug throwing the knife to the contact.

Oh, God. Oh, God.

The contact smiled, his lips thinning cruelly. The blade in his hand gleamed, the edges looking lethally sharp. His rest of his face was just as malicious as the look in his eyes. Cold-blooded killer. She shivered hard and he laughed low and vicious. The goon smiled as he slapped the blackjack menacingly. Both men were sweating like Daniel.

She was drenched. The only sound in the room was Daniel's harsh breathing and the sound of her own frantic heartbeat in her ears.

"You will tell me what I want to know. If you do not, I will cut you. Be a shame to disfigure that beautiful face. You're going to need those lips to smile."

His voice was cold and flat and as he spoke. The goon used the blackjack to give her stinging slaps on either side of her face.

"Who are you?"

She looked at Daniel, but he was staring into space. She could barely contain her panic. He was dying and there was nothing she could do for him. She was on her own. Stall. She had to stall. "Special Agent Kinley Cooper, Petty Officer Second Class. United States Coast Guard."

The contact snorted and turned to look at the goon. "You don't look like no agent to me. What the hell is the Coast Guard doing in Cuba?" He slid his hand against her knee and pushed up her skirt.

"I'm telling the truth," she hissed, trying and failing to move away from him. She was immobile.

"Maybe I don't need to cut you after all. I can think of something much more interesting."

"No!" The shout came from Daniel as he lunged up from the floor and slammed into the contact, who lost his balance and in turn stumbled into her, knocking her over. Her head hit the floor, stunning her. The breath was knocked out of her. She'd landed hard on her shoulder. Daniel was fighting like a madman, his fists punishing.

The goon went to him and dragged Daniel off and shoved him back, then shot him point blank.

The two men disappeared from her view. Tears filled her eyes at the horror of watching the life drain out of Daniel's eyes, made it hard for her to breathe as fear clutched her by the throat. "No," she sobbed.

The contact materialized, cutting off her view of Daniel. He grabbed her by the hair dragging her face close to his. "What are you looking for?"

"Diego Montoya," she rasped out between sobs. "We're looking for a picture of him to identify him. We think he's in the US after hijacking a Coast Guard cutter," she said, quickly.

The contact looked up at the goon. "Bastard is a dead man. He's in the US."

She tried to breathe, her gaze darting to Daniel, so pale, so still. Just like her father. The blade glinted in the light from the hallway.

The contact shifted the knife to her throat.

And then he wasn't there.

Two shots sounded in rapid succession, deafening blasts in close quarters. The contact jerked away from her and the knife clattered to the floor in front of her, followed by the splattering of blood and the sound of two bodies falling.

The goon was screaming. Someone else shouted something she couldn't make out through the ringing in her ears. She couldn't see anything but the knife, blood and Daniel.

The contact was dead, she had no doubt, and she was trapped. She tried to pull free, then froze as a dark shadow passed overhead.

The goon's screams turned to gasping sobs. She heard a struggle, heard the loud crack of bone, then the screams were silent.

Shadows moved and a chill went down her spine. *Let it be Beau.*

Please let it be Beau, she thought, the words bouncing around her brain as every breath became harder to draw. The smell of blood filled the air, and a sob of pure panic broke free from her throat. She couldn't breathe, and her arm felt like it was breaking with her full weight on it. She tried to turn her head.

The shadow passed over her again, stealing the faint light, plunging her into utter darkness. A man bent over her. She could feel the weight of his presence, hear his breathing. Oh, God. If it was someone else after information… With a soft grunt, the man shoved the contact farther away. The faint stream of light from the hall returned, and she saw a bent knee and the drape of a blue shirt. She closed her eyes in complete and utter relief even as every muscle in her body hurt.

She wanted to talk, but her mouth was too dry as

she watched blood running across the floor, glistening in the low light.

"*Chérie*, I got you," he said. "I'll have you free in a second." His voice was rough-edged, rock steady.

Beau.

The second wave of relief made her weak. He sliced through her bonds, first her hands, then her waist and each of her ankles. Each cut was a single, swift stroke. She tried not to think about the blood on the floor, about what he'd done to save her.

But it was far too late for Daniel.

He pulled the chair away from her, but she couldn't move. Her arms and legs were numb. "Come on," Beau said, hauling her up to a sitting position. She slipped her arms around his neck, hanging on to him.

"You're safe. Stay put for a minute."

He went directly to Daniel and pressed his fingers to his neck. He waited for a moment and then sighed heavily. Silently, he closed Daniel's eyes.

He went and searched each man thoroughly, heedless of the bloody mess. Every movement was controlled, his actions swiftly executed and efficient. He had both men stripped of their possessions and was back by her side in less than a minute.

"You okay?" he asked.

When she didn't immediately answer, he cupped her chin and looked directly into her eyes. His were steady, warm, so beautifully blue. She nodded, a single, automatic movement.

"Good, that's my *chérie*."

The murmur of voices coming down the hall made him stiffen and spin toward the door. Her adrenaline spiked, and she tried to get to her feet. He grabbed her around the waist and helped her up, guiding her quickly through an opening in the wall where there once had been a door.

They retreated into the shadows, using the wreckage of the dark room for cover. The only escape route was the shattered window, leaving the interior open to the weather and the wind, blowing the smell of spicy food and the pungent odor of the ocean.

There was no furniture, just piles of trash and junk. Beau hadn't let her go, kept his arm securely around her waist.

She worked on getting her equilibrium back. She wished she had her gun. The sound of laughter in the hall indicated no threat. Probably some of those punk rockers from the party below looking for a place to do drugs.

She didn't let down her guard, though, not for a second because Beau was taut against her. Every muscle in his body was battle ready for whoever came through the door. She was so tense that she felt like she was going to snap.

In another couple of seconds, Beau's instincts were rewarded. A new set of voices came down the hall speaking Arabic.

She sucked in a breath.

Her blood ran cold. She would know that voice anywhere, in any language. She heard it in her nightmares, sneaking up on her in the dark, suffocating her in a blanket of white as he laughed and hunted her.

More voices joined in, more than she could distinguish from each other, all of them getting closer to the apartment. She and Beau were horribly outnumbered— and oh, God, he'd killed two of el Ajeer's men.

An arc of light sliced through the gash in the wall, and a man swore low and mean.

Without thinking she grabbed Beau's arm, dragging him toward the window. In the back of her mind, she felt sick at having to leave Daniel behind. It hurt like hell. Looking out she swallowed hard. The fire escape was intact, but looked far from stable. They had no choice—they were going to be discovered any moment.

Chapter 12

Beau followed Kinley out the window and swore, catching her as the structure wobbled beneath them. He had to give her credit for using their only escape route without hesitation and bravery, but this wasn't a viable option for long.

They were trapped and he couldn't go commando on the guys back there. So that meant they had to run. Again. The fire escape was a temporary solution.

But he couldn't risk Kinley. She was hurt and still feeling the effects of being threatened. She wasn't used to or prepared for this, but so far she'd held her own ground.

He hated like hell to leave Daniel behind. It didn't sit well with him to ever leave a fallen man. But in this case secrecy was their ally. He didn't want el Ajeer and *Las Espadas* to identify them and be hunting for them. They needed their anonymity to figure out another route to the doctor's identity now that Daniel's "contact" had turned out to be bogus.

If he'd been alone, he would have gone into stealth mode and taken out every one of them.

The whole metal structure swayed and buckled, grinding metal against brick as they fought for balance on the stairs as they moved down one by one. They had only gone down two floors before he decided that it was time to get off. They couldn't jump to the ground. They had come from the seventh floor and a five-story fall would probably kill them or injure them badly. There couldn't be much holding the stairs together the way they wobbled and rattled, and whatever was holding it together was probably really rusty. The suppressed shots from above him that pinged off the outside rail spurred him on. Yeah, it was time to bail.

He busted in a window, using his shoe to clear the glass away, hurrying Kinley through before he ducked inside. More gunfire erupted right near them. She clutched him, losing her balance. What a cluster.

Once she was stable, he grabbed her hand and avoided the hall. They moved fast as they jumped though openings in walls and through barely there doorways. Most of the walls separating the abandoned apartments had been at least partially destroyed. Others had doors in them. They had gone quite a ways before they hit the end of the line and had to chance using the hallway.

Kinley was quite a trooper. She'd proven herself competent, held out until he'd gotten to her, and those bastards—damn, he wanted to kill them all over again—had hurt her. The echo of the rage was still thick in his chest. As a SEAL he didn't go into battle with fury. He went into battle calmly collected.

But when he'd seen what they were doing, how they were threatening her with a knife and assault, he'd lost it. Even though Daniel was dead, he owed him gratitude for that last bit of defiance that had given him enough time to get there. The gunshot had led him right to her.

He needed to get a grip and keep his head in the game right now. He had to get his fiercely intense emotions under control. No matter that his heart had almost stopped.

He paused just inside the door and slammed his back up against the wall, his arms tightening around her waist.

A snick of sound at the back of the room had him whirling around with the HK leveled and deadly, his finger on the trigger.

Two kids stumbled out of the shadows, completely oblivious to the fact that their lives were dangling on a thread.

They'd been making out according to their flushed faces and disheveled clothes and Beau felt like his heart was in a vise.

"¡Váyanse!" he growled.

They didn't need to be told twice. Staring down the handgun's barrel, their eyes widened. The guy wrapped his arm protectively around the girl and they shot out of the room heading away from the searching *Las Espadas*.

The sound of men talking, searching, coming through the apartments behind them and down the hall was narrowing their options pretty damn fast.

He glanced towards the window, but they were still five floors up and that fire escape would be once again noisy and dangerous. He dismissed the idea of taking it as a route.

"Give me the gun," she said.

He turned to look at her. "What?"

"Give me the gun and I'll buy us some time."

"We're not splitting up."

"Yes, we have to. I'll slow them down. You find us a way out. It's the only way. We're running blind—el Ajeer—I want to…"

"What?"

"He's the one who killed my father. I would never forget that voice. I want to…"

"No." He holstered the HK and grabbed her by the shoulders. "Kinley, you can't go after him. We're outnumbered and outgunned right now. Escape is what we're after. Believe me, if it wasn't for the fact that we need absolute secrecy here, I'd be all for going after him right now. But, we can't. Promise me you're not snowing me here."

She bit her lip and looked away, her face showing her struggle with her emotions. "He killed my father and scarred me. I have a right—"

"I'm not arguing that point. You do. You have the right, but in this situation, we have to let him go. It's about the mission and it's far from complete. Daniel died for it and we can't let his death be in vain."

"We shouldn't have left him, Beau." She stood there looking so upset and he had to be tough.

"I know. A SEAL never leaves a man behind, *ever*. We're going to make sure he's taken care of. I promise. We had no choice. The DEA will take care of their own. I guarantee you. We'll get word to them as soon as we're out of this. But you have to stay focused on getting away, not going after el Ajeer. Agreed?"

When she didn't answer, he got a little frantic and had just decided to throw her over his shoulder and hightail it out of there blind or not when she said, "Yes. Agreed."

He had to rely on the trust they'd built up. She was tough enough to take on the terrorist, but not enough to wade through God knew how many tangos he brought with him.

"Hurry, Beau. Find us a way out."

"I'll be back. Stay here unless you have to move, then only move forward. If they hem you in…"

"Okay, I'll be careful. Go."

The hardest thing he'd ever had to do in his life was move away from her. She was being baptized in the combat fire and his only boost was knowing that she could handle it. Had handled it.

He skirted some debris and kept moving until he dead-ended and had to move into the hall. Just as he breached the door, he saw a shadow moving toward him. He ducked back into the room. They'd never make it that way. They were fanning out too much and pretty soon, the two of them would be trapped. He backed into the room some more and the floor went out from under him. Windmilling his arms and throwing himself forward was the only thing that saved him.

Breathing hard, he turned to find a hole in the floor that revealed another room below him. It was a drop, but he spied a mattress. Something to break their fall. At this point it was their only hope.

Without thinking about the ramification of a broken ankle or worse, he rapidly made his way back to where he'd left Kinley.

The sound of the HK discharging into the semiquiet of the apartment complex supercharged him and he swore, increasing his speed.

When he got close to where she was, he already had

his KA-BAR out and ready. Two guys were moving around to cut her off from him.

Oh, hell, no.

He didn't hesitate and ran full force into the two men. He made quick work with the knife and the guy was down before he could even draw his next breath and Beau grappled with the other. The guy brought his gun up and Beau jerked his hand, shoving it over his head. The gun discharged with a suppressed load and plaster and debris rained from the ceiling.

Beau jammed the knife into the guy's throat and jumped back as he fell. Snatching up the man's weapon, he darted into the room where Kinley was focused on returning fire. Bullets sprayed into the walls around them.

He grabbed her hand and pulled her with him. "I found a way out."

She squeezed off another round as he dragged her through the door. They ran full-out until they reached the room where he'd found the hole. She stopped and looked at him, her puzzled face flushed. "Where?"

He pointed down. She looked down then back up at him. "We're jumping?"

"Only way, *ma belle*," he said, crouching down and setting his hands on the lip of the opening. "I'll go first."

She immediately nodded, her head swiveling towards the door. "They're coming."

With a muttered oath, his hands tightening on a broken beam, he swung free and for a moment hung suspended in midair. Then there was a cracking, breaking sound above him. The wood and plaster beneath his fingers broke away and he was falling. He bent his knees and rolled as the floor rushed up to greet him. After many HALO jumps, this was a piece of cake.

"Beau, catch," she said as she dropped the weapon down to him. He watched as she swung over the lip. A man materialized out of nowhere and reached down to grab her wrist. Beau already had the suppressed weapon up and pointed, pulling off a round. It barely made a sound. The guy fell and hit Kinley. As Beau sidestepped the hurtling body, Kinley dangled for a moment, then she let go. Beau watched her as she fell, never taking his eyes off the prize.

She dropped into his arms and he set her on her feet and gave back the HK. Together they headed for the hallway. It would take a moment for them to figure out where they had gone.

With Kinley behind him, they raced down the hall, but Beau brought her up short. Two men were standing guard at the head of the stairs. "Wait here," he whispered. He sneaked up behind one and grabbed him around the neck. Within a heartbeat he brought up the suppressed weapon and put two slugs into the guy's buddy, then one into the temple of the guy he held, pulling off another head shot before the guy hit the ground. He looked down the stairs and swore. Two more tangos. Taking aim, he popped both of them.

They raced down four flights, bringing them back to the crazy, black-lit, neon-haired party that was in full swing. Threading their way through the dancers, Beau's hand tight around Kinley's. He could feel her other hand twisted in the fabric of his shirt.

This time Beau used the press of bodies and the chaos to make it to the outside stairs. Beau dragged her into the darkness and it swallowed them up.

Using the parking entrance to the hotel, they made their way silently across the concrete. The lights, dim and sparse shone down on her, limning her profile, softening her face and turning her skin into a silken wash of rose and pale peach.

Her eyes were dark, the downward cast of her gaze making it hard to figure out her mood. She was so quiet.

Too quiet.

Reaching the bank of elevators, they slipped inside. Beau breathed a sigh of relief as he pulled her against him. She cuddled him, setting her face into the hollow of his neck and wrapping her arms around his waist. They had gotten away clean. He was sure of it. Only the dead guys had learned Kinley's name. After a shower, rest and food, they were going to lie low until they discovered the doctor's name. Beau knew exactly where to look first.

They both looked worse for wear. Sweaty, dirty and one of the straps on her form-fitting top had broken and hung over her breast.

Damn. She'd wanted to go after el Ajeer. He wasn't sure if he was impressed with her guts or terrified of them.

What had happened to her when she was sixteen had destroyed her world. It was understandable that she would want to make sure the man who had shattered it paid. Having to tell her no hurt because he hurt for her. He didn't have the words to console her over the fact that el Ajeer was still breathing.

Revenge wasn't for the faint of heart and often, even after thinking about it and plotting it, the result didn't really satisfy, either. This wasn't about getting el Ajeer. It was about mentally figuring it out and either letting it go or letting it eat you alive. He would rather she found a way to let it go. It had already taken a big chunk out of her.

He knew about letting something eat you alive. He thought about his most recent stint in Afghanistan for NCIS. He hadn't gotten there in time to save the agent they'd sent him after. He had been so close, but the guy had been beheaded just as Beau had infiltrated the compound.

He'd done the next best thing, a snatch-and-grab of the warlord who probably hadn't ever heard of NCIS before he'd killed one of its agents. He wouldn't ever forget what it stood for now.

When they reached their floor, he was sure to check both ways. No one around. They exited the elevator and were soon inside the suite. He opened the doors onto the balcony to let the moonlight and the sounds of the city night in.

When he turned, she was standing against the wall next to the entrance exactly where he'd left her.

He unclipped the empty holster from his lower back and set it and the gun he'd taken on one of the tables in the living room as he passed it.

"I'm going to run a bath and we're going to get cleaned up."

She didn't respond as he went into the bathroom and started the water. As the tub filled, he took a moment to wash the grime and blood off his hands and arms. He pulled his shirt over his head and shucked out of the jeans.

When she didn't come into the bathroom, he shut off the water and went back out into the living room. She hadn't moved.

She put her hand out as he got close. "I need to… process."

He took a step closer and she said, more firmly, "No. Don't touch me. I can't think when you touch me."

"There's no need to think right now, Kinley. Let's get cleaned up."

Kinley tilted her head back against the wall, exposing the slender column of her throat, and he felt the heat of wanting her sparking deep inside him.

Mr. One-night Stand.

Mr. Temporary.

Mr. Never Engage His Heart.

Mr. Complete Dumbass.

He knew himself. He knew what this meant and getting his mind wrapped around what he had stupidly allowed himself to do was like a sledgehammer to his heart.

She was the most beautiful thing he'd ever seen, and he'd been chasing her his whole life.

"No. I've got to think about it, about Daniel and el Ajeer. All of it. Because it's too important to dismiss it."

He knew what it was to go that route. He knew what it was like. He'd seen it. He'd felt it. He'd been there, living in the badlands.

But he'd never lost a family member. That was…

Inconsolable.

She started to tremble all over as she clenched her fists. He saw it in her shoulders and in the way she wrapped her arms around herself, like she was trying to hold all the pieces in place.

Before the first sob broke free from her lips, he was there. As she folded in on herself, he was holding her against him.

"No," she said. "Don't touch me."

She was still backed up against the wall, her body so stiff, and yet shaking—everywhere, all over.

"D-don't," she repeated, not looking at him, keeping her hand over her face.

"Kinley," he said, wanting to help her and yet feeling so helpless.

"No." Another sob broke free, and then another, and she dropped her hand, looking at him, all of it, everything awful that had happened tonight.

He moved in closer. This was going to hell right now, and fast, but there wasn't any way to stop it.

Tears ran down her face in dark tracks of smudged makeup, and inch by inch, he felt her fall to pieces and begin to skim down the wall, her knees buckling. He held on and the reaction he was expecting happened.

She sobbed and pushed at him, and he didn't let go. Then she balled up her fist and hit him. He knew this was going to happen and he let it. It was what had to happen, the flash of fear and anger and anguish in her eyes, the tension holding her on the edge of the void. Hell, if that's what she needed, he'd let her vent again against his resilient muscles.

Everything was coming to a head, getting ready to demolish her the hard way, like a wrecking ball.

"You bastard. Why did you stop me?"

He didn't say anything, just let her vent.

He kept her backed up against the wall and he didn't have a regret in the world about using his superior strength against her.

She shoved at his chest. Ever since he'd laid eyes on her, he'd been locked on her like a friggin' tractor beam. He wasn't going to leave her alone like she wanted. She was going to a dark place and she needed him. He was going to be there every step of the way. Dammit. Whether she liked it or not, he was freaking staying.

"I was so scared…"

He had his hands on her waist, holding on to her, but she wasn't struggling to get him to let her go. She was struggling with that terrible dark well inside her, trying to make sense of it all, and she was struggling with herself far more than she was struggling with him. She was hitting him, yeah, but she was the one who was hurting. Oh, man, she was hurting bad.

She twisted against him, but not to get away, just to twist and writhe and ache with the pain.

He'd lived this, breathed this for eight years. He knew about how crap went down and how strongly it could affect someone. He knew how to find anything, complete any mission with a map, compass, weapon and target. Didn't matter how complex, how many countries he had to travel, how many enemies he had to neutralize, he knew how to make it work and get it done.

He knew what she was experiencing because through those countries, enemies and missions, he'd experienced the same things. He recognized them in her because they were also trapped in him. Process his ass. You didn't process this, you rolled over it and crushed it, let it mold you and make you stronger because that's what it took to get the job done.

So he knew what to do. He knew how to save her.

All he had was himself to offer to give her comfort and something to hang onto.

All in.

Just him.

He pressed closer to her and lowered his head to hers, resting his forehead on her brow, and he let her rant at him, let her vent her anger and her pain, let her pound on his chest until she was clutching his shirt in her hands and just holding on.

"Beau..." She whispered his name, burying her face in the curve of his neck. "Oh, Beau."

"That's, right, Kinley. I'm here. Completely present. You don't have to tell me what you need."

He kissed the top of her head, let his lips slide over the silken strands of her hair—and he pulled her closer.

"Beau…" She gripped him tighter, buried herself deeper, clinging to him. "Beau. Oh, Beau." She loosened her hold on his shirt, and her arms came up and around his neck.

Yeah, that was right—and so were the tears. She wasn't sobbing. She was just crying silently, nearly stock-still in his arms now. He felt the wetness on his neck, and it broke his heart. God, life could be so damned hard, more than a person could handle.

And yet, it had to be borne every day, in every way, over and over again until the end, and if a guy was lucky, every now and then he'd end up with a complicated woman in his arms, somebody who could turn him inside out.

Something he'd been missing for a long, long time. He hadn't really realized it until just this damn second.

Yeah, he was a bona fide freaking amazing genius.

These experiences were what made life worthwhile and she was the best freaking teacher he'd ever had.

"Kinley, sugar." He spoke her name, grounding her with it, bringing her back to him.

She slid her arms farther around his neck, and he kissed her cheek.

"I'm here, *chérie*. It's all you need, *ma belle*. Take what you need," he whispered in her ear and kissed her again, and she softened against him.

Comfort came in many forms and sex was just one of them, but if that's what she needed, wanted, he would comply. He wanted to make love with her, to ease her pain, to remind her there was life, always, the flame of it burning deep inside, to give her pleasure and ease her mind.

Yeah, he was so damned giving.

He wanted to take her so sweetly, to make her come apart in his arms, to make her his. He wanted to come so deep inside her, to claim her.

He opened his mouth on her neck and slid one hand down over the curve of her hip to pull her closer, to bring her up against him, and she turned her face into his neck and softly brushed her lips across the skin she'd made wet with her tears.

It was enough.

He kissed her neck, using his teeth so gently, licking her with his tongue and then sliding his mouth to hers and kissing her deep, angling his head to get more of her. Inch by inch, he hiked her skirt up over her ass, giving himself the contact he needed. When he had the skirt up around her waist, he slid his hand down over bare skin, over the softest skin he'd ever touched, over the perfect curves of her backside.

Right on. He'd been completely one hundred percent correct.

No panties.

Thong.

He needed the distraction because his heart was getting more and more wrapped around her. The taste of her, the way she held on to him, the way she looked at him, telling him how much his comfort meant to her.

A man could freaking lose his mind from this.

Chapter 13

To know how amazing it was to feel alive made his heart drop like a stone. Freefall without a parachute.

He hooked his fingers in that tiny scrap of lace covering what he wanted and pulled it down her legs, his eyes never leaving hers, wrapping his free arm around her thighs to steady her.

Moonlight caressed bare skin and the soft curls between her legs. Gotta love the way spandex stayed where it was placed: up around her provocative hips.

Leaning forward, he pressed his fingers to the hot center of her core, and he teased her, pushed her, felt her softly grind her hips against him and burrow her fingers through his hair.

"Beau…" His name was a sigh on her lips, her body silken, a force to be reckoned with in his arms.

He released her when he felt the pressure against his arm to allow her to spread her legs wider, and he slipped his fingers up inside her. She was so soft, so wet, so beautiful—electrifying, turning him on, getting him hot and hard.

"Beau…"

"Come for me, *chérie*." He wanted it so badly, to make her come undone, to make her feel so good. He wanted her to know he was her man, the one she needed, the one who could take her higher. But…the thought slammed into him…he needed her, too.

Her sighs grew rougher, more guttural, until he felt the contractions of her release rippling through her.

When she collapsed against the wall, he rose to his feet.

He took a breath. Her trust in him was in her eyes for him to see, and tenderness slammed into him as hard as a hollow-point bullet, shredding his insides.

Taking her mouth with his, he fitted himself to her and pushed up inside. No hesitation. No thoughts. It was mind-bending. She was so hot and slick, taking all of him on his first thrust, to the hilt.

"All in," he whispered on barely a breath, and her breathing hitched.

Her mouth was soft and wet, sucking on him, sucking on his tongue, then deepening the kiss. Between them, he felt her pushing at her top, and he did his best to get it up and off her. And then her breasts were exposed and so soft and full, and filling his hand even as he filled her, again and again, getting lost in her, mindlessly, so easily, following the heated warmth of her skin into pleasure so deep he never wanted it to end.

All he wanted was to be with her.

To be like this, driving into her, holding her to him. He had his tongue in her mouth, his hand on her breast, and his other hand wrapped under her thigh, lifting her leg around his waist, letting him go deeper and deeper. He thrust into her, and she took him every time, all the way, moving her hips with his, until the heat and the rhythm and the seductive softness of her body took him straight over the edge.

He pinned her up against the wall, his body rigid with the pleasure pulsing through him, her soft gasps of breath hot against his mouth. *Her.*

So perfect. Especially her. Hot and soft, and wet, and silky, turning him on and setting him off.

He pushed into her one last time, watching her face as he slid deep inside just to feel her, just to see her pleasure as she finished him off. Just to hear the small sound she made. God, he could do her all night long, but he didn't feel like she had the strength left to get to the bed.

So he held her and stayed inside her, just loving the way she felt, his heart still pounding.

She was so dangerous.

"You okay?" he asked after a few more moments had passed, brushing his mouth across her cheek.

"Yeah." She sighed, rocking against him, ever so slightly, and he sucked in a breath—it felt so good.

He pulled out, and in one powerful move had her in his arms. She snuggled up to him and there it was again. Damn, he loved when she did that.

He walked to the bathroom, a half-naked and totally boneless Kinley in his arms. He felt as if he'd just conquered the world.

He set her down on the commode and turned to the oval tub. Twisting on the taps and reheating the water.

Her eyes darkened when she looked at him and she rose, reaching for a washcloth. She dipped it in the bathwater and gently wiped at the skin at the top of his shoulder. It stung, but he was too busy watching the way she administered to him with that knee-buckling look on her face to care.

He cupped her face and rubbed his thumb along her tough little jaw. While she was attending to a couple of other nicks, he reached for the holder binding her hair. Pulling the elastic free, he started to unplait her hair, loving the thick silk as it unraveled as easily as he had. He reached for the skirt and shimmied it down her legs and off her.

His throat tightened as he rose and buried his face in her neck, breathing her in, filling himself with the warm and lovely scent of her skin. "I thought I had lost you."

"Oh, Beau. I knew you hadn't. I knew you would come for me. I knew it," she murmured, softening against him and running her fingers up through his hair—and he kissed her, moved his mouth to hers and played with her, sucking on her tongue, gently biting her lips, just trying to get more of her.

She was so responsive, teasing him, giving of herself—he felt it with every move she made.

He nuzzled her neck and she sighed. He glanced to see the tub was ready and left her to turn off the taps. He closed the door. The bathroom was filling with steam. He took her hand and drew her to the tub.

He climbed in first and then assisted her in. He settled into the steaming water. Pressing his back against the tub, he tugged her until she folded down against him, pressing her back to his.

"Lean back," he said and she did, just like that. He immersed her to her hairline in the water. "Now scoot up." She complied and he reached for the shampoo. Dabbing some into his hand, he lathered her hair, scrubbing her scalp. She sighed softly, her hand caressing his leg beneath the water, her thumb going to the top of his thigh.

"All in?" she said, her eyes downcast. She had to be looking at his tattoo.

"It's one of things we say. All in. All the time."

"I don't think I've met anyone like you, Beau, a man who so fully participates in everything he does. I love that about you. It makes me want to be like that."

"Like what?"

"Facing my fears head-on and dealing with them instead of retreating and letting them control me."

"Handling the fear in battle is the number-one thing that keeps you alive. Admitting your fear is all right. Totally. Handling it is the key. Because being afraid is a natural reaction to danger," he said tenderly.

"Even you get afraid?"

"Yes, even me. Now down again." He rinsed her hair out, lifted her back up, then applied conditioner.

"Scoot over and let me do you," she said.

"Mmm-hmm, I like the sound of that."

When she turned to face him, he was blindsided by her beauty, with her slicked-back hair leaving it stark and out there.

He kissed her mouth as he shifted so that his back was to her front. The water sloshed as there was a lot of displacement from his large body.

He didn't wait for her to tell him to dunk. He just did it. When he rose, she pulled him against her so that he was cradled in her arms, and he floated like that, enjoying the feel of her skin against his.

Finally she let him go and unlike her he had to tilt his head back for her to be able to wash it.

"Yeah, wasn't that you wanting to go after el Ajeer? Wasn't that you calling me a bastard and slugging me?"

"It wasn't about you," she said, running her hand over the nape of his neck.

He nudged her hands with the back of his head. "I know. Give me some credit, sugar. I knew you were hurting."

Her hands were so gentle on him, slipping through his soapy hair as if she couldn't get enough of the feel of him.

"He took everything." Her voice held the pain he'd seen in her tears and his heart squeezed at the sound of it. "For what? To make my father some kind of an example in his war of terror? What did he accomplish?" Her voice was getting bitter and angry. "Nothing. And my father died protecting me. I know it. He would never have run. He was a SEAL like you. He would have fought."

After dipping down and rinsing his hair and getting the conditioner treatment, he turned toward her. "I'm sure he did, Kinley, but you're wrong."

Her green eyes met his with the same pain he'd heard in her voice. "What? What do you mean?"

He cupped her face between his. "He didn't die for nothing. He died for you and the way we live our lives. Free and unafraid. If anything, he made a statement."

She closed her eyes as his words penetrated. Softly, she said, "He took my father's trident."

He stiffened and everything in him rebelled, heat whooshing over him, fury in his blood. "He freaking what?"

She opened her eyes, acknowledged his anger with her gaze. "He ransacked our home, trashed it and took it. My father kept it in his office, on his desk to remember to serve well in everything he did."

His lips thinned.

That just solidified this guy's place at the top of his hit list.

Beau wrapped a towel around her from behind and pulled her back against him, drying her off. She pushed at her heavy hair and sighed. Her gut still churned and she still felt raw and shredded from their ordeal in that ramshackle apartment complex. The place where Daniel had died and where they had had to leave him behind. She had seen it in Beau's eyes that it had killed him to leave a man behind, had heard it in his voice. But they hadn't had a choice.

Both of them had to call in. But she couldn't face that yet. She walked into the bedroom and sat down on the bed, leaning over and rubbing vigorously at her hair, then tossed the towel at her feet.

Beau came out of the bathroom looking like the battle-scarred warrior he was. God, he was beautiful with his broad chest, delineated abs, legs strong and muscular, his fingers nimble.

She didn't want to think about anything else, not about earlier, when she'd been crying in his arms, and not about the loss that would forever haunt her days, not right now. The ache was always with her. It never went away completely.

But with Beau, she had a chance for another small reprieve, and she wanted it, just a little more time with him, time to be held and cared for, and to get lost in his loving. It was crazy, something of the moment, intense and vital, sex and solace and salvation all wrapped up in Beau Jerrott with his sexy Cajun accent and his midnight-blue eyes.

She pulled the blankets down and gave him a sultry look over her shoulder as she settled on the mattress. He didn't need a verbal invitation. Every cell in her body cried out for him.

He was across the room, his damp, sexy hair framing his stubbled face. He put a knee on the bed and slid his hand over her ankle, brought it to his mouth and kissed it.

Just as she remembered the day her father died with the clarity that was born out of anguish, so would she remember until the day she died how Beau had saved her today, in more ways than one. No matter what happened between them.

"Beau," she murmured, and he moved up another inch and kissed her shin, then the inside of her knee.

Movement by movement he worked his way up her leg, stretching himself out on the bed, until his mouth was back at the hot sweet center of her desire. She lifted her hips against him in rhythm with the forays of his tongue, and she let herself sink into the loveliness of how he made her feel.

And so it went, on and on, his mouth on her everywhere and then coming up to take her in a kiss, hot and soft and deep, claiming her as he pushed up inside her. Everywhere she held him; she could feel the sleek, powerful movements of his muscles beneath his skin.

The world disappeared, every moment in his arms drawing them closer time and again—hot mouth, soft skin, hard body, thick muscles, the angle of his hips, warmth, eroticism, tenderness, falling…falling…falling into… Oh, God. Falling away and dropping hard.

She was a goner.

On his next thrust, he pushed up harder into her and held himself deep, and there he stayed, his breathing slow and even and sure, his body like iron.

He leaned down and kissed her, a fleeting touch of his mouth.

"You're hot, sugar," he said, smoothing her hair back off her forehead.

They both were. There was too much heat between them for them not to spark and catch fire. Their bodies were slick with sweat and he was teasing her, holding himself so still, second after endless second, until even the slightest movement nearly sent her over the edge.

"Beau...please."

He pulled out and pushed back in so slowly, his face so fierce, she thought she might lose her mind.

"Please..."

She strained against him, wanting him to take her there, to make her part of him, to give her release and power, and the life of him that he promised with each thrust.

"Please...oh, Beau."

He leaned down and kissed her again, and his next thrust came harder, and the one after that faster, each one stroking a banked fire deep in her core, until it caught and flashed into flame.

She clung to him, riding wave after wave of pleasure, hearing him groan on top of her, a guttural sound of need and satiation that echoed in her heart.

Beau, hard as nails, tough as granite, Beau. Her Beau had come undone.

Slowly their bodies relaxed as they breathed together, still locked in each other's arms, and dear God, he smelled good—all overheated male.

The gorgeous interior of him matching and exceeding the gorgeous exterior, Beau Jerrott, with his soft mouth and heartbreaking eyes.

By a twist of fate and a drifting Coast Guard cutter, Beau had dropped into her life. It was supposed to be temporary, but it didn't feel like it now. She knew why he was here. For whatever reason, the universe worked the way it did, and Beau Jerrott was a haven for her, a place to rest. She'd felt it instinctively when she'd first met him. She felt it in every cell of her body now. He was here, by her, with her, and she was safe.

She let her breath out on a soft, easy sigh, and he brought his forehead down to rest on hers.

"You okay?" he asked.

"Oh, yes. I feel so safe with you."

He smiled. "You are safe with me, *ma belle*," he said, resettling himself next to her.

Man, she could stay in his arms forever.

Wrapping his arm around her, he slowly rolled them to their sides, and he kept her close. He stuffed a pillow under his head and one behind her back and then he kissed her, slanting his mouth over hers and sliding his tongue in deep.

It was a hot kiss, lazy, thorough, missing nothing. Breaking off, he gently bit her lower lip, then licked her, then kissed her again, taking her mouth with his own. She explored him, not just his mouth, but the taste of him, the angle of his jaw, the weight of him up against her, the hard muscles in the arm around her.

She smoothed her palm over the broad curve of his shoulder and continued upward, tunneling her fingers into hair that she couldn't stop wanting to touch. She kissed him, one long moment after another, luxuriating in the sensuality of having him naked and close, and in the comfort she felt. Even the way he smelled made her feel safe.

She snuggled closer to him and kissed his chest and breathed him in, and after a moment, she said, "I know our next step."

"Sleep," he said. "Then we'll discuss that."

The sound of a clip getting shoved home woke her. She opened her eyes to find Beau standing near the closet in the bedroom dressed in tight-fitting jeans and a tropical shirt.

"Locked and loaded?" she said.

He gave her a sidelong glance, holstering the HK underneath his shirt. "Good morning, sleepyhead. Time to rock and roll. We've only got two more days before extraction." She rose to a sitting position and his eyes roamed over her. "I am damn sorry that I got up early," he said.

She gave him a sleepy smile and walked to the closet. Giving him a kiss, she opened the door and chose a pair of cropped jeans and a silk T-shirt that would also mask the weapon Beau had been able to snag.

"I ordered breakfast. It should be here any minute. I also contacted Chris. He said he'd take care of notifying the DEA about Daniel."

She nodded, the whole terrible night flashing back. Daniel's open, staring eyes. "I know I didn't give you a good impression of him, but in the end, he tried to protect me. He really did care about me."

He wrapped his hand around her nape and rubbed her hair and scalp. "How could he not?" he said softly. There was a knock at the door. "That's breakfast. You should call Stafford before we go. No telling what today is going to bring and whether we'll even have a signal."

She nodded and walked to the dresser. Grabbing underwear, she quickly dressed. In the bathroom she ran a comb through her hair and pulled it all back into a ponytail to keep it out of her way.

She picked up her cell from the nightstand and dialed Kirk. He answered on the first ring. "Are you all right?" he asked with genuine concern in his voice.

"Not great at the moment." He had always been a good boss and an even better man and she let just a bit of her guard drop. She'd never really trusted him, either, but he'd never let her down and had always believed in her as an agent. "It was a tough night."

He blew out a breath. "I can imagine. I'm sorry about Daniel, Kinley."

Her throat got tight. There had been absolutely no chance for them, not after she'd met Beau, but she was so sorry he was dead. Glad that she'd gotten a chance to hear his apology, since she'd been much too stubborn and hurt to open his emails before they had reconnected on this case. A sense of closure. She hoped that was true for Daniel, too. He'd died saving her from a sexual assault, giving Beau the added time he needed to rescue her. "So am I. The DEA will…take care of him? Right, Kirk?"

"Yes, they are making inquiries. Their intention is to get his body back."

She rubbed her forehead. "Keep me posted about that."

"All right."

"We might be cut off from communication. We're going to get that name that we need, no holds barred, and then we're going after that picture."

"Good luck and get back here in one piece."

"Yes, sir."

She disconnected the call. As she emerged into the room, the food was already on the table and she didn't hesitate to dig in.

No holds barred.

For her country.

For Daniel.

And lastly, for herself.

Chapter 14

"You know where we're going?" she asked, and Beau's eyes narrowed.

"Yes." He threw her the keys to the sleek black Mercedes coupe.

She got into the driver's seat and they drove off in the direction that she and Daniel had taken yesterday. Arriving in Cuba had been like descending into the 1950s with all the amazing vintage cars on the streets. Havana was the capital city, province, seat of government and major port of the island, and the architecture attested to its rich history. The buildings were beautiful and the city well maintained.

There was still a lot of lush tropical growth in and around the city, but she was under no illusion that the jungle beyond the metropolis wasn't filled with plenty of danger, least of all the snakes and crocs.

There was only one man on this godforsaken island who knew they were here.

The arms dealer.

"A bakery shop?" Beau said, eying the innocent and delectable-looking shop as she parked at the curb.

"Yeah, he's not just cooking up sweet things in the back. There are plenty of deadly weapons."

When they got to the front door, it was ajar and there was a smear of blood on the handle. Beau reached back for his weapon and she followed suit.

There was no one there and it wasn't lost on Kinley that there weren't any delicious smells coming from the kitchen. Yesterday, there'd been a warm cinnamon scent in the air when she and Daniel had walked through the front door.

Beau took a quick look around the counter. He stopped and pointed with the gun. There was a dead guy and a long swath of blood leading into the back.

"That's not the arms dealer," she said.

"Cartel?"

"That's the arms dealer's assistant. Looks like he was cartel."

He stepped to the kitchen door and pushed the swinging door open just a tad. He gave her a signal that she should follow.

When she pushed through the door she discovered the man she had spoken to propped up against the wall. He stared at them.

Gut shot. The trail of blood was his as he'd dragged himself back here.

"You."

She walked over to him and crouched down. "What happened?"

"They don't like loose ends. They left that guy out there to take care of me when I wasn't useful anymore. Got the drop on him with a gun I keep for emergencies under the counter. Even when you help them there's no guarantee you'll live."

She nodded. "I'm here for information. I think you know what I need. What I'm looking for. Because you were Daniel's contact. Weren't you?"

"How do you know this?"

"Daniel's contact sent us to you. I deduced you had to be him and was using this opportunity to make sure we were legit."

"It's true. I had to be cautious and make sure this wasn't a setup, but they got to my assistant in the bakery. He was one of them."

"The dead body out there."

"Those bastards killed my youngest son, shot in the street, so I was more than willing to help the DEA take them down. But then they took my oldest son for collateral to insure I wouldn't warn you. Even so they killed him…" He sobbed softly, his face contorted in pain. "They let me hear as he pleaded for his life. They are a blight on our country."

"Then help me now so Daniel's death will have meaning, so your sons' deaths will have meaning. The DEA won't give up. Especially now that the *Las Espadas* have killed Daniel."

He nodded. "I'm sorry about Daniel. He was a good man. It doesn't matter what happens to me now. The name you want is Dr. Miguel Costa." The arms dealer coughed. "He has a clinic just on the outskirts of town. You can find him there." He rattled off an address. "Take what you need from my shop." He recited the entry code. "You must hurry. It's possible my assistant has already passed this information on to the cartel or someone else. They are offering money for information. Like I said." His voice went weaker. "They have eyes

and ears everywhere. They are ruthless…my boys…"
He closed his eyes, his voice anguished. "My boys…
hurry…"

That was all he said as he suddenly stopped talking on a long exhale, and the life drained out of him as
he slumped over. She reached out and closed his eyes.

Together they turned away and Kinley led the way
over to a rack. She reached behind a metal support and
switched a button. The panel slid open and Kinley typed
in the code he'd given her.

The whole wall moved aside. Inside was an arsenal.

"Hoo-*freaking*-yah," Beau murmured enthusiasti-
cally, and Kinley turned to look at him. She huffed a
short laugh and walked to a large green zippered bag.

Beau wasted no time in grabbing a submachine gun,
another handgun and plenty of ammo, along with other
gear. Kinley went with her tried-and-true SIG along
with enough ammo. They loaded up the bag and left.

Once they were back in the car, she input the address and then checked the weather. It was habit. She'd
often done it before a tour at sea. "Oh, damn. There's
weather coming our way," she said. "A tropical depres-
sion. Not a hurricane luckily, though this is the season.
It could get really wet."

Before they left the shop, Beau called in an anony-
mous tip regarding the shopkeeper. His death was something else Kinley could use to keep her going on this
mission.

Fifteen minutes outside the city, the rain hit and
it was epic. Torrential, wind blowing and gusting. It
slowed them down to a crawl.

Beau had taken over the driving and she looked out
at the smeared and indistinct landscape. The windshield

wipers made a slapping sound as they crisscrossed, wicking away the moisture.

She looked over at him. "You said you were from Louisiana, right?"

His eyes lit up at the mention of his home. He nodded and smiled. "I'm used to driving in this kind of rain. We get quite a bit of it."

"Where exactly in Louisiana?" She reached out and absently rubbed her fingers along his forearm. He captured her hand and held it.

"I'm from Vermilion Parish in the heart of *L'Acadiane* or, in English, Acadiana. My family lives in Delcambre, a small town right on the bayou. It's the home of much of the local fishing industry."

"The bayou. What's that like, living near so much water?"

"There is no place like it anywhere. Lush ferns growing near purple iris beneath hardwood trees dripping with moss and some of the largest willows you'll ever see. Some brighter flowers like black-eyed Susans and daisies. It's a rich environment to grow up in. Some of the trees in the bayou are ancient. At night the swamp can be misty and dark, the water shining like black glass under a pale moon."

She shivered a bit. "Alligators, right?"

"Ah, me gators. The bayou can be beautiful, but it can also be dangerous."

"You said you have a large family."

"Yes, four brothers and a sister."

"There are four men as handsome as you running around?"

He smiled. "Yeah, we are similar. One of my brothers is a fisherman, one lives in New York City working on Wall Street, one is a firefighter and the last one is in the marines."

"And the sister?"

"She's in her freshmen year at Tulane. She's into chemistry."

"You must miss them very much."

His eyes got that faraway look people had when they were thinking about the past. "Miss them like hell. We were very close growing up, but I've been away from Delcambre for ten years. I go home as often as possible, but my tours were extensive and now that I'm based in DC for my job, I see my family mostly during holidays."

They fell silent as the GPS tracker gave instructions for a turn and Beau navigated the slippery road and the heavy rain.

"How about you, sugar? Where you from?"

"All over. I traveled with my father to all his billets. I lived mostly in Coronado because that's where my father was stationed. When he became a diplomat, it was London…and…well, after he was murdered, I went to an aunt's back in Coronado, then to a cousin's in San Francisco, another aunt's in Monterey. The cliffs there are quite magnificent, the ocean so turbulent."

"Why were you tossed around so much?"

"I was in demand until they realized that my inheritance from my dad was protected. Then they lost interest in supporting me. It was all in trust and I couldn't touch it until I was eighteen. It was a help when I was in school and for living expenses. My family wasn't as close as yours. When my father wasn't deployed, he was training. When he wasn't training he was on base."

"Your *mère*?"

"Does that mean mother?"

"Yes, sorry, mother."

"She died when I was one. My father didn't remarry. He had girlfriends who I stayed with and caregivers, but when he could, he took me with him. After he left the SEALs, he was always there for me."

"That's a tough life, huh?"

"No, not really. I didn't really experience that. My dad was great and all I needed. I was sheltered and protected."

"Why the Coast Guard?"

"I think it stemmed from my time in Monterey. I fell in love with the changing face of the sea. Because of what happened to my father, I knew I always wanted to do some kind of police work and protecting our coasts appealed to me."

"CGIS was always your goal, then?"

"Yes, I want to have my own team someday. If I can stop screwing up and getting myself tied up with seductive bastards who happen to be agents."

She hadn't meant for that comment to come out so harshly. It could be a result of all that had happened with Daniel, but Beau didn't deserve that. "I'm sorry, that was…"

"Honest."

"I was half of that equation with both you and Daniel and I had a choice with both of you, so I can't really complain. It's just that with our kind of lifestyle, it's really difficult to meet people and have a normal life. Mostly I meet guys on the job because I'm so often on the job. When I'm home, it's downtime for me."

"Kinley, I understand fully."

"Then what's up with the one-night stands?"

He didn't immediately answer. She was under no illusion that Beau had any long-term plans for them. This was a moment out of time. They'd been thrown together and they had an amazing connection. She tried really hard to not fool herself. When the mission was over, she expected they would be, too.

That brought definite regret. But Beau had made things clear from the start and just because she was falling for him, that didn't change a damn thing

She realized he'd tensed up and she didn't know how much she wanted him to confide in her until he spoke.

"I got...burned pretty bad and now I'm a jaded jerk."

"What happened?"

"Jennifer was ambitious and always gung ho about her job. She wanted to make admiral and that is a tough career path. I guess I thought she was willing to make room for me in her life. We had a lot of arguments about spending time together, mostly on my side. She suggested I go for SEAL training. I should have realized then that it was a way to put distance between us. I took the SEAL route and our correspondence waned, mostly because there isn't a lot of downtime in BUD/S. She didn't show up for my graduation and didn't return my messages. When I got home, she was gone... everything was gone. I was going to propose to her..."

Her chest filled and she squeezed his hand in sympathy. She wasn't sure what she'd expected him to say, but that caught her off guard. It would have been easier to hear that he was one-dimensional and a womanizer than it was to find out he'd had his heart broken. "I hate this woman already," she murmured. And she did. How could she have hurt Beau like that? He was... She had to get a grip, especially now.

"I don't use women. I just enjoy their company and then move on."

Well, he couldn't say it plainer than that, even though it hurt. She was a big girl and had known what...okay, she hadn't known exactly how amazing it would be with him, but she'd known his boundaries. She respected them and really it couldn't be better that he felt that way. It made it easier on her.

So why was her heart aching so hard?

There was no more time to worry about their personal relationship. The GPS tracker squawked and let them know they'd reached their destination.

The clinic was an oblong structure and Kinley realized that it was more of a health clinic than a place where people came for plastic surgery.

Beau parked the car.

"Kinley," he said. She loved the way he said her name with that slight accent making it sound incredibly exotic. There was way too much she loved about Beau.

"I get it, Beau. Don't worry about me. I understand and you were quite clear. Temporary. I've got my career to focus on. That's really what matters to me." She didn't want to examine her feelings for Beau anymore.

Whatever he'd been about to say died on his lips. With a stiff nod, he opened his door and slipped out of the coupe. There, that should allay his fears about her wanting anything…even if she did. But that was stupid fairy-tale stuff.

Her shoulders drooped a bit and she took a deep steadying breath. It was time to get this information from the good doctor and get the hell of out of Cuba.

Inside, the clinic was clean, neat and well maintained. The woman behind the reception desk looked up as they walked in. *"¿En què puedo servirles?"* She was very pretty with long dark hair and wide chocolate-brown eyes.

Beau smiled and approached the desk, introducing himself and including her. She smiled and said something in Spanish. Beau nodded. "We'd like to see him now. It's very important."

The woman picked up the phone and spoke, then hung up and motioned for them to follow her. They trailed her past the waiting area. The people in the waiting room were an odd mix. Some well dressed, others shabby. Clean, but it was clear they were quite poor. She disappeared through a door that opened up to a hallway with examination rooms on either side. When she got to the end of the hall, to a closed door, she knocked before opening it and ushered them inside.

Dr. Costa rose from behind his desk. He was a compact man, balding with a fringe of salt and pepper hair cut close to his scalp. He wore a white lab coat and a stethoscope was draped around his neck.

"Mr. and Mrs. Nadeau?" he said in beautifully accented English. "Welcome. Please be seated."

"This isn't exactly the kind of establishment I was expecting. But, at least it's clean," Kinley said, still playing her role.

"Sweetheart," Beau said in an indulgent way.

"My clinic serves many, Ms. Nadeau, and I am a certified doctor as well as quite skilled with cosmetic surgery. What can I do to help you?" His pleasant smile didn't waver even in the wake of her rudeness.

"I want some work done."

Dr. Costa studied her for a moment, and then sighed. "Are you certain, senora?" He came out from behind the desk and faced her. "May I?" he asked. She nodded.

He tipped up her chin and turned it both right and left, studying all the planes and angles. Then he released her.

"I cannot augment what is already quite perfect. You have the bone structure of a goddess and an uncommon beauty. I wouldn't touch your face no matter how much you paid me. I simply cannot help you."

"What?" she said, looking at Beau and laughing softly. "Goddess?" This isn't what she'd expected of a greedy man who took black-market jobs for the money. But nothing was ever as it seemed and ruthless men always found ways to get others to do what they wanted.

"Actually, Doctor, I have to agree with you," Beau said, steel replacing the bored-CEO look in his eyes. "Since you can't help with my wife's plastic surgery, perhaps there is something else you could help us with?"

He looked puzzled for a moment, going back behind his desk and sitting down. "What would that be, senor?"

"Diego Montoya."

Dr. Costa stiffened and sat forward. "I don't know anyone by that name."

The fear in his voice underlined the lie.

"Who are you people?"

"We're people looking for photographs of Montoya. The before and after, if you get my drift."

"Americans. CIA?"

He reached for the phone, but Beau pressed down on the receiver before he could lift it.

"We can do this easy, Dr. Costa, or we can do this hard. Me, I like the easy."

He sat back, torn and terrified. "Who did he threaten in your family, Miguel?" Kinley said, going with her gut.

He looked at her sharply and rubbed his hand over his bald pate.

"That…monster, that…criminal, threatened my beloved Maria. My wife. I had to do what he asked. But I destroyed all evidence of it just as he ordered. I'm sorry, but I cannot help you. I would ask that you leave my clinic and not return."

She planted her hands on his desk and leaned forward. "I know what it's like to lose someone to a terrorist. I don't buy it. You kept insurance."

His lips thinned.

"He's a threat to the United States. He's murdered innocent people. As a doctor, how can you let that sit on your conscience while he's free to perpetuate even more heinous acts on even more innocent people? Husbands, wives, children?"

He rose and went to the window, obviously torn. "I hate these men who make my country into a...a conduit for drugs, a place that shelters murderers and cutthroats. Men with money who think they are above the law." He rubbed at his forehead, his voice thick. "He came to me because I am the best. He threatened me when I refused, and when I still refused, he threatened her. I hate that he made me use my skills to mask him. To protect him from the law and the cartel who's hunting him like the dog he is."

"Dr. Costa. We need your help."

He turned back to them. "I can't risk her. She is everything to me."

"If you give us the means by which to capture him, he will no longer be a threat to you or your wife."

That made him pause. It was apparent that apprehending Diego Montoya appealed to him very much. Dr. Costa was no black marketer for hire. That was evident. "You are not only a very beautiful woman, but a very persuasive one. I must think about this and consult with my wife. That is the only answer I can give you at this moment. Come back at closing and I'll give you my answer."

"Dr. Costa…"

"Beau." She put her hand on his arm and he shifted his gaze to hers. After a moment, he stepped toward the door. "At closing, then. I know you will do the right thing."

Outside, Beau snagged her arm. "That was a nice bit of tap dancing in there, but I hope you know what you're doing. We're on a timeline here and if he decides to say no, we're going to have to push and he knows it. He could run."

"He won't run."

"How do you know that?"

"Because this is his home and he's dedicated his life to helping these people. He's nothing like we thought. Did you see the patients in that waiting room? They're local and they're poor. I'm banking that he's a good man caught in a bad situation. He'll do the right thing, Beau. Trust me."

It started to rain again as they got back into the Mercedes. Beau pulled his handgun from the small of his back, checked his clip and slammed it home, chambering a round and reholstering the weapon. "I'm going to watch the back. You stay here and keep an eye on the front. Call me if you see anything suspicious."

She grabbed his arm before he exited the vehicle. "Thank you."

"What for?" he growled, obviously frustrated that they had to wait around.

"Trusting me."

He flashed her a wry grin. "I just want to do this the easy way."

He slipped out of the vehicle and headed into the thick, dense growth of the jungle butting up to the rear of Costa's clinic.

It was only two hours before the clinic was set to close.

She changed into a pair of jeans and a dark T-shirt, donning slip-on canvas sneakers that she'd kept stored in case of emergencies. She wanted to be ready to run for the chopper when the time came. An hour of waiting had passed and the rain had gotten more intense. It was sheeting across the windshield when Kinley heard a number of vehicles turning into the clinic's makeshift parking lot, three Jeeps with four men in each of them, looking way too paramilitary for her comfort. One of them got out of the vehicle. Kinley ducked down, hoping the rain would obscure her inside. Luckily he didn't see her.

But she saw clearly the tattoo on his neck, right below his lobe.

Two crossed swords.

Holy crap. She hit Beau's number and when he picked up, she said, "*Las Espadas* are going in the front door."

As the men filed in, bristling with weapons, people started running out.

"How many?"

"Twelve. Too many."

"I'm going for the doctor. I can see his window from here. We'll be coming in hot."

"All right. I'll fire up the coupe and be ready." She reached for the green bag. She thought she'd grabbed… Yes, here it was. A tracker. She slipped out of the vehicle and was soaked in seconds. Running to the lead Jeep, she jammed her hand underneath the wheel well and stuck the device to the metal. The *crack-crack* of automatic gunfire mixed in with the sound of the pouring rain. The screams and sobbing of a woman filtered out to her. Backing up, she ran back to the car and started it up.

Before Kinley could put the Mercedes in gear, the front door opened and the men came out. They were dragging a sobbing woman. The receptionist.

Even as she watched them drive away, there was a weird stillness all around, an eerie calm. It seemed as if even the rain paused. It was a pulling sensation in the air around her.

Then the building blew apart, a great crashing, rending explosion that rocked the car and sent debris up into the air to rain down on the vehicle. Kinley was safely cocooned inside as the blast whooshed with such force it rocked the coupe, the diminished concussion rolling over her. Even with the downpour, fire erupted as the debris continued to fall in heavy, soggy clumps.

Oh, God, *Beau.*

He had gone inside to get Dr. Costa.

Chapter 15

"Beau!"

He came to, sputtering; rain running in a small stream off some kind of siding on top of him. He was lying flat on his back in the dark, buried under debris, with Kinley's frantic voice beating out even the rushing, roaring sound of the rain.

"Here," he said hoarsely, weakly, his ears ringing and his head vibrating like a frigging bell. What the hell had happened?

He heard running feet, but he couldn't move, still dazed, still reeling from getting mown over by hundreds of pounds of explosive pressure that had cleaned his clock but good.

The sound of the stuff on top of him being pulled away was coupled with her harsh, out-of-control breathing. Finally, he could see the sky and her face leaning over him.

"Oh, God, Beau. Are you okay. Are you hurt?"

"I'm okay. What happened?"

She reached in and helped him to sit up, her hands going over him, still pushing stuff out of the way. "They left and took the receptionist and then the whole building went up."

His chest hurt a bit, but everything seemed to be in working order. The blast had just knocked him out.

"Dammit," he swore. He should be damn glad he hadn't already been inside when the building exploded.

"You were right. We shouldn't have waited. It was the *Las Espadas*. They found out about Dr. Costa."

He rolled to his side, curled up and pushed himself to his hands and knees. He put one hand to his forehead before she helped him get unsteadily to his feet. He felt gut punched and behind that, bearing down on him like a friggin' freight train, was the anger. Beau did not like to lose or be outsmarted and outmaneuvered. "They took the receptionist?"

"Yes, she was not going willingly and she was crying hard."

Beau looked toward the building, pushing his wet hair off his face. Without a word, he started toward it, his head clearing. When he got to the wall that was now complete rubble, he put up his hand to ward off the intense heat of the fire. The rain was doing a good job of keeping it at bay. He stepped over the small lip of the wall that was intact and peered inside.

There was a body with a hole in the forehead. The lab coat was filthy and covered in blood, the stethoscope still around his neck.

He turned away, blocking the view as Kinley made it to him. "Dr. Costa is dead."

Her eyes stricken with guilt, she said, "Well, that's it then. We failed and it's my fault."

"What?"

"We failed, Beau."

"Not yet."

"What is that supposed to mean?"

"We go after her. They had to have taken her for a reason. She must know something." Water sluiced off his face and trailed down his arms. The jungle was going to be a muddy mess.

"What?" Her eyes widened and she grabbed his forearm. "Go into the jungle after an army of ruthless cartel goons? Are you out of your mind?"

"No. We can get her back. There were only twelve men. I can handle that."

She stepped back and glared at him. "We were expressly forbidden to engage the *Las Espadas*! We can't go after them."

"Do you know what they're going to do to her? They're going to torture her and once they get her to talk—and believe me, they will get her to talk—they're going to kill her. Are you seriously telling me we should walk away when the life of this woman and the security of the US hang in the balance?"

"They were orders, Beau."

"And that's enough for you to turn your back on a terrorist threat? I know that you care about terrorists because one murdered your father. In addition, you were just in the cartel's hands, helpless just like she is now." He had no way of knowing whether or not Montoya was a threat, but he was going to err on the side of caution. And, yeah, he was being a sumbitch. He knew it and, judging by the tightening in her face, she knew it, too.

"Orders," she repeated, her mouth tightening. "Using my father's murder against me is not fair, Beau." She bit her lip, the battle of her conscience and her experience warring on her face. "I'm not ignorant or immune to what I know they're going to do to her. But…orders are orders."

He ignored the emotion in her eyes. This was too important for him not to bring out the big guns. Her hair was plastered to her head. Her makeup was long gone. She had a bruise on her face from her ordeal yesterday. She was trembling and wired as tight as a drum. And all that emotion had to go somewhere. She'd never been more beautiful to him in her life.

"Where is that woman that wanted to take down el Ajeer? If we don't do this, Montoya is free to do whatever he wants, unleash whatever he has planned on American soil. Do you want that on your conscience? Do you want her torture and death on your conscience when we could have done something about it?"

"No, of course not! But it's suicide and career ending to go against orders, to go into an unfamiliar jungle in a foreign land after armed men without a plan or permission from our superiors!"

"Kinley, I've made a living going into unfamiliar places and taking down armed men. I'm not asking for permission. I don't ask for permission. I complete a mission, whatever it takes."

She folded her arms against her chest.

He didn't realize how much he wanted her to step out of her comfort zone and go with him. "Montoya might even have information on el Ajeer. He works for the cartel. He's their damn go-to guy. I bet he knows plenty about el Ajeer."

"I know what you're doing. You're playing on my emotions."

"All in, Kinley." He wanted her on this. He needed her on this all the damn way. Yeah, right, he was a goner for sure, even though he knew she was more interested in her career than she was in him. That had stung. He'd racked up all of three days with this woman, but somehow it meant something.

He'd been just about to spill his guts and she'd cut him off at the knees. He figured it was always better to know than to be in the dark.

She looked away. He shoved back his disappointment and started to walk toward the front of the building. "We're wasting time. Why don't you go to the extraction site and wait for me."

She grabbed his arm, trying to slow his forward momentum. Her small hands and petite body couldn't stop him, but the anguish in her voice did. He stopped and rounded on her.

"Damn you, Beau. I'm not going to leave and let you do this alone. We're supposed to be a *team* and we've already lost Daniel. We *had* to leave him. I'm *not* leaving you."

Her voice caught and he dragged her against him, hard. "Kinley, we can't waste time. I don't want to be insensitive." The truth of the matter was a world of feelings had opened up for him. Not because they were dancing on the edge of a knife, trying to complete a mission that just got damned-near impossible, but because with each moment he was showing her what was beneath his rock-hard shield. A side of himself he'd buried a while ago. She was giving him back something he'd lost.

She wiped at her eyes and stared at him. "Well, you're being an ass, but I'm in. *All in,*" she snapped with just the kind of attitude he liked. Fiery.

"Then get your all-in ass into the vehicle before we lose these guys."

She brushed by him, stalking to the car. "We won't lose them. I put a tracker on one of the Jeeps."

He huffed out a laugh and shook his head. Well, look at her thinking tactically like a damn navy SEAL. Damned if he didn't like it a whole helluva lot.

"Stop looking so damn smug and get your insensitive ass in the car."

Her confidence turned him on, right here, right now, in the middle of a crucial mission with her stepping completely out of her comfort zone. She'd been pushed hard for two days, seen more death in that time span than she had ever, he was sure. He strode up to her and grabbed her shirtfront and jerked her toward him. She made a little squeak as his mouth clamped over hers.

Kinley had kissed him before, but nothing like this. She swore her toes curled in her soggy shoes, and as his mouth slid over hers, her hands crawled around his waist. She held on. He was ferociously warm and tight against her. Not an inch of him soft, and all of it getting harder. Excitement coursed through her blood and cut at her composure. His mouth molded with a fragile pressure that was such a contrast to the man, and made her body tingle with expectation. He kissed her like she was his next breath and she returned the kiss like he was hers.

His tongue was bold and sweeping and her mind just melted into sensation. His hand slid upward. The backs of his fingers fluttered to her throat, gathering her fraying nerves as they went and making her unbearably greedy for more. His fingertips spanned her jaw, holding her as if she'd vanish. It was so damn sexy, and she wanted to get closer, unconsciously pushing her hips into his. He drew back a fraction.

"Damn," she whispered against his mouth.

He rubbed a thumb over her lips.

"Aren't we wasting time?"

"I don't care," he said, pulling her back against him and kissing her again.

He drew back. Something in his dark eyes sent a fresh pulse of awareness through her. This man made her feel so much at once, she couldn't pinpoint anything when he was kissing her. And suddenly she realized… her numbness. It was gone, replaced by a pulsating, supercharged energy that was all consuming.

"Okay," he said. "Now get in."

She huffed, but it had no impact as he settled in the driver's seat and fired up the engine. She grabbed the tracker and turned it on. It started to blip and Beau put the car into gear. Gunning the engine, he took off.

And he didn't slow down. The Mercedes was made to hug the road and it was a tank, enough to plow through rain and mud. When they came to a turnoff that made Kinley swallow hard, he gave her a reassuring glance.

It looked like nothing but a rutted road heading to the middle of nowhere. There were no signs that the rain was going to let up. Yeah, October was one of the rainiest months here.

"You ready for this?" he said.

"Let's get this done and go home and stop that bastard."

His grim, locked-and-loaded look said it all.

He turned onto the rutted road and they took off again. They probably shouldn't have been barreling down this road that was more like a poor excuse for a path at top speed. Branches slapped the windows, green and brown flying past. But they were gaining on the blip. It wouldn't be long before they were in very close proximity.

Then the blip froze.

"They've stopped."

"Probably for the night. How close are we?"

"About a mile or so." He slowed the car and came to a stop.

"We'll have to go the rest of the way on foot. We don't want to alert them that we're here." He did some maneuvering to get the vehicle turned around and pointed in the direction they'd come.

He reached back and grabbed one of the submachine guns and a utility belt, rapidly adding to it, totally in his element. He pulled the wicked knife he always carried out of his pants pocket. "Here, take this to cut her bonds."

"I cannot believe we're going to assault an armed camp of cartel goons against orders."

"We aren't. I am. You have your marching orders. Get in. Get her free. Get out. Get here. Got it?"

"You get all the fun," she said, saluting him.

He pulled down the visor and smeared his face with camouflage paint that they had picked up courtesy of the arms-dealer contact, then handed it to her. "Face and hands," he said "We have the element of surprise and I have the skills to handle them. You just get that woman out of there and hightail it back to the coupe."

He pulled the keys out of the ignition and handed them to her. "As soon as you get here, fire her up and be ready to go."

She nodded, smearing her own face. Her nerves were steady, as they had been on many a drug bust. She had taken down her fair share of go-fast boats and armed-to-the-teeth smugglers, and knew how to use the semiautomatic Beau shoved into her hands. "Only use that if you have to. Any gunfire is going to focus every tango in the camp on you. You need to be quiet and quick."

She nodded. He reached up and fiddled with the light in the roof of the car. When he opened his door, it remained pitch-black. He slipped out and Kinley followed suit.

He grabbed her arm and dragged her against his hard body, kissing her. "Do what you have to do," he said. "Don't worry about me."

"Beau." She pulled him back and kissed him, hard.

He started down the road and Kinley followed. There was a quarter moon and it didn't help her see the rutted and muddy road ahead of them. Stepping in pools of water, mud slippery and squishy beneath her sneakers, she did her best to follow. Beau moved like a commando, quiet, sure-footed and almost invisible beside her. If she was to assault an enemy camp of ruthless cartel killers, she couldn't have had better backup.

In the distance Kinley could make out a fire, and she heard the low murmur of voices filtering to her. Then laughter. The camp.

There were only two Jeeps parked near the tents and Kinley wondered where the third one was.

The terrain evened out and Beau grabbed her arm and pulled her off to the side, right behind one of the Jeeps. Beau's gaze went around the camp. "I'm going to do some quick recon. You stay put. Don't move a muscle until I come back."

Before she could respond, he was gone, melting into the jungle. She strained to see him, but it was impossible and she hunched down lower for the longest five minutes of her life. Suddenly her skin rippled with awareness and her head snapped to the right. Beau moved in as quietly as he'd left.

He bent close to her ear and whispered, "She's in the tent in the middle. I lifted up one of the stakes, which will make it easier for you to crawl under and then get back out. There is only one guard at the flap, so be as quiet as possible. Her hands and feet are bound."

He cupped her face and gave her such an intense look she felt it all the way to her soul. "Don't take any risks. I'll draw them away."

She wrapped her arms around his neck and squeezed him hard. "Be careful. Come back to me." When she released him, he flashed a confident grin. "This will be a walk in the park. Hooyah, *chérie*. Wait until you hear my signal."

"Wait. What is your signal?"

He flashed that same cocky grin. "Oh, you'll know it when you hear it."

He disappeared like he had the last time and Kinley moved silently toward the middle tent, keeping low.

She waited, every nerve taut. Then she heard the explosion. She ducked under the flap and put her finger to her lips as the woman's head whipped around. She drew out Beau's knife and cut the woman's bonds.

"¿Quién es usted?"

"Do you speak English?"

"Yes." Her eyes widened. "Oh, I recognize you. You're that haughty woman who insisted on meeting with my husband today."

"Your husband? You're Maria?" Kinley sliced through the rope binding Maria's feet and then the one around her hands. "Follow me."

"Yes, I'm Maria. Th-th-they killed my husband when he refused to help them. Who exactly are you?"

As they were getting ready to go under the flap, a hand grabbed the back of Kinley's shirt and hauled her to her feet, backhanding her across the face. She reeled away and hit the tent pole. Her eyes watered and she worked her jaw, tasting blood. At least this time she wasn't tied to a chair.

"You cannot escape." He stepped close and she put her hands up, the knife folded and concealed in her hand.

"Okay, okay, no punching! Maybe we can work out a deal." She moved to him, her expression giving new meaning to the words, *Come on, honey. I'm yours*. "Just you and me."

He smiled as if she were already conquered.

That's all she needed. She grabbed his wrist, dug her thumb into the apex of his finger and thumb, and twisted hard, forcing his arm and elbow backward. His scream of pain was drowned out by the gunfire and another explosion.

He reached for her, but Kinley threw her weight into it, lowering him toward the floor. Then she slammed her knee into the side of his head. He dropped like a stone. She stepped back and slashed his throat.

She tried to ignore the sick feeling at the sight of the blood, but he would have killed her without a thought. "Let's go."

"Where?"

"I think you know where, Mrs. Costa."

Her lips thinned, her eyes going dark with the thought of revenge. "Diego Montoya. Yes, I will help you."

They slipped under the flap, the rain obscuring them in the already pitch-black night. Kinley took her hand and they were running full out down the rutted road, kicking up mud and water. She could only hope she didn't break her stupid ankle, running like this in the dark.

After going less than a mile, Kinley heard someone coming up on them fast. She pulled Maria into the underbrush.

Not wanting to give away their position with automatic gunfire, Kinley crouched. The man stopped as if sensing them nearby. Staying perfectly still, barely daring to breathe, she waited, but when he started to methodically check the brush beside the road, she knew she had to…take him out.

Kinley silently removed the semiautomatic from her back and handed it to Maria, whose eyes grew wide. Then she nodded firmly. Kinley gave her a supportive look and pulled Beau's knife out of her pants pocket. She unfolded it and crept around behind the guy, giving him a wide berth. Rising, she wasted no time in jumping on his back, reached around and stabbing the knife into his throat, jerking it.

With a gurgling sound, he fell and lay still as her stomach twisted and coiled with revulsion, his wet blood rushing over her hand. She pulled the knife out and wiped it on his shirt, folded it and put it back in her pocket, trembling.

She made her way back to Maria and they were on the run again.

When they made it to the coupe, Kinley pulled open the back door. "Get in. Hurry," she said. Beau had to be on his way there. Still reeling and trembling inside from the close-quarters kill, Kinley shoved the keys in the ignition and turned over the engine. She shifted over to the passenger side and rolled down her window. She strained her ears while watching for any movement in the rearview, but could see nothing. "Oh, God, where is he?"

Maria was tense, sweat dripping off her chin as Kinley felt her own sweat slide over her skin, her heart still pounding. He said not to worry about him. But that didn't mean she was leaving this place without him. She wasn't and he could take those orders and shove them...

"Miss me?" he asked, materializing right at her window.

She jumped and reached out and shoved him as he laughed and ran around to the driver's side. "Got some bad news for you, *chérie*. That last Jeep is on its way here. I disabled the other two." He put the car into gear and stepped on the gas.

Chapter 16

He cursed the fate that had led that damn Jeep to do recon right at the time that he wanted to disable all three. At least two were out of commission, along with eight of the twelve guys who had grabbed the woman.

"This is Dr. Costa's wife, Beau." His eyes went to the sad and haunted eyes in the rearview. Damn, she must have been right there when they killed her husband. "This is Special Agent Beau Jerrott with the Navy Criminal Investigative Service and I'm Special Agent Kinley Cooper with the Coast Guard."

"NCIS, like the TV show?" Maria said, her eyes widening. "I saw it when I was visiting Florida."

Beau shook his head. "Oh, man, that show has done more to elevate our profile than our work. Nice to meet you, Mrs. Costa."

"Maria, please."

"Where exactly are we going?" Kinley asked.

He hadn't missed the blood on her hands. "How many did you take out?"

"Two," she said, her face grim.

"That's all eight, then," he said.

He would have to ask her what happened later, but the dark shadows in her eyes were something he intended to find the time and peace and quiet to soothe.

"As fast and as far away from that Jeep as we can get." He glanced in the rearview and said, "You planning on helping us out, Maria?"

"Yes, I will help. My husband gave his life to protect mine. It must mean something. Take me to our residence. I know where my husband kept his insurance policy. Diego Montoya is ultimately responsible for getting my husband murdered by those thugs. If he hadn't forced my sweet Miguel to perform those surgeries to change his appearance, he'd be alive today. He was such a good, good man." She dropped her head into her hands, sobbing.

Kinley reached back and squeezed her shoulder and rubbed her arm. "We're so sorry about what happened."

Maria raised her head and wiped at her eyes. "There was nothing you could have done. There are many of them. They breed like vermin."

"You okay?" Beau murmured, looking at Kinley.

She rubbed at her hands and he cringed. Damn, she'd killed tonight, and it looked like it might have been at close quarters. Baptized in blood wasn't exactly what he'd wanted for her, and he'd dragged her on this mission, manipulated her with that terrorist comment he knew she wouldn't be able to ignore. He felt like a jerk, but he had no intention of failing on this mission. No NCIS agent or SEAL would ever give up. Orders or not. He didn't give a damn what the Commandant of the Coast Guard said. He knew what Chris expected of him and it was going to the max and then pushing past that. National security and protecting every man, woman and child in the US was a mission he took seriously. Without even having to ask Kinley, he knew it was her mission, too.

He reached out and slipped his hand over hers as they twisted in her lap. Her head came up and she curled her fingers around his hand, sliding her hand up his forearm.

"I'm so proud and impressed," he said quietly.

She squeezed her eyes closed and took a deep breath. "I would never want to let you down."

"Couldn't happen," he said.

The bobbing headlights that appeared behind him had him flooring the Mercedes. They were already going way too fast for such a narrow road, the vegetation slapping against the windows as they rushed by. But the Mercedes performed better in the mud than he'd hoped.

"Hang on, ladies. We have company."

It wasn't long before they hit the blacktop of the main road, but his sharp left had Kinley's head snapping around.

"Beau. Havana is the other way."

"Well aware, backseat driver," he muttered as he saw the headlights of the Jeep swerve onto the road and gun after them. "Yeah, that's right, come on, you bastards."

Her hand was clamped to the side door, holding on.

He'd done a bootleg turn before, but that was in the middle of the bayou with plenty of space to maneuver. And it had been in a tricked-out Mustang. He'd also been professionally trained, as all agents were, in tactical and dangerous driving. He was booking it, his speed way too high on a slick, rain-washed road. They were hemmed in by a mountain of dirt on one side and a sloping roll into dense jungle on the other.

He was about to find out if the driver of the Jeep had nerves of steel, too.

He glanced at Kinley. Even with her hair falling down, stuck to her neck and her face, sweaty, dirty, bloody, she turned him on. He wanted her, with her damned red hair, and those deep green eyes, and that mouth beckoned him every time he looked at it. But if he didn't start thinking with his head instead of with whatever was going on below the belt, he would get them all killed, and he couldn't do that because that would mean he wouldn't get to have her again. And that wasn't acceptable.

Finally he found what he was looking for. The road opened up ahead with a passing lane. It was time to turn the tables. Naw, it was time to flip that table and turn it into a turbocharged bullet.

"Get down, and stay down." He rolled down the window.

"What exactly are you planning?" she asked, giving him a wild-eyed look.

"Power slide."

"What? On this road in these conditions? You are crazy."

"Only a little," he said. "The rest is mad skills. Now get down and hold on."

"This is your plan?" Kinley asked, her voice definitely nervous.

On the fly and in his head it sounded damn good. He'd done this many times—pull up on the parking brake, turn opposite the slide while downshifting to ride the controlled drift, until the car snapped around in a 180-degree breakneck maneuver that would spin the car in the other direction. If all went well, he'd full-throttle the coupe from zero to sixty in two seconds flat and power the Mercedes back to Havana.

Going all out, and getting all in.

If luck was on their side, the Jeep would pass right by them and not even realize it. Best-case scenario.

He noticed that Maria had followed his order, but Kinley was still looking at him.

"Kinley, do as I say. Trust me. I'm going balls to the wall. Get ready. Keep that beautiful red head down. If this doesn't pan out, there's going to be some shooting, and they'll be shooting back. Hang on."

He pushed the coupe even harder, thundering around the curves, trying to get as many seconds ahead as possible so that the chasing Jeep didn't see him do the bootleg. The acceleration was enough to convince Kinley there was going to be some power sliding happening in just a few seconds. Out of the corner of his eyes he saw Kinley duck down.

"Oh, my God. This is your plan."

"Yep, sugar, this is my plan. Hang on!"

He checked his rearview again, and when he saw no headlights, he worked the clutch and downshifted. Then the white lines of the passing lane started slipping beneath those beautiful, traction-for-days tires, and he executed the maneuver. It was textbook perfect.

The vehicle spun around, tires screeching, brakes heating. Beau hit the lights and slid her right up against the dirt wall like greased lightning. The car came to a complete stop. All that sounded in the interior was their hard breathing as they all caught their breaths. They skulked on the muddy and slim shoulder of the road, silent and dark, waiting for the Jeep to zoom by.

Damn. His heart raced as sweat soaked into the neck-
line of his shirt and collected beneath his arms. His
heart was in his throat, but he didn't waste a second.
He reached for the submachine gun and laid it across
the open window. The Jeep flew past, a buzz of sound
and color.

He released the brakes working the clutch and rolled
the vehicle back onto the road. It was all downhill from
here. He punched the lights on and hit the gas. A quarter
of a mile later, he swore as another Jeep passed them,
squealed to a halt and started to turn around. No bootleg for him, just a three-pointer.

Damn them. Communication must have gone out
once Beau and Kinley had assaulted the camp, and
they'd called for reinforcements. There would be no
quarter if they caught them. None. They'd kill him and
Kinley and take Maria again.

Not friggin' happening.

The headlights were soon in his rearview and that
other Jeep was probably on the way back.

A spitting, cracking *ding-ding-ding* and the explosion of the driver's-side mirror left no doubt in his mind
that they were running for their lives. Bits of glass flew
as the mirror fragmented, leaving nothing left.

Ah, damn, they weren't going to get their deposit
back.

The Crossed Swords Cartel was out for blood and the
whole group had been alerted. Well, they were going to
be very disappointed.

Beau stomped the gas. Their only hope now was to
outrun them, but as Beau came around the next curve,
he hit the brakes, fishtailing the Mercedes and sending
them all forward as the Jeep tapped them from behind.
Beau wrestled with the wheel to keep the Mercedes on

the road and from rear-ending a freaking outmoded camel bus, a hitched cab and trailer full of people in his lane. A red truck, loaded down with produce—pineapples, melons, tomatoes and a starchy plant called malanga—was approaching from the other direction, both of them moving way, way too slow. He braked, swore, braked harder, then swore harder still before slamming them, shaking the back end of the car violently as he went from bat-out-of-hell ballistic to turtle-slow-as-hell.

They were dead unless he could get them around this mess and quick. The trucker's timing sucked. It slowly rumbled forward, blocking off any escape. Kinley raised her head to see what was going on and her face blanched when she saw the scenario and realized they were trapped.

There was no time to do anything at this point. The Mercedes was rolling way too fast. The Jeep crowded his tailpipe and another burst of gunfire ripped into the side of the car. In the distance, Beau saw the other Jeep catching up.

Suddenly, Kinley grabbed his semiauto and rolled down the window. Leaning out, she opened up on them, sending the cartel boys ducking. The Jeep swerved and dropped back.

Everything was happening in split seconds. He held the wheel in a death grip, worked the brakes and prayed and cursed at the same time. Just a millisecond from impact, the trucker rolled far enough past the camel bus to create a Hail Mary pass, and Beau grabbed Kinley's shirt and jerked her back into the vehicle as he shot through. The fit was so tight that the rear lights of the truck went by him less than six inches from his window. The shattered remains of the car's side mirror were sheared off completely.

The trucker overreacted and the heavily laden vehicle skidded, produce flying everywhere, smashing into the windshield of the pursuing Jeeps, sending them careening and swerving to miss the truck as it slewed sideways. The trucker came to a safe stop, but effectively blocked any possible pursuit by the second Jeep.

Beau gunned the Mercedes and put as much real estate between them as they could. As soon as they hit the outskirts of Havana, it started to rain again, a lashing storm that would help to effectively slow down any pursuit. It'd probably keep the cartel boys out of their hair, at least for the night.

"Do they know who you are, Maria?" Beau asked.

"Yes, I'm afraid so. When Miguel couldn't tell them where the pictures of Montoya were, I had to speak."

"Why?"

"Because he didn't know." Tears welled, spilling over and down her cheeks, her voice clogged with emotion. "He gave them to me as collateral. That's why he had to talk to me. He gave me the choice." She sobbed softly. "I thought I could save his life, but Miguel refused to be used against me. He attacked them and they shot him. They blew up his clinic as a way to show everyone they cannot stand against *Las Espadas*."

"Where are the pictures?"

"At our residence, but I refused to tell them anything, so they still don't know. But they will go to my home and search. I'm sure of it."

"They probably have already been there," Kinley said.

Beau nodded. "Agreed."

"Where do you live, Maria?"

She gave him her address and directed him. He drove and parked a block over from her house.

"Tell me where it is and I'll go get it."

"It's in a floor safe in my sewing room. The curtain hanger on the farthest window is the release mechanism." She gave him the combination.

"Kinley, get in the driver's seat. Any sign of trouble, you get the hell out of here. Text me if that happens and we'll rendezvous."

"The key is in the planter right beside the front door."

He nodded. Before he could get out of the car, she grabbed his arm. "Please, there is a picture of me and my husband on a table in the sewing room. Could you…"

"Yes. I'll get it. Do you want anything else? We will have to travel light." He reached back and grabbed her shoulder. "You'll have to come with us. You know that, right? We can't leave you here. We can offer you asylum in the US."

Her face crumpled and she rubbed over the moisture there. Nodding, she squeezed his forearm. "Thank you for saving me. I have no illusions they would have let me go like they promised. I would have just ended up in some shallow grave." After a moment, she said, "My passport is in the safe as well as ten thousand American dollars. That's all I need. We have off-shore accounts and Miguel has provided for me quite diligently." Her voice caught on a sob.

Beau exited the car. It was dark and raining hard, the wind plastering his clothes against his skin.

As he crossed through yards as a direct route to her house, he could see there was no need for a key. The front door was open and when he got inside, it was trashed. Their belongings strewn everywhere. Most of the valuable stuff was already looted.

He searched and found her sewing room, hurrying. It might be dark and stormy, but he couldn't be sure they wouldn't come back or had paid one of her neighbors to watch out for activity here.

Using the face of his phone to light the way, he found the curtain hanger and pulled straight down. He heard the release and swung his phone that way, crouching to minimize the illumination.

He flashed the light and quickly worked the combination until it snicked open. He grabbed a brown folder and pulled it out. Opening it, he saw that it was the information they needed. He took pictures with his phone and sent them to Chris. He reached in and grabbed the money and Maria's passport. Lastly he located the photo she had described. The glass was broken. With a quick trip to the kitchen, he found a plastic baggie and slipped the brown folder and the frame inside and zipped it closed.

Tucking everything under his shirt and into the waistband of his jeans, he headed back out into the rain, staying low.

Back at the car, Kinley moved over as Beau knocked on the window and slipped back inside.

Pulling out the package from his waistband, he handed everything to Kinley who stowed it into a small backpack.

"Mission accomplished. I sent everything to Chris with instructions to alert Stafford."

Kinley breathed a sigh of relief. "What now?"

"I know where we can go," Maria said.

Beau and Kinley turned to look at her. They needed

a place that was safe where they could eat and sleep. Tomorrow they would be heading for the extraction point.

"We have a safe house. Miguel again. It's under a bogus name, not far from here."

"Okay, we'll go there if you're sure it's safe."

"I'm sure. We've never even been there. Miguel hired people to furnish it and paid cash for everything. He was very careful."

When they pulled up to the safe house, Maria got out of the vehicle and Beau turned to Kinley. "Take over here. After we get the garage open, drive it inside."

She nodded and Beau caught up to Maria, who was reaching around an exotic plant, presumably for their spare key.

She unlocked the door and rushed to the back of the house and through the kitchen as he followed close behind. She opened a door and punched a switch and the wide door started to lift. As soon as it was possible, Kinley drove the vehicle inside and Maria punched it closed.

"Come inside and I will get you something hot to drink, get cleaned up and into some dry clothes."

She led the way back into the house and upstairs, where she pulled towels out of the linen closet and drew them into the bedroom.

Kinley was carrying the bag with their changes of clothes.

Maria wasted no time and grabbed clean, dry clothes out of the closet. "Use the shower in here and I will take the one in the hall."

"That will be fine," he said, unbuttoning and shrugging out of the dirty and muddy black shirt.

Kinley was pulling stuff out of the bag.

"We're going to have to lay low here until we get

close to extraction. It's too dangerous to be out in the storm. Lucky break for us as it should keep the cartel buttoned up until the storm passes."

"After our showers, we'll go back downstairs. I'll make us something to hold us over and some good coffee."

"That sounds heavenly," Kinley said, heading for the bathroom.

Maria turned to go and he said, "We'll be down in just a few minutes."

She nodded, and then looked to the bathroom door. "Kinley was quite fierce and deadly, but she is also kind and gentle. Thank you both."

He squeezed her shoulder. "You're welcome. We're sorry about your husband."

She nodded and left.

When he entered the bathroom, she was just standing there at the sink looking at her reflection, but he knew that wasn't what she was seeing. When he touched her shoulder, she turned and wrapped her arms around his waist.

"You were amazing," he said quietly. "A freaking Amazon warrior."

"Who says so?"

"Maria says so. And…I say so. So you killed a couple of guys, huh?"

"Yes, and it was completely awful. I know that they would have killed me in a heartbeat. I didn't underestimate them, but they underestimated me. I took their lives to save us both and that was that."

"Exactly, *chérie*. That is that."

He really had pushed her hard, he thought, and he admired her resilience.

"I'll wait until you're done," he said, retreating.

When she vacated the bathroom, he ran the water

and got in to scrub off the grease paint, the sweat and the blood.

Kinley was waiting for him when he got out, sitting fully dressed at the foot of the bed. It took everything he had to keep his hands to himself.

She rose and they embraced. "I wish we were alone," she said, putting her hands on his shoulders. He slid his hand heavily down her spine, in a soothing caress.

"Me, too," he murmured.

Her smile was bone melting and he swept his palm from her throat to her cheek, molding her flesh, his gaze lingering over her. Her eyes held awareness of her power—her shape like an hourglass, plush and ripe, wrapping him in her scent and sensation. Beau felt privileged, every moment he'd ever spent with another woman obliterated as if those faceless, nameless women had never existed. She touched his face, slid her thumb over his lips. It was a simple thing, but he wanted more of it. He wanted to connect to her deeply and seal the connection tighter.

He slid his hand up her side, crushing back the need to bury himself inside Kinley. Out of respect for Maria, he reined in this wild hunger for her.

She was more than under his skin. She was inside him. And when she wrapped her arms around his neck, she took him with her, away from danger and isolation, ignoring everything about the mission.

"Beau," she said, almost choking on his name. "Please just a kiss—" Her fingertips ran over his face, her breath hot in his ear. "I need you."

His feelings tumbled over each other.

Kinley sighed when he groaned and drew in air through clenched teeth. A deep heavy heat coiled through her body as his mouth rolled over hers, drawing her into him. She held him tighter.

"Beau," she breathed, wanting his heat, his energy, the life of him pulsing through her. Her hands swept over his contours, her fingertips molding to curved muscle and man.

"I'm a mess," she whispered in his ear, his big hands pushing back her hair.

"So am I," he growled.

He was an experience—something from the tightly guarded places she'd rarely visited. His kiss alone twisted her up in a net, tying her tight. In knots. She didn't know if she wanted to keep him as close as possible or turn in the other direction.

She cupped his face, devouring his mouth, thrusting her hips a bit, and he grunted and cursed, then nudged her thighs wide and stood between them. She took what he offered, and a million thoughts ran through her mind, nothing sticking long enough to make sense. She felt freed, her need beyond passion, beyond control.

Kinley stared up at him, never expected to see this man humbled by anything. Yet he was, she could see it in his eyes, his expression as if he was questioning everything he knew, and her throat tightened. The world, the enemy saw strength and deadly skill. Kinley saw need and unguarded man. She loved the exquisite intensity of his gaze trapped in hers.

His breath shuddered, almost gasping. "You have no idea what this is doing to me, do you?"

"How can I not?" she said, brushing her fingers across his hair, caressing down the side of his face. Gently she laid her mouth over his, licking the line of his lips slowly before sliding her tongue between them and making them both crazy.

Her whispers mingled with the sound of the rain, their secrets bared and unspoken drifting between them.

"Coffee's ready," Maria called.

He wrapped his arms around her and held her, and she clung to him. Tomorrow was going to be precarious, dangerous and might just take their lives. But she had found something here that had changed her, changed her so profoundly, and she hadn't even begun to scratch the surface. It also frightened her more than going into battle, more than losing her life. It scared her down to her soul, to the core of her heart where she had loved so unconditionally, she hadn't been able to get over it. Now there was another man, a man that meant as much to her. How could she open herself to that again? How could she take it and feel completely sure that she wouldn't go through the same kind of agony?

When they left the room, Kinley saw that Maria had pulled out the photograph of her and Miguel smiling with their arms around each other. Her heart broke for the woman who had obviously loved the man who had been taken from her. She couldn't stop that fear again. It was raw and real and scored her insides.

"I suggest we all sleep in the same room, close to an exit. I like the family room. Two couches and a chair, sliding-glass door and closer to the garage."

He followed Maria into the kitchen where she poured the coffee. She then started pulling things out of the refrigerator. As she started assembling a meal, she said, "This asylum. Am I able to keep my belongings and my assets?"

"Yes, asylum just means the US is accepting you as a refugee. We don't strip people who are already displaced. Do you have family here?"

"No. My family is gone. I only had Miguel. As I am

sure you are aware, I am much younger than my husband. We've only been married for a year. I met him when he was called to the hospital where I worked in Emergency. He performed an operation on a victim of a terrible accident and what would have been a disfigurement. Miguel is…was a genius, so talented." She wiped away her tears. "We planned on having children…"

Kinley came around the counter and wrapped her arms around Maria as she started sobbing. "I'm so sorry. I can only hope we got the bastard who killed him."

She raised her head. "You did. He was my guard. The man you killed. So if you feel any regret for your actions, you can rest at ease. Thank you, again." She put the cover on the skillet and said, "Excuse me for a moment."

When she left the kitchen, Kinley turned to Beau. She just stood there, her heart broken and bleeding for Maria. She'd had a terrible, horrible loss and it was devastating her from the inside.

She trembled when she looked at Beau, feeling vulnerable and crushed. His hair was a mess after the shower, curling around his face, his bangs heavy on his forehead. His midnight-blue eyes a deep well into which she could fall and never find her way out. His sympathy for Maria was there, too, in those eyes that were so expressive, sometimes full of steel and at other times full of her, as if he was a mirror that reflected her image so that she could feel completely whole.

And the fear she'd been pushing at with both hands since their recent lovemaking rolled over her, swamping her, jumbling up her emotions. She felt like she was in that fog again, waiting for the moment she'd heard those shots and knew with certainty that her father had just died. Feeling it as the life left his body. She'd never felt safe again…

Not until now.

Maria's situation had reminded her of what happened when love was lost suddenly, a hollow gulf so wide there was nothing to bridge it, so deep it ripped out whatever made you whole. And when it went, when the person you loved went and you were left behind… it *hurt*. A can't-catch-your-breath, I-think-I'm-going-to-die agony.

Beau was like a force of nature, like the energy of atoms splitting, cosmic and unexplainable, and they connected just like that sexy chain around his biceps with the empty link.

Getting into his orbit was dangerous, but she couldn't fight it. She closed her eyes when he cupped her face and drew her against him, murmured to her that it was going to be okay. But she knew it wasn't and knew he was also lying to himself.

He would understand why she walked away.

He would understand why she couldn't stay with him. Because he'd been burned. He'd felt that same loss. And decided that he was better off without it.

And she understood herself so much better. Understood why she'd always kept herself behind that protective fog, a barrier between her and any man she thought she could love. The main reason she couldn't give him everything. The fear of loss.

Even as she buried her face into his throat and slipped her arms around his broad shoulders, she knew this was the beginning of saying goodbye.

And Beau would let her go.

He'd let her walk away because his fears were just as powerful as hers.

Wouldn't he?

Chapter 17

After the food was consumed, Maria set them up with blankets and pillows, and they settled into the family room. Maria took one couch and Kinley took the other. Staying vigilant, Beau took the chair with the perfect tactical view of the entrance to the street and a panoramic view of the backyard. He'd been trained to go without sleep and he had no intention of being caught off guard. They had fulfilled their mission and he was getting them out of here in one piece. The storm still lashed the vegetation surrounding the house, the wind making a keening sound in the rafters. Sometime in the night, Kinley settled against him. She curled up to him, exhaled long and low and in moments fell asleep, her hand on his chest. Beau set his weapon on the table, the safety engaged, and settled next to her. He sent his hand into her mass of hair, burnished in the dancing ambient glow from the security light burning in the backyard.

He stretched his legs out and snuggled her more comfortably. It felt good, her compact body wrapped around his. He was pretty shocked how good. But he cared deeply for her. He wasn't sure how it would work between them.

He recognized the look in her eyes so well. He used to get it with women after one night, and that was all it would take. He was either gone the next day or trying to get gone. But…damn, he was thinking things he hadn't thought since Jennifer.

Settling down.

He wanted that with Kinley.

Kinley's barriers had fallen right along with his, revealing something surprisingly vulnerable and open when she'd given herself to him. Now, even as she got close to him again, her barriers were there, wholly back in place, and they'd been reinforced.

That left him hanging on the edge of a cliff. He'd committed with Jennifer. He'd been all in. He'd tried to be patient and understanding. He'd tried to talk to her and make her understand how much he loved her, but in the end, she'd simply left. He'd come home to an empty apartment, his belongings piled into the corner and everything else…gone.

He wanted to hold fast to the knowledge that while Kinley might now be busy backing off and constructing walls, in that moment when she'd looked into his eyes, there had been confusion and longing plainly there for him to see. And that said otherwise. There was something else going on here, whether or not she could tell him, whether or not she'd even admitted it to herself.

He wanted to figure it out.

He wanted to be *all in* with Kinley.

But the remembered pain of being abandoned, as

Jennifer had simply cut him out of her life, was still there. He wasn't sure pushing her or getting her to try to understand how he felt about her would do any good.

The conclusion: the all-in had to come from her and if it didn't, it would be best if he just let her go. Let her walk away. Less pain now, no more empty apartments and emptiness he tried to fill with shallow women who he picked because they responded to his charm and his looks. He closed his eyes and rubbed his hand deeper into her hair.

Suddenly, a snippet of conversation came back to him from his partner at NCIS, Amber Dalton. *One of these days, Beau, a woman is going to come along and knock that Cajun charm of yours right on its ass. When that happens you're going to be humbled by actual feelings. I want popcorn and a front-row seat for that.*

Aw, hell, Kinley filled that emptiness with a genuineness that he couldn't deny.

Her hand shifted to his stomach and Beau felt his muscles instantly flex. He moved her hand away from the danger zone.

The dark night transformed into a gray, rain-washed day, but to Beau it was their wake-up call. The chopper that was going to take them out of Cuba would be at the rendezvous at 0800. Kinley woke slowly, and he loved watching her face as it crinkled. She stretched a little, then opened her sleepy green eyes.

She looked up at him with parted lips, looking like she was still caught in a dream, and all that bull he was thinking last night tugged at his heart.

They had to get moving. That chopper wasn't going to wait for them. Maria made a quick breakfast and they packed up the green bag, leaving everything else behind except Maria's meager possessions.

"Mind if we take that Lexus sedan in the garage? Would be best to keep the Mercedes out of sight," Beau asked as they prepared to leave.

She shook her head. "No, I don't mind. Miguel gave it to me as a birthday present."

Suddenly the sound of a vehicle motoring into this quiet section of the neighborhood had Beau striding to the window.

"Damn!" he muttered as two Jeeps filled with more cartel goons pulled up to the front of the house. It was easy to see the tattoos.

"I don't know how they found us, but these guys are really not going to give up Montoya. Time to bug out, ladies."

They raced to the garage and Beau settled behind the wheel, handing the bag back to Maria as she settled into the backseat. Kinley shot him a look as she softly closed the passenger-side door.

"Buckle up."

"I take it we're not going to raise the door."

He started the car and twisted his body around. Giving her a grim smile he said, "You locked and loaded, *chérie*?"

"Hooyah," she said.

"Watch your six." He gunned the engine and hit the gas.

The Lexus punched through the garage door like it was tissue paper. Gotta love a car that drove like a dream but was as indestructible as a tank. The cartel contingent was already out of the Jeep and just starting to surround the house as Beau flipped the car into first and peeled out, burning rubber.

As he shifted to second, Kinley already had her window down and she sent a burst of rapid fire across the lawn, cutting down some while others dove out of the way of her hot lead.

Beau sped through the street, swerving around traffic and heading for the main road where he could open the vehicle up and leave those tangos in the dust. He banked the turn, downshifting to check his speed, then the tires of the car hit the asphalt.

Kinley kept her eyes on the side-view mirror, the submachine gun in her hands at the ready. When the Lexus growled and Beau shifted, she swung her eyes to him. He drove like a freaking race-car driver. She was still awed at the maneuver he'd pulled yesterday to get them away. He handled the vehicles like he handled everything else—with hot, sexy, mad skills.

He shifted into second gear. Third, fourth and fifth in rapid succession, each gear forcing a quantum leap in their acceleration. Her heart jamming in her throat, she watched the speedometer climb.

Sixty miles an hour was much closer to zero than she thought. Seventy flew past so fast, it didn't register.

Eighty was a memory.

Ninety, and she white-knuckled the door handle.

One hundred.

She glanced up, and he flashed her a grin, the wind whipping at his hair, one hand easy on the wheel, the other on the shifter.

One hundred and ten.

One hundred and twenty and oh, damn…they were flying. The sleek car low to the road, roaring.

They left those Jeeps in their dust as Beau never hesitated, navigating around anything in front of him as if they were standing still. She could smell the ocean as they got closer to a long spit of land, buried in thick jungle growth. From what she'd been told, there was an opening in the trees, perfect cover for egress.

Beau was slowing down when he saw them and he swore. He swerved off the road as the tires kicked up gravel and dust, then they were skidding on the vegetation as he sent the Lexus fishtailing, careening for the opening in the trees.

But a different Jeep barreling down the road in the opposite direction saw them even as they passed each other. Bad luck and good communication between the cartel lackeys. A few more minutes and they would have been able to stash the car out of sight and made the chopper. The driver slammed on the brakes even as they skidded over the vegetation.

Kinley spilled out of the car, hearing the muted whirling blades of a Black Hawk as it screamed across the sky, heading for the edge of that spit.

Beau practically pulled Maria out of the car and Kinley started running as automatic gunfire cracked behind them. She turned and backed up as she depressed the trigger of the machine gun in her hand. The goons ran behind the Jeep for cover.

"Run!" he shouted at her as one of the cartel goons yelled at everyone to hold their fire. Of course they would want Maria alive and with two women, the cartel couldn't be sure which of them was which. Their caution gave them an opening to get to the chopper. Kinley turned and ran, but one of the goons had not stayed with the Jeep and had run around to outflank them. He was heading straight for their tightly formed group.

She brought up the machine gun, but the clicking noise told Beau she was out of ammo.

The man hit Kinley and Beau, knocking them all to the ground.

* * *

Beau hit his head and was stunned for a moment. When he could focus again, he saw Maria hesitate. "Run, Maria! Now!" he screamed. With an agonized look on her face, she whirled and took off.

Looking around for Kinley, he saw her fighting off the thug.

He rose and headed for the struggling pair. Delivering a hard kidney punch that would have the guy pissing blood for a week, he followed up by locking an arm around the guy's neck.

Her attacker let Kinley go and Beau shouted at her to run as the Black Hawk touched down. More members were catching up to them as Beau faced the guy. There was no time for a prolonged battle.

When Kinley scrambled away, Beau slammed his foot behind the goon's knee, taking him down. After a quick boot to the face, Beau pelted after the two fleeing women. He saw Maria make it to the chopper, but with a cry she turned.

It looked like the cartel's patience was at an end when they realized they were going to lose them to the waiting chopper. A spurt of gunfire sounded behind him and to his horror Kinley turned around and started running for something bright reflecting the light. She bent down and grabbed it, crying out as she grabbed her side and collapsed to the ground.

Hot lead whizzed past his head. Something molten punched into his side and he gritted his teeth at the pain, stumbling. He regained his footing and pressed forward, heart pumping, chest tight, his eyes never leaving her crumpled form. Scooping her up over his shoulder, he ran the last few feet to the chopper.

Once they were out of the line of fire, two marines

opened up on the cartel members. One of the marines slipped out of the chopper, running for him, laying down defensive cover as Beau hit the open door to the chopper, propelling them both inside.

As soon as they were on deck, the Black Hawk powered up off the spit of land and accelerated away from the cracking gunfire, but Beau was oblivious. He was frantically clawing at Kinley's shirt, panic shredding him. *Oh, God, no, no, no!*

Blood covered her stomach and he swallowed hard.

In her hands, she held the picture of Maria and her husband.

With her face contorted in pain and the medic trying to shoulder Beau out of the way, Kinley reached over and handed the frame to Maria, who sobbed and clasped Kinley's hand as she passed out.

When Beau woke up in the hospital after collapsing in the chopper from the wound to his side, the doctor assured him that Kinley had been tended and released. Her wound was superficial. The Black Hawk had landed on top of the medical center to get Beau the treatment he needed.

Shortly after that, Ken came into the room. "Good to see you awake." There was a sadness in his eyes Beau understood.

"I'm sorry about Daniel."

Ken nodded. "He was a good man and he died a hero. They're going to release his body to me tomorrow."

"That's good to know. The cartel?"

"Still a threat, but they don't know who you are, so you and Kinley are safe. Maria Costa will be protected until we finish working with Cuba to dismantle the cartel. There's already been some nasty infighting in the ranks so it's a sinking ship. Also, thought you would want to know that Umprey Thompson's little girl and grandmother have also been sent to the States under protective custody with new identities."

He nodded. "Kinley?"

"She's on her way here now that you're awake. She's been debriefing the DEA…ah…wait, there she is now."

Kinley came into the room and gave him a smile, but he got a bad feeling when she stayed a respectable distance. It wasn't like she could kiss him or anything, but he just wanted some reassurance that…what? That she cared for him enough to want to take the next step in their relationship? His feelings for Jennifer had been laid to rest, but the memory of the pain was something that still plagued him.

His attention shifted from her when Ken pulled out the laptop from the case he was holding and opened it. The display winked on. The screen was taken up in thirds by the director and his boss, Chris, the commandant, and then SAC Stafford.

"Good to see you're recovering Special Agent Jerrott."

"Thank you, sir."

"To fill you both in, Diego Montoya has been identified by his photograph and his residence in Norfolk was raided. He was so confident he'd gotten away with it, he'd not only bought a house and settled in the city, but applied for a driver's license. He and his two bodyguards are in custody and charged with the murders of Cameron Dixon, Mark Levin, Pete Samson, David Walters and Umprey Thompson along with the nine National Defense Force members and the three Coast Guard crew. In addition, they were charged with hijacking a vessel at sea. The ballistics proved that Dudley Martin had been shot and killed by Umprey, presumably when he had been betrayed.

"Montoya's DNA locks him in at the scene. To get a lesser sentence, Montoya agreed to testify against the cartel. He told us that he'd had his face altered by Dr. Costa and had cashed out his bank account and secured a shipment of cocaine to finance his getaway. He intended to hide out in the US until he could neutralize the danger he was in. He'd already had Umprey on his payroll, but had Martin trick the Americans into thinking they were going to film a movie about the Coast Guard to get them on board for the sole purpose of deceiving any CG vessels they might come across. Worked like a charm. As for you two…"

"Here comes the ass-chewing," Beau murmured and Kinley didn't say anything. He didn't like her silence.

"What exactly was it that you didn't understand about engaging the *Las Espadas*, Special Agent Jerrott?" The commandant demanded.

"I take full responsibility as lead," Beau said immediately. "Kin…Special Agent Cooper got dragged along in my wake. She wanted to follow orders and request permission."

"I commend her for that."

Beau breathed a sigh of relief, but tensed up as she opened her mouth. "Sir…"

"And I commend you, Special Agent Jerrott. We thank you both for an exemplary job in taking the initiative and handling this mission to a successful outcome. A dangerous man is behind bars and will answer for his crimes. Job well done."

Chris shook his head. "You are unbelievable, Jerrott. As soon as you're well, get your can back to DC. I don't want to see you in the office for two weeks, though. Take some time off."

"Thank you, Beau," Kirk said. "Kinley, I will see you when you land."

"Yes, sir," she said.

Ken powered off the laptop and slipped it back in the case. "I'm ready to take you to the airport whenever you're ready, Special Agent Cooper."

She nodded. "I'll meet you downstairs."

After Ken left, she cleared her throat and stood there awkwardly, not meeting his gaze. That wasn't like her.

"Are you okay?" he asked.

She nodded. "It's just a flesh would, but oh, boy, did it hurt." She lifted up her shirt and he saw the stiches.

"Be careful," he said softly, "or you'll end up as battle scarred as me."

"I consider it a badge of courage." She smiled.

"So, you're heading back to Norfolk, now." He so wanted to tell her how he felt, but with her closed expression, the words died in his throat.

"Yes…Beau…" She wrapped her arms around his neck and placed her mouth over his. She kissed him fiercely, and then let him go. "You are a wonderful, amazing man. Thank you for everything." She swallowed hard and turned away.

"Kinley."

"No. We both know it won't work. You have your job and I have mine. Take care of yourself," she breathed, her voice thick.

He nodded like an idiot as the woman of his dreams turned away and left, the door shutting quietly with finality after her.

Maria sat in the plane seat next to her. She would have a new life in the US. Too heartsore to talk, with the pain medication taking some of the sting out of her

wound and making her drowsy, she closed her eyes
and fell asleep. She woke up as the plane landed. As
they made their way through the terminal, both of them
were quiet.

Kirk Stafford was waiting at the curb and when he
got out of the car to wave to them, he took one look at
Maria and got this completely blindsided, shell-shocked
look on his face.

He came around the hood and opened the door for
her, introducing himself softly and tucking her inside.
Then he glanced at Kinley.

"I should have known that sending a SEAL would
get the job done, but also stir up a hornet's nest."

Just thinking about Beau hurt far worse than her
wound or any reprimand Kirk was going to mete out.
"Beau doesn't care about getting stung. He was so focused on getting the job done. He's..." she had to pause,
"...quite persuasive and persistent."

Kirk shook his head and got into the driver's seat. He
quickly had them back at Naval Station Norfolk where
Maria was taken to a conference room with some State
Department types. Kinley reassured her that she was
in good hands.

Before Maria left, she hugged Kinley hard. "Thank
you both for what you have done for me. I will always
remember you. Please extend my thanks to Beau as
well."

Kinley accepted her tight hug and then, with tears
forming in her eyes, Maria raised her head high and
walked off.

"Come on, Cooper. Let's get you home," Kirk said.

Kinley walked with him, blinking back the tears
that had threatened since she left Beau in the hospital
in the Bahamas. She thought she could get away scot-

free, but that wasn't happening. She felt *shredded. Devastated.* She forced herself to keep walking. *It will get better tomorrow.* It was exactly how she'd shut down after her father's death. Every day she told herself the next day would be easier.

And, although the pain dulled over the years, she would always miss her father terribly.

She pushed back the pain, swallowed back the tears, and made sure she was in control as she pushed out of the NCIS Office and slipped into the passenger side of Kirk's car.

He drove while giving her looks. "You look like hell."

A wry laughed bubbled out of her. "Thanks."

"You did a good job. I knew you would," he said as he pulled up in front of her house and they got out. Kirk followed her up the walk.

Once inside she settled onto the couch in the living room.

Kirk sat across from her. "The DEA has recovered Daniel's body. They're sending it to his parents in Spokane, where he's from. The Cubans are pissed about the covert op, but the DEA is glossing that over and engaging in talks about the *Las Espadas.* Hopefully they won't be terrorizing the island or being a conduit for drugs and terrorist drug money in the near future."

"That is really good news."

"Daniel's memorial service is next week. You hereby have leave to attend."

Her throat spasmed and her chest filled. She covered her eyes with her hand. Kirk made a soothing sound and switched to the couch, sending his arm around her. She leaned into his shoulder. Yeah, he was a guy she could trust and it was shocking how easily that happened. She thought of Beau, her heart breaking. All she had to do was take the risk. Could she?

"I'm sorry. I know this is hard, but I need to tell you." His voice was sad. "While Daniel was in Cuba, he sent me an email and cc'd his boss."

"What?" Kirk looked grave through the blur of her tears.

"The email basically laid out the incident that got his partner killed. He took full responsibility and he told us that you took the blame because he let you."

She couldn't help the soft sob.

"It exonerates you and your disciplinary action has been revoked, your record expunged. With your performance on this mission, you're being promoted two ranks. The one you were originally at before the death of Daniel's partner, and the one you deserve and should have been granted eight months ago."

She cried harder.

He rubbed her back. "The commandant wants you in DC leading your own team."

Her head came up and she just stared at Kirk. "What. I…I… Oh, God…I don't know what to say. He saved me…"

"I know. It was in the report Beau gave to the DEA when he called in about Daniel. Are you going to be okay here by yourself?"

She took a deep breath and nodded. "I'm going to need more time off. I've got something I need to do. Visit my father's grave at Arlington Cemetery. I haven't been there in a while."

He nodded. "Take the time you need. You might as well look for an apartment while you're there."

She nodded again. "Thank you, Kirk."

* * *

Beau walked through the halls of the CIA, a visitor's badge clipped to his shirt. He'd been discharged from the hospital and even though he wasn't 100 percent, he was following through with his plan.

He didn't bother to knock at the door to an office marked "Steven J. Giles" before letting himself in.

The man behind the desk looked up with a startled expression on his face. Then he laughed and stood up and laughed again. "Ragin' Cajun!" he said as he came out from behind the desk and gathered Beau up in a bear hug.

Beau laughed. "Even Steven. Put me down, you moron," Beau said, using his nickname from the SEALs.

Steven let him go. "I haven't seen you since we were both discharged. What the hell you been up to?" He punched Beau on the shoulder.

"NCIS."

"No way! You're a copper, kicking ass and taking names. I guess you know what I'm doing."

"Working for the CIA, yeah."

"Nah, I don't work for the CIA," Steven said with a grin. He walked to the door and closed it. "I'm no spook."

"Right."

"What brings you here?" He sat on the edge of his desk as Beau settled into a chair.

"High Value Target List."

The smile faded from Steven's face.

"What number?"

"Two."

"You're kidding!"

"Kaamil 'The Assassin' el Ajeer, the leader of Sons of the Republic."

"The CIA has been after him for a long time, over fifteen years, but he's been elusive, a real ghost. But if you know where he is…"

Beau sat back and folded his arms.

"I don't like that look."

"Remember in BUD/S when you were working your ass up over that damn wall during PT?" Beau leaned forward. "You know, the one where you almost gave up and rang out?"

Even Steven rubbed the back of his neck. "Oh, geez."

He'd gotten his nickname because the man was fanatical about paying his debts, keeping everything even. Beau had told him he'd collect someday. "I was that grunt who grabbed your hand and hauled your ass through that obstacle course. It's time to pay the piper."

"What do you want?"

"I want to go after him."

"What the… Are you crazy? The CIA won't sanction a former SEAL and current NCIS agent a pass to go wherever el Ajeer is and take him down."

Beau rose. "All right, then I'll find a way myself."

Even grabbed his arm. "Wait! Dammit, Ragin', you're putting me in a tough place."

"I need to take this guy down."

"Why?"

"It's personal. He's got one of our tridents."

Even stiffened, his brows folding down and outrage lighting his eyes. "Whose?"

"Paul Cooper's."

"Oh, yeah. Killed in London. Hey, he has a daughter…Kinley. She's about…um, twenty-eight. A real looker I hear." He gave him a sly grin. "You dog."

"It's not like that. She deserves to have closure on this."

"Oh, man, this is personal. Look, I could lose my job over this."

"Steven, we're in, we snatch-and-grab and we're out." He rubbed at his forehead. "What do you say? You in?"

Steven laughed and shook his head, putting his hand up for Beau to slap. "Yeah, Ragin', I'm all in."

Kinley stood at her father's grave in Arlington Cemetery in DC, the second grave she'd visited in the past two days. Fog misted over the gravestones almost like it was paying homage to her father. She liked that as she not only had made peace with his death, but with the fog that had sheltered her and saved her life.

Daniel had been laid to rest with his family and friends attending. It was a large turnout. Kinley made her peace with his death, but was still struggling over what he had done for her.

She had thought that the pain of saying goodbye to Beau would have diminished by now, but it hadn't. She was still raw, missing him terribly.

She knelt down in the grass and set the dozen roses on his grave. "Hi, Daddy," she said softly. "I haven't been here in some time and I'm sorry about that. I thought staying away and trying to block out everything would make it easier. But, of course, I was wrong."

She rose and finally let the pain go. Let it drift over his grave and fly away on the wind. Beau. He was responsible for this. She had to be accountable for her own inner guidance. Everything she needed was deep inside her. She'd run a mission with a tough former SEAL and kept up with him. Not only had she learned to trust him, but more importantly, she had learned to trust herself.

He made her feel so safe. She closed her eyes. She

looked across the full expanse of Arlington Cemetery, remembering what Beau had said about handling fear. Admitting it took away its power. She wanted to do that because she wanted to overcome this fear. Beau's office wasn't far from here. It was her next stop.

Suddenly, without warning, strong arms encircled her from behind. She didn't have to turn around to discover who it was. The memory of his scent was locked deep inside her.

Beau.

He breathed in deep, sending waves of shivers down her spine and over her skin.

"Miss me?" he said hotly against her ear.

She turned in his arms. "Yes, and you know it."

He grinned and took a deep breath. "Back in Cuba, I made a big mistake. I thought that it wouldn't change your mind to tell you how I feel about you. To tell you that from the moment I met you, I have been feeling you here." He placed his hand over his heart. "I thought that I couldn't say anything that would affect you and make you want to take a risk with me unless you already wanted to. But I was wrong. SEALs don't give up and I didn't even try."

He pressed his forehead to hers. "I found a name for the last link in my chain." He pushed up his sleeve and Kinley's throat got so thick and tight. Her name was etched into his skin, still rough and swollen from the recent application of red ink.

"It's you, *chérie*, for *being* my world." Tears spilled down her cheeks and he rubbed at them with both thumbs. "I love you, Kinley. Enough to risk my heart again. Enough that the pain of living without you and saying nothing was something I couldn't live with."

"Oh, Beau, I was so afraid of losing someone else

that I used my job as a barrier with every man I met. Just when I thought I could maybe let go, Daniel betrayed me. It wasn't until you came along and opened me up and showed me that it was worth it." She kissed his mouth, pressing her lips against his, that sense of urgency subsiding.

"You helped me to not only make peace with my father's death, but you helped me to make peace with myself, to trust myself. I love you, too, Beau."

He pulled something out of his pocket. The gold of it caught the light and she recognized it right away. Her breath caught.

"You're giving me your trident? Beau…"

"No, it's not mine. It's…your father's."

She cupped her hands around his, her heart so full of his love for her. "What? How did you…Ohmigod. You went after him, didn't you?"

He pressed his forehead against hers. "I went back and I ran that bastard to ground. He wouldn't give up, so that's one more dead terrorist we don't have to worry about anymore. I got this back for you. I went there not because he was on the watch list but for a brother in arms and for you, Kinley, for your justice and your closure."

"Thank you," she said, wiping away fresh tears, her throat so tight. She buried her face into his throat and wrapped her arms around his neck, squeezing him close. Then she kissed him, his mouth responding to hers just as frantically, with the same need.

When they parted, he took a deep breath. "So, I hear you got promoted and got your own team here in DC. I'm guessing you might need a place to live."

"Was that the little bird who also told you where I would be today?" she said, smiling through more tears.

"Taking the Fifth," he said. He gave her a sly, slick salesman look. "Well, there's this amazing apartment in this old building with so much charm, overlooking this amazing city. The view is breathtaking. There's only one small problem."

"What's that?"

He gave her a pained look. "Well, it comes with this guy, this annoying gung-ho dickhead that might make you get up and run with him every day and make love with him every night."

"Hmm, those sound like pretty good perks."

"Oh, really?" He chuckled.

She slipped her hand into his hair. He really did need a haircut. "Where is this amazing apartment?"

"Well, I could take you there right now, but I have to warn you, he might have to see you naked to make his final decision to let you stay."

She frowned and said, "What an ass."

He pressed his hand into hers, laughed and started to walk. "So, Kinley, I have one last question for you."

"What is it?"

"Are you in?"

She stopped and wrapped her arms around his neck, kissing him again, and murmured against his mouth, "Yes, Beau—*all* in."

Epilogue

Kinley held on as the old truck they were in rattled its way down a rutted and barely there path. It was reminiscent of that harrowing drive through the jungle, both going in after Maria and coming out again once they had her.

Only this time Beau wasn't driving. It was his grandfather, or as Beau called him, his *grand-père*. He was speaking in what Kinley was beginning to understand as Cajun French. Proficient speakers used both French and English. *"Nous avons pêché tout le temps. C'était la façon de garder nos bellies pleins. Ces buggers rouges étaient notre groupe alimentaire de base. Nous avons well mangé presque tous les jours et vendu ce que nous ne pouvions pas manger ou nous l'avions donné à des gens moins fortunés."*

Beau translated for her, his mouth sending tingles down her spine. "We fished all the time. That was the way to keep our bellies full. Those little red buggers were our basic food group. We ate well almost every day and sold what we couldn't eat or gave it away to less fortunate people."

Beau was sitting on the other side of her and she was sandwiched between the two men. The affection Beau held for his grandfather was evident as she'd been here in Delcambre for just under a week.

Six months had passed since their mission to Cuba. Word had reached them that the *Las Espadas* leaders had all been killed and the cartel had broken up. The SEALs had done a job on the rest of el Ajeer's followers with reports of many deaths and the rounding up of the rest to face international charges. Diego Montoya had been convicted and would be sitting in a federal prison for the rest of his life.

And Maria and Kirk were…well…they were an item. He'd fallen for the Cuban beauty and had given her a shoulder to lean on, cry on and finally to hold on to. Kinley was so glad that her boss and Maria had found each other. Talk about silver linings.

She lived with Beau in his apartment, just as he'd described it. When Beau had invited her down to the bayou to meet his family, she'd jumped at the chance. His family was huge and didn't only include his four very handsome brothers and his very pretty, very smart and very sassy sister, but his mother, father, aunts, uncles, cousins and friends. Kinley couldn't keep track of them all. It was so strange to be welcomed so warmly into his family when hers had been so cold. They were loud and spoke in a broken English/French language, listened to a lively music, the joy showing in their eyes so clearly that Kinley soon felt at home.

Now Beau and his grandfather were taking her craw fishing in the bayou. She was so excited.

They parked on the shoulder of the road. It was a pretty spot, the stream itself narrow and shallow with low muddy banks and a thick growth of water weeds and flowers. A perfect haven for crawfish, or so she'd been told by Beau.

A young couple was there trying their luck. They waved as Beau and Kinley and his *grand-père* got out of the truck. Kinley waved back as Beau handed her a pair of rubber knee boots to wade in while stamping into his own. Grabbing several cotton-mesh dip nets and three folding lawn chairs, he headed down toward the water with the nets tucked under his arm, carrying a cooler of bait in his other hand.

Beau's *grand-père* tucked her arm through the crook of his and they both made their way down the bank. In his heavily accented voice, he said, "You listen to my *petit-fils*. You'll be fishin' like you were born to it. You gonna then eat yourself some crawfish, you. You so little, I could pick you up over my head."

"Who you kidding, *grand-père*?" Beau said, dropping the bait and the nets near the water and turning toward him, giving him an indulgent look. "You could pick *me* up over your head without any problem."

"I will if need be. I might have to show him who's boss, me." He chuckled when Beau shivered in fear. "I'll do it, smart aleck, ha."

"I have no doubt," Beau said with affection in his eyes.

He motioned her over and she leaned up and kissed his cheek.

He opened the bait cooler. Reaching in, he baited the nets with shad gizzard and chicken necks. They each took a net out into the water, spacing them a good distance apart. Beau worked quickly and methodically, the ritual obviously second nature to him. Kinley kept stumbling over tangles of alligator weed entwined with delicate yellow flowers and water primrose. The spot she had chosen to drop her net was choked with lavender water hyacinth that kept getting snagged on it.

"Ah, sugar," Beau said indulgently, reaching around her, enveloping her in his warm male scent. "You havin' a bit of the trouble, you," he said, his accent as thick as his grandfather's, and Kinley giggled.

Beau helped her set the net and supported her as she waded back to shore. She lost her balance and Beau caught her against his hard-muscled, solid body. "Getting your sea legs?"

"Was this part of your craw-fishing plan? Get me to stumble around out here so you could be my hero?"

"Yeah, what of it?" he said. "It was a solid plan."

She set her arm loosely on his shoulders, playing with the hair on the nape of his neck. The sounds and smells of the bayou wrapped around her. It was as beautiful as the man it had nurtured.

When he smiled, his charm, his love for her, was evident in his face. It was evident in everything he did for her, in every moment that they interacted, even when they were arguing. She loved him so much that sometimes she got scared, so scared. Then she'd realize that he was dedicated to her. Committed so fully. Loving him was everything.

"Yeah." He leaned forward, setting his forehead against hers. "I love you, too, *ma belle*."

"Is it that evident?"

"It is, and it makes me feel like the king of the world."

"Well, you're king of mine."

He laughed and roared, picking her right up out of the water, carrying her to shore without one stumble. Damn him.

When they got home and he'd delivered the crawfish to his mother for dinner, he dragged her up to his room under the pretense of showering and changing before dinner.

As soon as the door closed, his hand slipped heavily down her spine, cupped her rear and meshed her hips to his. She felt his hard, broad erection through his jeans, the heat and pressure. She crossed her arms over her chest and pulled off her shirt, then stripped him of his.

His gaze was direct, hot and lazy.

He bent to taste her, pushing down her bra strap and exposing her. "So sexy."

His gaze slipped down over her plump breasts, smoothing the roundness with his hand, and then he leaned down. His lips closed warmly over her nipple and he drew her into the warmth of his mouth, watching her expression of pleasure. Her head fell back, her body bending to his. The motion ground her warm center to his erection and she thrust back as he licked and scored his teeth over the soft underside. He held her gaze as he ran a finger inside the edge of her bra cup, then pulled down. Her nipple spilled into his mouth. She gasped and closed her eyes as he devoured her.

Picking her up, he took her to the bed, licking slow heavy circles around her nipple. Kinley was breathless, her body hungering for his. She ran her hands over his sleek sculpted muscles. Then wrapped her hands around him, slid her finger over the moist tip, and laughed softly when he groaned, drew in air through clenched teeth.

"Damn," he said and clasped her hands above her head, "I love you."

"Prove it," she said, and for the next hour, he did.

Later on, after a feast of fresh spicy crawfish, dirty rice and green beans, Beau turned to her. "I have something I wanted to give to you."

Her breath backed up in her throat. "What?" she said.

He pulled something out of his pocket and handed it to her. The tension released in one breath. It wasn't the ring box she'd expected.

She opened it and held it up so his family members could see. They started hooting and hollering.

"He gave her a knife," one of his brothers said.

"Yeah, that's Beau for you," another said.

"Means he loves her," his sister said.

He looked over at them, then smiled. "I do love her. More than anything."

"You got me a folding KA-BAR."

He looked back at her. "I do have something else for you." This time he did pull out a ring box.

"Ohmigod," she whispered.

"Kinley, I don't need another six months or a year to know what I know now. I love you. I want to spend the rest of my life loving you. You are my world. Will you marry me?"

Tears stung her eyes and a soft sob escaped her lips. "Yes, I will. You know I will. I love you, forever."

He opened the box and she looked down at the exquisite square-cut diamond.

"There's an inscription," he said.

She tipped the ring and read it. *All in.*

She kissed him as he slipped the ring on her finger. "You and me, *chérie*. All in. All the time."

She breathed a soft sigh against his mouth.

"All the time. Forever and ever."

* * * * *

If you loved this novel, don't miss other suspenseful titles by Karen Anders:

DESIGNATED TARGET
SPECIAL OPS RENDEZVOUS
AT HIS COMMAND
FIVE-ALARM ENCOUNTER

Available now from Harlequin Romantic Suspense!

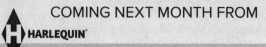

REQUEST YOUR FREE BOOKS!
2 FREE NOVELS PLUS 2 FREE GIFTS!

H HARLEQUIN®

ROMANTIC suspense

Sparked by danger, fueled by passion

YES! Please send me 2 FREE Harlequin® Romantic Suspense novels and my 2 FREE gifts (gifts are worth about $10). After receiving them, if I don't wish to receive any more books, I can return the shipping statement marked "cancel." If I don't cancel, I will receive 4 brand-new novels every month and be billed just $4.74 per book in the U.S. or $5.24 per book in Canada. That's a savings of at least 14% off the cover price! It's quite a bargain! Shipping and handling is just 50¢ per book in the U.S. and 75¢ per book in Canada.* I understand that accepting the 2 free books and gifts places me under no obligation to buy anything. I can always return a shipment and cancel at any time. Even if I never buy another book, the two free books and gifts are mine to keep forever.

240/340 HDN F45N

Name _____ (PLEASE PRINT) _____

Address _____ Apt. # _____

City _____ State/Prov. _____ Zip/Postal Code _____

Signature (if under 18, a parent or guardian must sign)

Mail to the **Harlequin® Reader Service:**

IN U.S.A.: P.O. Box 1867, Buffalo, NY 14240-1867
IN CANADA: P.O. Box 609, Fort Erie, Ontario L2A 5X3

Want to try two free books from another line?
Call 1-800-873-8635 or visit www.ReaderService.com.

* Terms and prices subject to change without notice. Prices do not include applicable taxes. Sales tax applicable in N.Y. Canadian residents will be charged applicable taxes. Offer not valid in Quebec. This offer is limited to one order per household. Not valid for current subscribers to Harlequin Romantic Suspense books. All orders subject to credit approval. Credit or debit balances in a customer's account(s) may be offset by any other outstanding balance owed by or to the customer. Please allow 4 to 6 weeks for delivery. Offer available while quantities last.

Your Privacy—The Harlequin® Reader Service is committed to protecting your privacy. Our Privacy Policy is available online at www.ReaderService.com or upon request from the Harlequin Reader Service.

We make a portion of our mailing list available to reputable third parties that offer products we believe may interest you. If you prefer that we not exchange your name with third parties, or if you wish to clarify or modify your communication preferences, please visit us at www.ReaderService.com/consumerschoice or write to us at Harlequin Reader Service Preference Service, P.O. Box 9062, Buffalo, NY 14269. Include your complete name and address.

HRS13R

SPECIAL EXCERPT FROM

H **HARLEQUIN®**

ROMANTIC suspense

*Noah Scott inherited a fortune from his biological
father, who was murdered. With his best friend
Rachel's help, Noah must find the killer, but will her
secrets destroy their growing attraction?*

*Read on for a sneak peek at HEIR TO MURDER
the latest in* New York Times *bestselling
author* Elle James's *THE ADAIR AFFAIRS series.*

Tonight, Rachel would tell him the truth. If he couldn't
forgive her or trust her after that, well then, that was the
end of the time she'd spend with him. She swallowed hard
on the lump forming in her throat. She hoped and prayed
it wouldn't come to that. In the meantime, she would look
her best to deliver her confession.

In her bathroom, she touched up the curls in her hair
with a curling iron, applied a light dusting of blush to her
cheeks to mask their paleness and added a little gloss to
her lips.

Dressing for her confession was more difficult. What
did one wear to a declaration of wrongdoing? She pulled
a pretty yellow sundress out of the closet, held it up to her
body and tossed it aside. Too cheerful.

A red dress was too flamboyant and jeans were too
casual. She finally settled on a short black dress with thin
straps. Though it could be construed as what she'd wear
to her own funeral, it hugged her figure to perfection and
made her feel a little more confident.

As she held the dress up to her body, a knock sounded
on the door.

"Just a minute!" she called out. Grabbing the dress, she unzipped the back and stepped into the garment. "I'm coming," she said, hurrying toward the door as she zipped the dress up.

She opened the door and her breath caught.

Noah's broad shoulders filled the doorway. Wearing crisp blue jeans and a soft blue polo shirt that matched his eyes and complemented his sandy-blond hair, he made her heart slam hard against her chest and then beat so fast she thought she might pass out. "I'm sorry. I was just getting dressed and I haven't started the grill…"

He stepped through the door and closed it behind him. "My fault. I finished my errands earlier than I expected. I could have waited at a park or stopped for coffee, but…I wanted to see you."

"Hey, yourself. I'm glad you came early." And she was. The right clothes, food and shoes didn't mean anything when he was standing in front of her, looking so handsome.

He leaned forward, his head dropping low, his lips hovering over hers. For a moment, she thought he was going to kiss her…

If you loved this excerpt, read more novels from *THE ADAIR AFFAIRS* series:

CARRYING HIS SECRET by Marie Ferrarella
THE MARINE'S TEMPTATION by Jennifer Morey
SECRET AGENT BOYFRIEND by Addison Fox

Available now from Harlequin® Romantic Suspense!

And don't miss a brand-new **THE COLTONS OF OKLAHOMA** *book by* New York Times *bestselling author Elle James, available September 2015 wherever* Harlequin® Romantic Suspense *books and ebooks are sold.*

Love the Harlequin book you just read?

Your opinion matters.

Review this book on your favorite book site, review site, blog or your own social media properties and share your opinion with other readers!

HARLEQUIN®

A *Romance* FOR EVERY MOOD™

JUST CAN'T GET ENOUGH?

Join our social communities
and talk to us online.

You will have access to the latest
news on upcoming titles and special
promotions, but most importantly,
you can talk to other fans about your
favorite Harlequin reads.

Harlequin.com/Community

 Facebook.com/HarlequinBooks

Twitter.com/HarlequinBooks

Pinterest.com/HarlequinBooks

THE WORLD IS BETTER WITH

Romance

Harlequin has everything from contemporary, passionate and heartwarming to suspenseful and inspirational stories.

Whatever your mood, we have a romance just for you!

Connect with us to find your next great read, special offers and more.